Lucy Greene

Published by Mission Point Press
2554 Chandler Rd.
Traverse City, MI 49696
(231) 421-9513
www.MissionPointPress.com

ISBN: 978-1-950659-68-5
Library of Congress Control Number: 2020913027

Cover image, obtained from the historical archives, depicts
one of the many patient cottages on the Traverse City State
Hospital grounds in the 1960s.

Printed in the United States of America

Lucy Greene

Richard VanDeWeghe

Mission Point Press

Preface

THE THREE BOOKS IN THE TRAVERSE CITY STATE HOSPITAL SERIES explore poignant time periods in the life of the asylum. The first book, *Jimmy Quinn*, takes place in the early 1950s, and it chronicles the demise of the successful patient-run farm program that was pioneered by the hospital's founder, Dr. James Decker Munson. This second book in the series, *Lucy Greene*, takes place in the early 1960s, at a pivotal time in our nation's history, when the winds of change were blowing from many directions. The third book, forthcoming, is set in the 1980s, during which time the last patients left the Traverse City State Hospital—not ironically, at the same time that the homeless population grew in the streets of the city and across the country.

The Traverse City State Hospital (formerly the Northern Michigan Asylum) had many admirable qualities and some serious problems. But it was a place that, in most respects, served as a true "asylum" from the harsh realities of a world that offered no humane alternatives for the most unfortunate and helpless of our citizens. The hospital, located in Traverse City, Michigan, served over 3200 patients and employed roughly 2000 employees. Its founder and first medical superintendent, Dr. Munson, had left a solid imprint on the institution, which you can read about in this novel, by the time he retired in the mid-1920s.

Today, the "Village at Grand Traverse Commons" is home to a vibrant residential and commercial community on the grounds of the former Traverse City State Hospital. Visitors will find restaurants, retail shops, a winery and a brewpub, a park and hiking trails. The original hospital buildings and grounds are being restored by The Minervini Group (www.thevillagetc.com/about-us/) in one of the largest historic preservation and redevelopment projects in the country. Historical tours of the asylum grounds are available daily and are very popular among the thousands who visit the "Village Commons" each year.

In keeping with Dr. Munson's philosophy of beauty, nature, and work as therapy, the hospital farm (as depicted in *Jimmy Quinn*) has been repurposed as a public park, with a botanic garden, labyrinth, healing garden, community garden, and event venue in the restored Cathedral Barn. Thousands of visitors also enjoy the daily tours of the Botanic Gardens as well as its gift shop and numerous hiking trails.

Set on the former asylum grounds, *Lucy Greene* is a work of fiction. Any relation to any real person is purely coincidental, with two exceptions. Dr. Munson is alluded to in the book as the hospital's prime mover behind its *moral treatment* approach to patient care. Father Fred also appears. He was the hospital's chaplain who raised money to build the first *interfaith* church on the campus, All Faiths Chapel (1965), and he served as chaplain from 1959 to the closing of the hospital in 1989.

That said, the footnotes appearing in most chapters are not fiction. I intended that they provide historical background to the events of the narrative. They too are important as they broaden the events of the novel and connect them to events that were transforming our nation at this crucial time in history. Reading the footnotes in context will underscore the multiple ways activism and social justice in *Lucy Greene* anticipate many events of a similar nature that we witness today.

Such is the interplay between history and fiction in historical fiction. Historical fiction derives its narrative energy from the tension that exists between history and story. To the extent that it is often difficult to separate out one from the other is the genius of the genre, as any good storyteller knows, including you, as you have no doubt told stories from your own past. Sometimes you got "the facts" right, sometimes not. But always, it was the story that mattered most.

Prologue

IMAGINE A DREARY MAY MORNING, RAIN IN THE FORECAST, GRAY CLOUDS low in the sky. Sister Lucy Greene sits in her kitchen in her rented flat, just a few blocks from the asylum over on Pine Street. She holds in her hands the letter from Father Pete that convinced her to come north to the state hospital in order to find a home for her dear friend and fellow nun, Sister Anna Jorgenson.

Like Lucy, Sister Anna is also a member of the Society of St. Joseph, their religious order. Both in their late twenties, the two nuns' friendship began in their parochial grade school in Kalamazoo. It continued on through high school and then through their years in convent and college. The Sisters of St. Joseph were among the first generation in the 1960s to give up wearing the religious habit. They dressed in everyday clothing, and except for the small cross that hung from their necks, they were indistinguishable from the laity. As with so many progressive nuns in the S.S.J., these two eschewed the title "Sister," though, out of habit or respect, many people still called them by their religious titles. It was difficult to break old semantic habits.

Lucy gazes out her tiny kitchen window, recalling the tortuous months downstate trying desperately to provide for Anna's medical and emotional needs following the tragedy in Alabama. She recounts the long and difficult drive back to their home convent in Kalamazoo, followed by

Anna's aged parents' befuddlement over how they could possibly take care of their daughter now that they were well into their seventies and infirm themselves. She relives the heroic efforts by the convent nuns to accommodate Anna's needs, and the Mother Superior's difficult final decision that the convent simply was not equipped to support Anna.

Writing to Father Pete was a shot in the dark. Lucy hadn't spoken with him since she was in high school when he was the assistant pastor at the parish as well as the girls' basketball and softball coach. He had since been moved around the diocese, and she learned he had become assistant chaplain at the state hospital in Traverse City. When she wrote to him, she minced no words about Anna's piercing headaches, her alternate bouts of raving madness and comatose inwardness. And the doctors' inability to distinguish between suspected brain damage and extreme psycho-emotional trauma. As one doctor said of Anna, "She's as bad as any of the soldiers I treated who came back from the concentration camps in the Pacific."

When Father Pete wrote back, he offered hope. In his letter, he described the centerpiece of Dr. James Decker Munson's legacy as founder of the hospital:

"No institution is perfect," Father Pete wrote, "but this one has had a philosophy of humane patient care dating back to the 1880s, and it boasts a corps of nurses, trained right here at the hospital, whose dedication and concern for the patients is just superior. Wait until you meet Nancy Brownell, the head nurse, for whom I have the highest regard. You will quickly come to love and admire her very much. Trust me when I say she will take a personal interest in Sister Anna's welfare and hopefully, her recovery. All the nurses will."

Father Pete wrote glowingly of what Lucy could expect were she and Anna to come to the hospital in Traverse City:

"You will be amazed at the beauty of this place. There are hundreds of acres, giant expanses of lawn where patients can stroll at will, hiking trails in the wooded hills to the west, more trees than you can imagine, and until about ten years ago, a huge farm program where supervised patients worked the fields and tended the livestock and greenhouses. There is even a miniature golf course!

"You asked about having a job to help make ends meet. Good news there! I think we can find a way for you to support our ministry here at the hospital. You would certainly be an asset should you come. And I urge you to come!"

When Father Pete gave a glowing account of what Anna's life might be like when treated by mental health professionals in a loving environment, and when he intimated what kind of work and advocacy Lucy could do there—her decision was made. And a huge burden removed.

She would take Sister Anna to the Traverse City State Hospital. She would make sure Anna received the best care, and she would assist in hospital ministry. As "new nuns," she and Anna had purposefully entered into community in Alabama, and they found their ministry there, in the school where they worked and in the struggle for justice in the state. She would likewise enter into community in Traverse City—sadly, by herself this time. But that would be all right. She would be a familiar face to doctors, nurses, and staff throughout the asylum, and she would become a trusted friend to numerous patients who needed love and comfort. She would find her way. She always did.

Chapter 1

ACTIVITIES IN WARD 3 HAD BEGUN BY THE TIME SISTER LUCY GREENE peered through the wire mesh window in the hall door. Patients in various stages of dress paced restlessly back and forth in irregular patterns, while other patients sat in rocking chairs, gazing at nothing in particular. Some patients stood in the doorways to their rooms, peeking this way and that. Attendants in white uniforms mingled with patients throughout the corridor, or stood alone, watching. Nurses scurried here and there helping the older or less able women get dressed for the day or lined up for meds.

Every person on Ward 3—patient or attendant, doctor or nurse—knew Sister Lucy. They noticed how she attended daily to Sister Anna, the careful ways she helped dress her friend, the low songs she sang to ease Anna's suffering. At every visit, Lucy would stop by to visit with two or three other patients "to bring grace and blessings," as she was fond of saying. She also brought lollipops and apples when she visited, judiciously distributing the goodies throughout the ward. Every face brightened when Sister Lucy entered the ward.

The smiling face of Nurse Bennett popped into the window. She was the one who had called about Anna's troubled night. She raised one finger to signal *just a minute*, and then she escorted away two patients who had huddled before the door. She returned to push the door open for Lucy.

Lucy first heard the gravelly voice of Dr. Gordon, a

kindly old gentleman for whom Ward 3 was a routine stop on his daily rounds. He knew each patient better than any other doctor at the hospital knew these women, and, likewise, the patients knew him better than they knew other doctors. He had a special way of gently coaxing even the most obstreperous patient into a modified version of good behavior.

Which was exactly the case this morning when Lucy entered. Dr. Gordon stood just a few feet away, crouching to bring himself eye to eye with a wild-haired, pock-marked woman in her mid-40s who stood before him tearing bits of cardboard in a frenzy of anxiety.

"I just can't take it anymore!" she yelled at him. "They all hate me! And they all want me to be dead! I wish *they* were all dead; they make me so mad!"

"Now, Amanda Lynn, I know just how you feel. Sometimes I feel the same way, like everyone is against me. But then when I calm down, why, I can see better that they don't *all* hate me. Some like me a lot, just like they like you. Don't you want to be calm too? Would you like to feel calm?"

"Yeah, but I don't like that medicine. I don't trust red pills."

Dr. Gordon saw his advantage. He took Amanda Lynn by the hand and led her to the nurses' station, where pills were dispensed.

"Tell you what, Amanda Lynn. If *I* take a red pill, will you take a red pill too? You can trust me, right?"

"Yeah, I can trust you, Dr. G." Her voice had come down a few decibels.

The nurse behind the glass handed Dr. Gordon two paper cups with one red capsule in each and two glasses of water. Keeping one pill for himself, he handed the other to his patient.

Count of three. One, two, three, and into his mouth it went. She studied him for a moment and then popped the pill in her own mouth. They both gulped down their water.

"There now," said Dr. Gordon, "You'll feel better in just a little while. Now, why don't you go back into your room and lie down for a while. I'll come by in a few minutes to play a game of slapjack with you, okay?"

"Okay. Bye, Dr. G. Don't forget the cards."

Amanda Lynn disappeared into her room opposite the nurses' station as Dr. Gordon returned to where Lucy had observed this scene.

He smiled as he approached. He opened his mouth and with one finger worked free a red capsule lodged between his rear lower gum and cheek.

"It's called *tonguing your meds*. Some patients do it when they *pretend* they're taking their meds. Then they spit them out and go about their day unmedicated. Those are the ones we started giving injections to instead of pills. They can't very easily tongue an injection. Amanda Lynn there, she just needed someone to pay her some attention until she could get her anxiety medication to bring her down from her state of high alert. She was indisposed this morning and missed her morning meds, which she usually gets before everyone else—to curb the heebie-jeebies before they become a full-blown anxiety attack. If she doesn't get her medication, well, you can see what we can expect. She'll be fine by the time we whack the first slapjack.

"Now then," he said to Lucy, "Back to rounds. Oh, and by the way, good morning, Sister Lucy."

"Good morning to you, Dr. Gordon. I am amazed at your skills."

"Why, thank you." He turned and opened the door that Lucy had just passed through. She looked out over the activity in the ward.

"Mornin', Sister Lucy," echoed from down the hall as Lucy stepped in. She nodded a friendly smile and waved to each greeter. Nurses were at room doors announcing that it was time for medications. Some women went willingly to the nurses' station; others had to be coaxed. Two or three had to be forcefully escorted by male attendants.

"Nothing's changed with Sister Anna," Nurse Bennett said. "She's resting now. I'm so sorry if my call worried you. She's comfortable now. But it was a hard night. I mean, *hard*." Her smile had faded into a worrisome look as she glanced over her shoulder and looked down the ward toward the nurses' station at the other end. When she looked back, there were tears in her eyes.

"I came right over," Lucy said. "I would come no matter the urgency. You don't have to apologize."

Nurse Bennett, a prim 24-year-old and the youngest nurse on Ward 3, had completed her nursing education program just a short six months ago and was in her probationary period. She wanted more than anything to do the right thing, and to earn the respect of fellow staff. Most importantly, she strove to develop that delicate balance seasoned nurses had between compassionate care and skilled practice.[1] She had been warned that some patients feign

---

1. "Great pains have been taken to instruct the [nurses] in those principles which are deemed of the greatest importance in the care of the insane. The necessity for patience and kindness, for habit of close observation and for personal regard toward each person under their charge,

illness or exaggerate symptoms just to get attention or to play pranks on the newer nurses. Nurse Bennett had been cautioned not to be manipulated, so she constantly had her guard up. New to the daily interactions with women who suffered from a variety of mental conditions, what she lacked in self-confidence she made up for in imaginative mothering.

"I got warm wet towels to put on Sister Anna's forehead, but she threw them off. I tried singing to her and then humming. She tossed and turned and then thrashed all about. So, I just rubbed her hands real gently and sang some more until she got a little calmer. Poor Sister Anna, she just clung to my hand and mumbled over and over something about getting away, but for the life of me I couldn't make it out. I'm sorry, I just couldn't understand her. It was just me and Sandra on duty, and she was trying to calm Alice down in her room, and with the others all yelling and crying, I didn't know for sure what to do. Then Dr. Gordon *finally* got here and gave her something to make her sleep. And I just, I just wanted ... oh Jiminy, Sister. I never had someone so, so ..."

Lucy stepped forward and put a calming hand on the nurse's shoulder.

"You did just fine," she said, "I wouldn't want anyone other than you to be there for her. You'll make a fine nurse. You already are a fine nurse!"

Wiping her eyes, Nurse Bennett let out a long sigh as

---

has been especially dwelt upon. It has been said that the [nurses] are the eyes and hands of the physicians in the care of the insane ... " (James Decker Munson [founder of the Traverse City State Hospital], *Report of the Board of Trustees of the Northern Michigan Asylum at Traverse City*, September 30, 1886, as reported in Heidi Johnson, *Angels in the Architecture* [Detroit: Wayne State University Press, 2001] 77).

she thanked Lucy for her kind words. Then she turned her head and pulled a thumb over her shoulder. She pointed it to the first door on the right.

"Sister, would you mind peeking in at Alice first? She's awfully worried about Anna and you could give her some comfort. She's asked for you since she woke up. We had quite a night here, but Alice was especially upset because of, you know, the baby."

"Of course," said Lucy. "I'll step in right now."

What Lucy liked most about Nurse Bennett was the way she spoke with the women on the ward who suffered from dementia, patients who had little understanding of what they were doing there. Many, like Alice, believed they were still living in their original homes. Some had been committed because they could no longer be trusted to turn off the smoking frying pan on the stove, take their medications, or find their way home if they went for a walk. Their memories decayed; some no longer recognized family who came to visit, while others mistook strangers for their children or husbands.

All nurses treated the ladies with patience and tried to keep them busy with hangman and bingo games, fiber and paper crafts, manicures and hairdos, and television game shows. But not all nurses had the same core belief about how to care for patients whose dementia caused delusions. They were split as to whether or not they should let *truth* enter into their daily interactions with these women.

Some—the sympathetic *truth tellers*— believed that delusions should not be allowed to flourish. So for instance, when a demented woman asks for her husband, she should be told that he had died, and then they should console the grieving widow. If another patient asks to go see her sister

6

across town, she should be reminded that she lives in a state hospital, far from her hometown. Delusions should not be encouraged, they argued at staff meetings. Lying to patients is wrong, they claimed.

Others, however—the sympathetic *truth twisters*—believed they should tell the poor woman her husband is still working in the fields or is at the office and will be home later, and then interest her in some alternative activity. Or if a woman picks up her purse and says she's going to catch the bus to go visit her sister, that nurse might walk with her to a bench outside and wait there until time passed and then announce that the buses have stopped running for the day and it's time to return to the ward. By then, the poor woman would likely have forgotten the purpose for catching the bus in the first place.

For the truth twisters, feelings were more important than facts. Their role was to enter into the emotional world of the patients and validate their feelings from *their* perspective. For them, it was not lying; it was intimate caring.

Lucy was definitely in the camp of the compassionate truth twisters. For her, lying to deluded patients had nothing to do with morality. It was a pragmatic and empathic form of ministry. Fascinated by the imaginative and sympathetic ways she had observed Nurse Bennett talk with Alice, Lucy naturally followed suit.

With Nurse Bennett looking over her shoulder, Lucy peeked into Alice's room. Gray-haired Alice, late 60s, sat on her bed, legs dangling. She wore a beige shift and a blue button-up sweater. A rosy-cheeked baby doll wearing flannel pajamas and wrapped in a small white blanket was cradled in her arms. She looked up at Lucy, a broad smile erupting and bright eyes beaming as Lucy entered. She held up her doll for Lucy to see. Her own broad smile beaming back at Alice, Lucy stepped through the doorway. The nurse followed, stood off to one side.

"Look, Sister," Alice said, "Baby Sally said her first word today. She said 'Mommy'— clear as day. Isn't that something? She's only a baby and she said my name, didn't you, Baby Sally?"

Lucy gave her a thumbs up. "That's just wonderful, Alice. You're such a good mommy. And Baby Sally is such a good little girl. You should be very proud of her."

"I am a good mommy, yes I am," said Alice. "And ... and, I got seven other kids too and they all love me and I love them. They're around here somewhere, I don't know where. Maybe they're playing outside or in the woods. They'll be back for supper, though."

Nurse Bennett pulled on Lucy's arm as she moved easily around her and closer to Alice's side. It was time for medications, she announced. She could bring the baby.

"Where are the other kids?" Alice asked.

Nurse Bennett glanced at Lucy and then at Alice. "Why, they're all at school, Alice. Gone for the day. C'mon, let's get you taken care of, honey."

Alice didn't move. Her feet bobbed from the side of her bed as she turned her face this way and that; a scowl came across her features.

"It was bad last night," she said, "Sister Anna was screaming and that woke up Baby Sally. I tried to find my husband to help out, but he was gone somewhere, I don't know where.

I was calling for my husband—what's his name again?— to go help her."

"Well," Nurse Bennett said in a calm, reassuring tone,

"his name is Paul, and he had to work an extra shift last night. He came home late, darling. Now, let's get along and get your daily meds. Okay?"

"And I'm going to help Anna too," Lucy reassured her. "So, don't you worry about her, okay?"

"Okay," Alice said as she slipped off the bed. She put her doll on her shoulder, patted its back as if to burp it; she followed Nurse Bennett out the door. Lucy stood to one side. As they passed, the nurse gave Lucy a wink, and lips pursed, whispered, "Thank you for giving our girl the kindness she deserves."

"They *all* do," Lucy said as Alice and the nurse turned toward the nurses' station for morning medications. At Anna's room, in the middle of the ward, a stout female attendant named Gina stood like a sentry at the door. Blond-haired and ruddy-faced, she looked Scandinavian. Hired from the local community, attendants went through on-the-job training and then a probationary period at half pay before becoming fully paid employees. The hierarchy on the wards was doctors first, followed by nurses, and then attendants. As an *advocate* at a time when there were no official advocates, Lucy stood outside the pecking order.

Gina had been an attendant since her youngest child graduated high school and went to work delivering for Sears. Her years of raising a brood of five had paid off in her knowing just the right ways to comfort the upset or infirm.

"She had a rough night, Sister. I worked a double shift just to be sure she got good care, but those headaches had her in a real tizzy. When she wasn't throwing up, she was flailing about on her bed. We took away anything she could throw, and I held her down just to protect her from hurting herself. My middle one, Sammy, was like that when his temp hit 104 with the scarlet fever. Held him down for hours, I did, with my husband swathing him with cold towels. All night that one lasted. But he pulled through once he got on the right medicine. That's why I knew what to do. Anyway, Doctor Gordon gave her a sedative and that worked. Thank God she finally slept. I was going to call you after that, but then she calmed down with the medicine, so I didn't. Then I found out Nurse Bennett called you, so that was that. I'm glad you're here. I'm going off shift now."

Lucy handed Gina a chocolate bar she had in her purse. "It's not much," she said, "but it's something you might enjoy on the way home. Thank you, Gina. God bless you. It would have been okay if you would have called me. But no harm done. Go get some rest, dear."

Gina leaned in close and spoke in a low voice. "I heard that they might move her to Hall 5—you know that ward, right? It's for the most disturbed women patients."

"I do, and I hope to persuade someone to not allow that to happen. There must be some other solution."

Gina looked past Lucy and scanned the hall to check on their privacy.

"Maybe there is. Doctor Gordon, last night, he said Dr. Turner knows of a new drug that's getting good results in patients like Sister Anna. I don't remember the name, but we expect Dr. Turner to be here this morning. He's the one who'll decide.

"I'm not supposed to share medical information with anyone," she continued, glancing around again, "but with you it's different."

"Thank you again, Gina. You're a treasure."

Lucy took in this new information soberly. Since her

arrival at the asylum, she had not approved *any* drugs to be administered to her friend. She had done her research—hours spent in the library at Western Michigan University proved to her that no drugs that she knew of could treat trauma. Could a tranquilizer calm an out-of-control patient? Yes, but sedation was not treatment. It was only a temporary symptom reducer. She felt it was a dangerous course—a slippery slope where one medication leads to another—to conflate removal of symptoms with treatment. Could Dr. Turner convince her otherwise? Might he know something different? She was skeptical.

That last question hung in the air as Lucy sat in a chair next to her friend and held her hand in both of hers. She gingerly wiped beads of sweat from Anna's brow and pulled matted strands of brown hair back from her forehead.

Anna was a mere shadow of the athletic, animated young woman she had been just two years ago when she was a teacher at a grade school in Alabama. Then, she could race a gang of elementary kids around the schoolyard and never tire. She had captured the trust and affection of her special needs students through corny jokes that only eight-year-olds could relish. In the classroom, her students cuddled next to her while she read to them, their hands sneaking up to touch her smooth face and stroke her rosy cheeks. None of her students had ever touched white skin before. Anna loved her students as much as a mother would love her own children. Given that Anna (and Lucy) had taken the vow of chastity, this would be the closest she would ever come to having that motherly instinct satisfied.

But now her skin was ashen, and her cheeks shrunken as she had thinned measurably, often refusing to eat or go outdoors for fresh air. Since her arrival, Lucy estimated she had lost twenty pounds. The vivacious animation that once marked her interactions with everyone had now dwindled to an empty stare and occasional hollow monosyllables. Only with Lucy could she muster enough strength to communicate basic needs or respond to rudimentary questions, if at all. Otherwise, she was enveloped in a world of her own.

Patients walking the hall peeked in, waved a little greeting and crossed their lips with a free finger to signal quiet.

Chapter 2

ANNA WAS STILL ASLEEP WHEN DR. TURNER, ASSISTANT MEDICAL SUPER-
intendent and supervisor of all medical staff, appeared on
the ward mid-morning, a stethoscope dangling from his
coat pocket, a clipboard under one arm. Under his white
coat, he always wore crisply starched white shirts with gold
cufflinks and colorful neckties. Sticking out of the breast
pocket of his doctor's coat was a matched Montblanc foun-
tain pen and pencil set that must have set him back a few
hundred dollars. His expensive-looking gold Rolex wristwatch seemed incongruous with someone who earned an
institutional doctor's salary, Lucy thought.

Dr. Turner dressed better than any doctor she knew at
the asylum. He had taste, she thought, and apparently, he
could afford it.

He was on rounds, but he wished to take a few private
moments with Lucy about Anna's "case." Could Sister
Lucy step outside to a bench where they could talk privately? Of course. He escorted her through the halls to a
side entrance. Once outdoors, he pointed to a bench under
one of the giant oak trees that lined the sidewalk leading
toward Cottage 21, where "acute" female patients were
housed.

They sat in silence for a few moments as a line of attendants pushing patients in wheelchairs passed by. The attendants nodded a greeting as each passed; the patients stared
in silence. A small downy woodpecker tapped furiously on a

tree limb directly above them. Amused by the bird's industry, Dr. Turner pointed up and remarked, "We have a lot to learn about tenacity from a character like him," which was mostly lost on Sister Lucy, who had other things on her mind.

"I realize she's not doing so well lately," she began. "The headaches. And the thrashing in the night, probably from vivid dreams. The nurses can't get her to eat a regular meal and I'm afraid I'm not very good at getting food down her either."

Dr. Turner's eyes followed the woodpecker as he sat silent, waiting for Lucy to continue.

"My aunt Jen suffered from migraines," she said. "She lived up the street from us in Kalamazoo, a single woman with a career, but then she had to quit her job when the headaches got so bad, and my mom had her come live with us. I was pretty close to her when she was well, but when the headaches started, it was like she was possessed. She was miserable and so hard to be with when they came on."

"Did *she* get any medical care for them?"

"Yes and no. The doctors gave her a new drug that was called Ergat or something like that."

"Ergot. Technically, ergotamine tartrate. The wonder drug of the 1940s."

Dr. Turner was a walking encyclopedia of pharmaceuticals. He pronounced Latinate terms with precision and pride.

Lucy deferred. "Not in her case. It had no effect on her. I read that Ergot helped some sufferers but not all. In her case, it gave her nausea and vomiting, which only made things worse. Then a new drug came out—DHE it was called. She tried that too, but no luck. Not only did the other side effects continue, but she developed severe diarrhea too."

"Ah, dihydroergotamine mesylate—DHE—it works the same way as Ergot but lacks the dependence factor."

"Well, she didn't stay on it long enough, so that never mattered. She died—of cancer—before she found any relief from the migraines. With Sister Anna, I don't want to see her on daily sedatives; sleeping through her day is just not acceptable. I understand the trade-off one must make between suffering and calm. But a sedative is no cure. It was okay as an emergency precaution last night, given the circumstances, but I cannot allow her to be sedated all the time, if that's what you were considering."

Dr. Turner realized he was not talking with one of his subordinates. Here was a woman, he figured, who did research before coming to a conclusion and who grasped the complexity of medical science. In his experience, medicine—virtually all the sciences for that matter—was primarily a man's world, though increasingly women were being added to the ranks, albeit the lower ones. Thus, the gender discrepancies between nursing schools and medical schools. Sister Lucy struck him as a curiosity—not his equal, to be sure—more as an engaging conversationalist.

His eyes followed the woodpecker as it flew off to another tree across an expanse of grass and bushes. Those eyes alighted on Lucy momentarily, and then glanced at a passing car as he spoke.

"No one believes a sedative is a cure," he began. "But the fact is that your friend is suffering. Sister Anna's pain is causing her great distress, and I'm very sorry about that, but there is a bigger picture here, you see. Her distress is causing problems on the floor. Ward 3 has mostly women who suffer from old age and senility, but they can be riled up easily when there's a commotion. We can't have Sister Anna upsetting others on the floor. That would cause a whole new set of problems. We have to do something about that, I'm sorry to say. It will be like a chain reaction—once one gets started, well, the others start up too. Dr. Gordon suggests we move her to a ward where the staff are more prepared to support her."

"Hall 5?"

He blinked his surprise but then figured she was smart enough to know where the likely transfer *might* be. "We have limited choices," he said, "and we do have to think about *all* our patients on Ward 3." He said this with a pronounced tone of resignation, implying that he didn't want the solution to be Hall 5 either.

"I understand," she said. Determined to remain calm and objective, Lucy looked up at the woodpecker who had returned to the spot above them. She was inspired by the bird's determination to get to those beetle larvae and ants it *knew* were just beyond the bark.

"But there *must* be another way," she said.

"There *is* another option," he said, his voice taking on a more optimistic bent. "I sense you have reservations about medications, and for good reason, given your aunt's experience. But she had migraines, not trauma." He paused long enough for the contrast to settle in. Then, "There *is* a new drug that we might try."

It was unusual that Dr. Turner or any of the asylum doctors would have had this discussion before administering a drug to a patient. Virtually all patients had been committed by family members who signed an agreement allowing the medical staff to make treatment decisions *without* family approval. There were, of course, exceptions, such as when a patient needed a surgical procedure for a life-threatening condition. But by and large, the psychiatrists and medical doctors had free rein over making medical and therapeutic decisions for patients.

"Before we get to the particulars," Dr. Turner began, "I want to emphasize that, as a man of science, I have complete faith in the wonders of modern medicine.[2] We live in a remarkable era of pharmaceutical interventions that, just a decade ago, were unfathomable. Ten years ago, we had just one antipsychotic drug, Thorazine, that was used to treat schizophrenia and associated mental disorders. That one drug revolutionized medical treatment of the mentally ill. Most of those treated with this drug were able to return to their homes and function in their community without the need for further asylum supports."

Sister Lucy sat quietly, listening intently as the doctor gave her a mini-lecture on the accelerated evolution of "wonder drugs"—and she wondered why. Why was he spending so much energy convincing her of the value of treating mental illness with pharmaceuticals? The only thing she could think of was that he had a large amount of ego invested in wonder drugs. After all, miracle drugs *were* increasingly considered the most efficient, most effective way to return the mentally ill to their families and communities, cured, quote unquote. He made a point of

---

2. "I think that the future looks entirely different than it did two years ago: that psychiatry is finally coming of age. But to see patients who were formerly untreatable, within a matter of weeks or months become sane human beings, means that the wall has been breached" (Senate testimony reported in "Wonder Drugs: New Cure for Mental Ills?" *U. S. News & World Report*, June 17, 1955, 78).

saying he was "a man of science." That was curious too. *Of course*, he's a man of science; *all* doctors are. It goes without saying. So why emphasize the point? She found his use of words fascinatingly odd.

Why didn't he just say, "I think we should start Sister Anna on X drug. Monitor for side effects and proceed slowly." That would have been a normal expectation. But he seemed to be going overboard on rationale—and giving her a history lesson to boot.

Sister Lucy thanked him for taking time to explain his views, and she half meant it.

"I understand that Thorazine can cause horrible neurological and emotional side effects like trouble reasoning, severe anxiety, even trouble doing common, everyday tasks. I read that it can rob a person of what makes them a whole thinking human being. It was hailed as the wonder drug of the *1950s*, the alternative to lobotomies even, but … "

Surprised by her informed awareness once again, he interrupted her. "Now, now, Sister. Don't get all upset over that. Trust me, I'm not a fan of Thorazine either, though I have seen some miraculous recoveries when it is administered properly. In fact, most of the reported cases of Thorazine problems stem from overmedicating a patient. Used properly and under controlled conditions, it can be very effective. But rest assured, that is not the treatment I have in mind."

She sensed his condescension when he said, "Now, now," as if she were an agitated child. And his "Don't get all upset over that" sounded suspiciously like "Don't get your dander up because doctor knows best." But she knew the importance of keeping things on a respectful level, for Anna's sake.

This time at least.

"What do you recommend, then?" she asked. Deferential, a neutral tone.

"A trial of a new neuroleptic, just now on the market. It has broad applications for a number of disorders, including reducing the swelling of blood vessels in the brain that cause intense headaches like Sister Anna's. It's called Progrol, and the medical journals are giving it rave reviews. We could begin it today."

Lucy pressed her spine into the back of the bench and raised her legs to stretch them out before her. Dr. Turner sat back too, allowing a moment of silence to capture the thinking time Lucy needed. *Rave reviews* smacked of *wonder drugs*. She could not shake her skepticism any more than she could shake her worry about Anna.

Lucy recalled one day the week before, sitting in the crowded dining hall with Sister Anna when her friend was overcome, for the second time that day, with sudden, head-splitting pain. The headache seemed to come on in seconds. She was sitting there poking a fork at her green beans and the ham Lucy had carefully cut up into bite-sized pieces. She sat upright suddenly and grasped both sides of her head. She pounded one fist on the table and then swept her other arm across the table, knocking plates of food and dinnerware onto the floor. She picked up a plastic glass of milk and threw it at a patient walking by. She fell backward off her chair and hit the back of her head on another table. Attendants rushed over to restrain and secure her as she flailed and began pulling out her hair in clumps. She scratched at her temples until she drew blood. The whole scene transported Lucy back to her childhood when the cries from her suffering Aunt Jen filled the house.

Sister Lucy had never seen such anguish, and she was willing to try anything that might offer relief for her friend. Cautiously, she asked questions.

"This Progrol, has it been researched for people who suffer from trauma? War veterans, for example, or victims of violent crimes?"

"The clinical trials are still ongoing," he said, "but the early results show that Progrol promises to be widely applicable to a range of mental conditions. Like the way aspirin can treat headache, muscle ache, toothaches, even the common cold. Some believe it can even prevent heart attacks. Progrol is being touted as the aspirin of the 1960s!"

Lucy noted that he did not answer her question directly. She asked about side effects.

"That's hard to say," he responded. "Some people have neurological or muscle-related side effects, usually hyperacusis, narcolepsy, or parasomnia. But that's only about 15 percent. We would have to monitor for oxidative stress, you know, check the biomarkers. We wouldn't want to see any negative signs of reactive oxygen species. But, generally speaking, we should see a lessening of the pathogens that cause her suffering as the blood vessels stop swelling and the headaches lessen in intensity."

Lucy glanced at him sideways. Since her aunt's migraines sent her to doctor after doctor—smart young Lucy usually in tow at her mother's side—she had noticed that doctors often used an excess of medical language when they talked to patients. In hindsight, it would be easy to say that they just forgot to translate special knowledge into common language. So when she studied linguistics in college, she thought a lot more about how doctors talk. She began to wonder, *is there more to it than simply forgetting the uneducated person with whom they are talking? And if there is*, she wondered, *what is it?* Could it be that they talk in terms that a layman cannot understand, so they sound very learned? And if so, why?

She noticed that when the patient or family member started to ask questions for which the doctor had no known answer, he was reluctant to say, "I'm stumped by this," or "I don't understand X." Instead, he used medical terms that made people feel inadequate to the occasion. Most people just assume the doctor knows what he's talking about; and the doctor, on his side, just assumes most people trust him for definitive answers. Certainly not indecision—and *never* self-doubt. She couldn't recall a time when anyone she knew challenged a doctor's diagnosis or questioned his knowledge or decisions. She herself had never challenged any doctor.

Lucy had been informally studying doctors' ways of talking for a long time, ever since her aunt's struggle, then in college, and a lot more since Anna's accident. What began as mere curiosity had evolved into a rudimentary theory about how doctors talk, one that involved science, language, ego—and power.

But this was not the time or place to make waves. She had to stay on course.

There were no other options presented. Lucy doubted that other options had even occurred to Dr. Turner. He was, after all, a man of science, and so he only endorsed *scientific* ways to treat illness. Apparently, he didn't put much stock into the "natural treatment options" some people believed in. Other than pray for her friend and comfort her, Lucy didn't know what else to do. But she knew she could *not* do nothing.

She gave her reluctant okay. There was no need to sign anything. The hospital operated on the honor system.

On her way back to Anna's room, Lucy was met at the entrance to Ward 3 by two male patients sitting quietly next to one another on stiff metal chairs. A paper bag sat between their two chairs. They rose as Lucy approached. The older one looked to be in his fifties. He had the rugged lines of age that traversed his face, and bluish veins extending from temple to mid-cheek. He wore thick glasses nestled in round brown frames. Black electrical tape wrapped around the bridge likely kept the glasses from coming apart. When he waved one hand at Lucy, she noticed his fingers were crooked and twisted, and the thumbs curved inward at the joints—two clear signs of crippling arthritis.

The other man looked to be in his mid-forties. Hair the color of a fire engine, it stuck out in every direction as if he had been attacked by a swarm of cowlicks. He kept his fingers busy by licking them and then trying unsuccessfully to pat down a cowlick here, a cowlick there. But he had a broad smile that invited the same, and he rose, as did his companion, as Lucy paused before them.

"Hello," Lucy said.

"Hell ... hello b-back," responded the older man, rising and stretching a gnarled hand in Lucy's direction. "I'm Georgie, and I'm a-a-a weaver." This h-here's m-m-my ... C'mon Harold. S-s-speak for yourself."

He pointed to his companion, who now rose but then tottered a bit on one foot. He righted himself and put out his hand her way.

"Hi, miss. I'm Harold and I'm a weaver too. And a

weaver's assistant (wink at Georgie; a wink back). Pleased to meet you. We been waiting here for someone to come by who's going into Ward 3. We're not allowed to go in ourselves and the attendants won't pay us any mind, so we just waited for someone else to come along. I guess that might be you?"

Lucy found both of them irresistibly charming in odd ways. What they wanted with her, however, was a mystery.

"I suppose that might be me," she said, "depending on what you have in mind. My name is Lucy Greene. I'm sort of an assistant too, on this ward. On all women's wards, actually."

Georgie reached over toward his chair and grabbed the paper sack. He pulled out a gorgeous wool rug that must have measured three by two feet. Solid gray with a bright orange circle that looked like the sun setting on Lake Michigan in late August. All around the edges were orange fringes. Lucy gasped; it was so lovely.

"Where? Did you ... make this?"

Georgie beamed. "I did, miss, but not without help from my weaver assistant Harold here." Georgie held up his gnarled fingers. "I g-got little movement in these old timers any m-m-more, and my eyesight isn't so g-g-good anymore. So Harold here, he's my extra set of eyes and hands. He's my *handyman*. Get it, h-h-hand-ee-man? See, I know how to imagine what a r-r-rug will be like when it's d-d-done. Harold sets up the yarn on the l-l-loom and he keeps t-t-track of the warp and the weft. I can w-w-work the shuttle and the heddle. And the foot pedals."

Harold chimed in. "We're a team, miss. We make rugs, table runners, towels, all sorts of things for people. In the shop, they call us the Weaver brothers. We're kind of proud of that. Sometimes we stitch Weaver Brothers on a weaving, sometimes not. You go around the wards and cottages, you'll see table runners and rugs everywhere. Well, guess where they come from? The weaver's shop, you know, behind the warehouse, over by the paint shop. This here one, it's sort of a cross between a rug and a blanket 'cause it's so thin, the weave I mean. We thought it would be better as a blanket, for some pretty tiny creature."

He winked at Georgie. Georgie winked back.

Lucy's eyes opened wide. "A weaving shop? Here? I didn't know there was such a place! But oh my," she said, running her hand over the smooth warp. "This is just lovely. Georgie, Harold, you do excellent work. Just beautiful. But what ... I mean, why are you sharing all this with me? Do you need something?"

Harold sat back down, stretched his feet out in front. "We figured some kind soul would be by before long and this here rug would find its way into Ward 3. See, we been making things like this for, golly, long as I've been here."

Georgie broke in. "1948, Harold. You and me came t-t-together, same m-m-month in '48." He turned toward Lucy, spoke to her in a low voice, "Harold had a b-bad business l-l-loss and he just fell apart. Depression. Real bad. His wife sent him up here. She don't visit anymore."

"I'm so sorry," Lucy said.

"N-n-no need," Georgie responded. "He's happy now, w-w-well, happier now that he's my hands and he makes beauty. He-he never had beauty in the c-c-c-car business. Me too, for that m-m-matter, since I got that sickness in my brain. Time w-w-was I never stuttered. But that's a long time a-a-ago and I don't ... I don't want to think about then. Besides, I got no family to s-s-speak of anyway.

Harold's like my b-b-brother and my son and my uncle all r-r-rolled into one."

Harold stood again. "And Georgie's like a dad to me, so we get along just swell. But we'd like to ask you to do a favor. See, there's a lady in Ward 3 here, lady we heard from Nurse Bennett needs some cheering up, so since we can't just go in there, it being a women's ward and all, can you give this to, um, what's her name, again, Georgie?"

"Alice s-s-something or other."

"Yeah, Alice, that's it," said Andy. "Nurse Bennett says Alice could use a nice blanket to lay her baby down on, so here it is."

Georgie's outstretched hands held the weaving. Lucy graciously accepted it.

"I know Alice very well," she said, "and I can promise you she will love this beyond anything she can imagine having. Her Baby Sally will love it too, and will sleep on this next to her mother every night. Thank you two, so much!"

Georgie and Harold nodded their appreciation. "Thank you, Lucy Greene," Harold said.

"L-L-Lucy Greene," said Georgie. "That's a n-n-nice name. You're a n-n-nice lady."

The two men started down the hall. Harold turned to look back at Lucy, who stood there feeling the threads of the weaving.

"We'll meet again, Lucy Greene."

"I'm sure we will, Weaver brothers," Lucy said as she knocked on the ward door for permission to enter.

Anna was still asleep. She tucked a sheet under Anna's chin and wiped her brow. She lingered over her long enough to whisper a short prayer. Anna breathed heavily, deep in sleep.

On her way out, she looked in on Alice, who was seated on her bed again. She wore her faded blue nightgown. Her bare legs dangled over the edge of the bed. She stared at the passing clouds outside the window and then turned to look at Lucy. The doll lay face-down on the floor as if it had been tossed there. Alice's stare was hollow; it hinted at no recognition this time. Mucus dripped from her nose and fell on her nightgown. Lucy picked up the doll. She placed it on a pillow on the bed. Alice's eyes followed Lucy's motions, but she didn't otherwise move.

Lucy placed her hand on Alice's shoulder, said she would visit her again tomorrow and bring a special treat for Baby Sally. Alice opened her mouth as if to speak, but no words came out. Lucy leaned into her as she gave the woman a hug. Alice then scooted the doll off her pillow and back onto the floor. She lay down and closed her eyes.

Lucy gently placed the woven blanket next to Alice, retrieved Baby Sally from the floor and laid it on the blanket, which she doubled over the doll next to its mother, as if to keep it warm.

At the door, Lucy looked back. Alice now curled up on her bed in a fetal position, one arm stretched out and covering Baby Sally.

Chapter 3

A<small>T THE CORNER OF</small> E<small>LEVENTH AND</small> E<small>LMWOOD,</small> L<small>UCY PAUSED TO CATCH</small> her breath. The day was unusually humid. Her short red hair sprouted unruly curls that proliferated in humid weather. Five feet tall and a bit chubby by women's magazine standards, she used to think letting her hair grow long would make her look slimmer, like the cute girls in *Seventeen* magazine.

When she entered high school, she let it grow long. But in her sophomore year, when the spring humidity set in, her curls extended laterally in all directions, like electrodes sticking out of those barrels on telephone poles. The kids in English, where they were studying mythology, started calling her Medusa. In the myth, Athena changed Medusa into an ugly monster with snakes for hair. Lucy would have no part of that legacy, although she was attracted to the part where people who stared at Medusa were turned into stone. So, at the ripe age of fifteen, Lucy developed a concentrated stare—she would turn *others* into stone! And she cut her hair short again.

Her hazel eyes looked right through people when she narrowed them in an inquisitive pose. Those same eyes lit up like the lighthouse beacons on Lake Michigan when she laughed. Her stare, she believed, could be a weapon if she used it at just the right time and with just the right duration, and so she practiced in the mirror, squinting this way and that, narrowing them for effect, or opening them wide like an alien in the movies.

As for chubby, she said she didn't care what anyone thought. But a part of her did care, really. It was hard to escape the cultural lie about slim bodies that was beginning to influence teen magazines and that anticipated the "Twiggy" look later in the decade. The other part of her, however, was proud of her body no matter what image the teen magazines put up. Father Pete, her softball coach, told her that her weight helped her batting average: "The few extra pounds are sheer athletic muscle," he said. When she batted .390 in her junior year, Father Pete's assessment sealed it: she had muscle and she was proud of it!

Today, she dressed in the styles of the late 50s—pleated skirt and plain blouse, knee socks and blue canvas shoes for informal wear, though she often wore white anklets and sensible leather shoes for dressier occasions. Her walking gait had a slight skip to it when she was in a hurry. Which was usually the case because there was always so much to do in her job, so many patients to visit and never enough time.

She checked her wristwatch and picked up her pace as she crossed Elmwood Street. Three days had passed since Anna had started on the new medication, and she'd had no return of traumatic symptoms. That was good. But it came with a price: Anna spent most of her day either sleeping in her room or staring at the television in the hall.

Lucy was not pleased. But she was willing to give the new medication a trial period. She hoped the sedating side effects would soon wear off. It was worth the try. She would check in on Anna before she began visiting other patients in the women's cottages. She had a purse full of miniature candy bars and apples to pass out on her "rounds."

The majestic three stories of Building 50 rose before her. She slowed when she saw a commotion unfolding in front of the ornately carved wooden doors of Old Main, the principal entrance to Building 50. Two men stood with their backs to her as she approached. She recognized them both—Dr. Al Turner, Assistant Medical Superintendent; and Mr. Tom Oakes, Director of Community Relations.

Dr. Turner and Mr. Oakes were dramatic opposites in their appearance. Dr. Turner, clean-shaven, tall, handsome some would say, hair stylishly combed back like Dick Clark on American Bandstand, his sport coat and slacks impeccably tailored. On the other hand, Mr. Oakes clearly cared little for outward appearances. His crew cut was sadly grown out and in need of a trim. His glasses continually inched down his nose, which meant he continually pushed them back up. His corduroy slacks (winter had long passed into summer) sagged in the seat, the cuffs hanging over his brown oxfords that hadn't seen shoe polish in months. Turner's body mass suggested athletics, fitness, and three-to-five helpings of vegetables and fruits daily. Oakes' appearance suggested lethargy, hours in a recliner in front of a television, and one too many slices of chocolate cake.

Dr. Turner caught sight of Lucy approaching and waved her over.

"Top o' the morning, Sister," he said, a cheery lilt in his voice.

"Same to you, Dr. Turner."

Tom Oakes said, "Mornin', Sister. On your way to Ward 3?"

"I am, Mr. Oakes. I ..."

Mr. Oakes put up one hand as a stop signal, as if to add emphasis to what he was about to say.

"I would like to get started on that article about you, Sister. Both of you, I mean. I'd like to have that conversation we talked about. When it's comfortable for you, of course."

Before Lucy could respond, the double doors of Old Main exploded open with a loud crash. A tall, wiry male patient who looked to be in his mid-50s burst through. He wore undershirt, underpants, socks and black leather shoes. He stopped, faced Lucy squarely, and, eyes alert as a deer's, put a finger to his lips and said, "Don't!"

Then he let out an eerie laugh and rushed away, heading toward Willow Pond on the Great Lawn.

The three spectators stood speechless. Before any of them could react, the doors sprung open again as two attendants in white garb and three uniformed security guards leapt down the stairs and ran toward the still-laughing, nearly naked man who by now had sprinted past the miniature golf course and splashed his way across the pond. He dashed across Eleventh Street and crossed more lawn before he disappeared into the thick, overgrown brush on the opposite side of Silver Drive.

"What was *that*?" said Mr. Oakes.

"Watch," said Dr. Turner, smiling knowingly. "This won't take long."

Lucy lingered with the two men, her curiosity piqued, her intention to get to Anna momentarily suspended as the drama before her unfolded. The posse of attendants and security guards shot across the lawn, and when they reached Silver Drive, they split up, each taking a different direction in the general vicinity where the patient had disappeared into the tall brush, wide green bushes, and mounds of weeds.

Security cars roared down Eleventh Street and screeched to a halt on Silver Drive. Officers emerged and stood next to their vehicles.

From the field of thick brush, shouts from one pursuer to another went up from various locations, though they themselves were hidden in the overgrowth. The recently arrived security guards stood at the perimeter, smoking cigarettes.

Minutes later, a dirty angular-faced patient now wearing just one white sock and shoe and underclothing—briars and bushy twigs clinging to them—emerged from the brush, two hospital guards escorting him, a firm grasp on both his arms.

Security escorted the patient back toward Building 50. Dr. Turner, Mr. Oakes, and Lucy stood aside as they approached. She recognized the patient—Mr. Frederick, a polite man who attended Sunday mass and who always sat in the front pew. Mr. Frederick slowed the pace of his entourage as he came opposite the trio. He stuck his head in their direction and spoke in an odd, high-pitched but clear voice, "No pills. They make me a stupid zombie! Don't let them! Don't!"[3]

---

3. "It is very hard to describe the effects of this drug and others like it. That is why we use strange words like zombie. In my case, the experience became sheer torture. Different muscles began twitching uncontrollably. My mouth was like very dry cotton no matter how much water I drank. My tongue became all swollen up. My entire body felt like it was being twisted up in contortions inside by some unseen wringer. And my mind became clouded up and slowed down" (From testimony before the U. S. Senate, Committee on the Judiciary, Subcommittee to Investigate

An attendant on either side of him, Mr. Fredericks was led through the heavy wooden doors of Building 50.

As the doors slowly closed behind them, "A stupid zombie!" resounded through open windows as Mr. Frederick yelled it this time. He and his escorts would make their way back to Ward 6, where this time, the patient would get an injection that would sedate him for the rest of the day. He'd be "on watch," in case he had any intention of bolting again.

The excitement over, Lucy excused herself, stepped toward those same doors. Before she entered the building, she paused and turned back to where Mr. Oakes and Dr. Turner stood.

"Yes, Mr. Oakes. About that article, we *should* talk. I've been thinking about that."

Then she turned, disappeared inside.

"Old Frederick," chuckled Dr. Turner, leaning toward Mr. Oakes, "He loves nothing more than to create a scene with his game of escape. All pretty harmless stuff, in my opinion, but it sure causes a ruckus when he does it. Happens every so often. Poor fellow claims he gets these persecution hallucinations, but then it just becomes a game of catch-me-if-you-can."

Mr. Oakes was curious about what he had just heard. "Seems contradictory to me. If he has a persecution complex, why'd he laugh? He seemed to enjoy this little caper."

Dr. Turner smiled. "Trust me, Tom, I'm with these folks every day. I know them better than they know themselves. They're just full of contradictions. If you spend

---

Juvenile Delinquency, *Drugs in Institutions*, 94th Congress, 1st Session, 1975, as reported in Robert Frederick, *Mad in America*, [New York, Basic Books, 2002], 177).

enough time with them, you'd see contradictions right off. Some are straight out insane and totally unpredictable. Others are far more predictable. We have more than three thousand here, no one like the other. Some are almost a delight much of the time—polite to staff, a good sense of humor, helpful, placid, almost normal. Others? Sad to say it, but they tax one's patience with their ornery attitudes and their outright hostility. Chemical interventions have changed everything, thank goodness. We credit the medications for a radical change in the entire dynamic of this institution. Why, it's like a miracle here."

Tom Oakes took out a little pad and pen from his breast pocket. "*It's like a miracle here!* That's a good line. I can use that. I'm sure we can find quite a few patients who fit that bill, don't you think? I like the religious aura of *miracle*."

Dr. Turner patted his colleague's shoulder. "That's why you're the writer and I'm the doctor. I'll find you the miracle patients; you find the miracle words."

Tom Oakes smiled. "I take it Mr. Frederick won't be one of them?"

"You never know," said Dr. Turner. "Let's see what he's like an hour from now."

Chapter 4

Mr. Frederick's "They make me a stupid zombie!" echoed in her mind as Lucy started down the long hallway toward Ward 3. From her left, a door opened suddenly, and a nurse backed out carrying a stack of manila folders and a black notebook. Lucy swerved to avoid her. The nurse pushed the door closed with her foot as she backed into the hall.

It was Nancy Brownell, long-time director of nursing at the state hospital. Nurse Brownell was a stately figure who exuded dignity and deliberation in every stride. Her dark brown hair had streaks of gray; her high cheekbones and simple makeup suggested Lana Turner or Ava Gardner. She had a reputation for winning over even the most oppositional patients—male and female—with her warm eyes, her calm voice, and her captivating smile.

Nancy Brownell, Lucy knew first-hand, was a fierce champion of patients' emotional wellbeing. She had devoted her life to one central principle: Mental illness would never be fully understood, and so it was imperative that comfort, patience, and love be the first line of treatment.[4] Other

---

4. "So many of us [nurses] cared, really cared about our patients and their lives. They were near and dear to our hearts, and although we tried not to take our work home with us, many of us did anyway. I remember one special little old lady named Ruby. ... She just loved to be outside. None of the other attendants wanted to take her out because she was such a handful. But I would ... Ruby would squeeze my hand tight and off we would go. I almost always took her to the same place—the gated area behind Building 50 ... and then just allow her to run around all

34

treatment modalities would come and go with the times or with the latest discovery, but the essential human touch would never lose currency. It was Nurse Brownell herself who was there when Anna was admitted; it was Nurse Brownell who guided Anna to her assigned room in Ward 3; and it was Nurse Brownell who made sure that Anna was greeted with fresh flowers in lovely vases and a welcome card signed by the ward's nurses and attendants and a number of patients. Nancy Brownell, Lucy felt certain, was most certainly a main reason the Traverse City State Hospital had acquired its reputation for humane patient care; it was that reputation that influenced Lucy's decision to bring Anna here.

"Oh my, I'm so sorry," Nancy said, turning abruptly. "Oh my heavens, it's you, Lucy. I could have knocked you over; tells you where *my* mind is today!"

Lucy offered to take some of the load off her hands, but the nurse declined.

"Just dropping these off down the hall; I can do just fine. Come, I'll walk with you. I'm so sorry I wasn't paying attention," she said with a laugh. "I'm rather preoccupied this morning. And, to be honest, a bit distressed."

Lucy asked why. Distressed, Nancy explained, over a new memorandum from the assistant medical superintendent, Dr. Turner, informing staff that there would be a meeting with representatives from some new pharmaceutical company next week. Mandatory attendance for all directors and supervisors. A new line of medicine would be unveiled.

---

she wanted. She just loved that!" (Recollection of Bonnie Witkop Hajek, former nurse, as reported by Heidi Johnson in *Angels in the Architecture* [Detroit: Wayne State University Press, 2001], 163).

"So, why does that distress you?"

Nancy stopped, turned to face Lucy. An attendant pushing a cart full of boxes approached and then hurried past them. He nodded as he went by. Nancy waited until the man was farther down the hall.

"Because of what that means," she continued. "More drugs, *more improved performance*, they will claim, and new regimens. Which means some medicines will be combined with others for better results. I have sat through so many of these briefings, for years now. What is no longer talked about are the natural treatments—art, exercise, games, hobbies, field trips, talk therapy, everything I believe is vital to the wellbeing of so many people—for one simple reason: medications are not for *everyone* here. For some, yes. But so much of what is being presented as *fact* or *proven* is just experimental. And our patients are the ones on whom the experiments are being performed. As an institution, I think we've lost a sense of balance—between the medical and the natural. You've heard me talk about this before, Lucy, so I'm sure my skepticism comes as no surprise. But, you asked, so there you are. I actually feel better having said this to you."

"I know," Lucy returned. "I share your reservations. But you know so much more than I do. It must be very hard, having to find balance."

Nancy stopped before Room 114 and waited as Lucy opened the door for her.

Nancy hesitated.

"Let's have coffee some time, off the grounds. We have … some things to talk about." Her back disappeared as the door closed behind her.

Some things to talk about? Lucy thought. Puzzled, she continued on her way toward Anna's ward.

Halfway to the door at the end of the hall, she approached two attendants swishing wet mops on the tile floor. Each worked his mop from the wall toward the center of the hallway, and they talked to one another as their mops swung from side to side. She knew them both, and she knew their being here *would* delay her yet more.

"That's not the way it happened," muttered Williams, the black man. Six feet tall, with a slight paunch, he sported a thin black mustache and sideburns longer than men his age were not to don for yet a few years. He wore a white T-shirt with the sleeves rolled up into cuffs and white tennis shoes with black laces.

"There were other women before her," Williams said, "At least three or four. They refused to go to the back of the bus."

The white man—Smit—leaned against his mop handle, shaking his head. Of average weight and height, Smit wore his hair parted neatly on one side in the preppy style of the day. Angular facial features and deep blue eyes graced a clean-shaven face and unusual movements of his nose when he joked or feigned ignorance. He wore a hospital white pullover shirt and slacks; his white tennis shoes completed the hospital uniform for attendants.

"No," Smit said. "Rosa Parks was the first one to refuse to move to the colored section on that bus, and she was arrested, and that's what started it all."

By most standards, both men were good-looking and carried themselves with confidence. They disagreed with one another in friendly tones and teasing gestures. When they spoke, it was evident that they had assimilated the language patterns of the educated.

Lucy paused, her eyes darting between the two men. She knew them only by their last names—Williams and Smit—and she'd had one or two brief conversations with them since her arrival. They were recent college graduates, roommates downstate somewhere. They seemed like two bright and articulate fellows, but why they worked at low-level custodial jobs at a state hospital instead of pursuing legitimate careers puzzled her. They seemed always to be together on a job, and they seemed always to be bickering about something or other from history or politics.

They knew her too—just from the way word gets around in the asylum. They knew she and Anna were nuns. They heard that Anna had suffered an accident somewhere in the South, and that the two women had been active in the Civil Rights movement. Something to do with that accident brought Sister Anna here as a patient. Details were as sketchy about Lucy and Anna as were details about their own histories. So it sometimes is in a busy place where everyone is in a hurry to get somewhere, which was usually the case with Lucy. But not so for Smit and Williams, neither of whom had anywhere to rush to.

Both men now leaned on their mop handles and faced her.

"Perfect," said Williams, "You came along at just the right time. Can you spare a minute?"

"Not really, Williams. You see, I ... "

"Only a minute, I promise. Here's the thing. Rosa Parks. And the Montgomery Bus Boycott in '56.

"'55," Smit corrected.

"Mid-1950s then," giving Smit a roll of the eyes. "Was

she the first Negro to refuse to give up her seat, or not? I mean, historical fact."

She put her hand on her chin and gazed at the ceiling, thinking. "I honestly don't know. If there *were* others before Rosa Parks who refused, and if they, too, were arrested, I can't say. But with Rosa Parks, it was different. She went to jail and then she was bailed out. She was the one the newspapers wrote about. That's what I recall anyway."

A broad smile swept across Smit's face. He tossed his head in Williams's direction. "Did you hear that, Barrister Williams? Third party corroborates my version of history."

"Correction, counselor," snapped Williams. "Third party corroborates neither version. She doesn't know." Then, to Lucy, "Rosa Parks is one of our great civil rights heroes. The first one-day bus boycott in Montgomery happened on the day of her trial. We like to rehearse important things like that while we work. It helps to pass the time."

Smit said, "Sorry to take up your valuable time, Sister. Not many people around here would give us the time of day, being attendants and all, not to mention enter into one of our occasional ... disputes."

With a smile and a shake of her head, she said, "I'm happy to help. But I must be on my way."

She glanced from one man to the other and said, "Gentlemen, that is my testimony. Good luck to you in resolving your dispute."

She started on her way again, but Williams glided over toward her, and in a quiet voice as she stopped next to him, said, "Sister Lucy, if there's anything we can do to help, you know, help you with Sister Anna, just say the word. Something she might need to comfort her. Extra blankets, pillows, you name it, we know where to find anything in this place. Same goes for you, whatever you need, we're ... you know, we sorta feel a connection with you and Sister Anna, you know what I'm saying?"

Lucy smiled warmly as her head cocked to one side slightly and her eyes slowly moved from one man to the other—it was the look that said *We do have a connection.*

"I appreciate that," she said, "very much. You're both ... very kind. Knowing I can count on you, that means a lot. Sister Anna and I, we always prided ourselves on our independence. That was bred in us in the convent. But now, well, she needs all the help she can get."

Smit chimed in from his mop. "I've heard about convents, and I've seen a couple I suppose, from a distance. But I never even talked to a nun before I met you," he said. "And, I don't know how to say this, but you're just like *anybody.* I mean, no uniform, and no baubles hanging all over."

Smit had this quirky way of mixing up words to make people laugh. He knew what to say, but part of his personal charm was the way he deliberately made words go wrong. And to underscore his feigned ignorance, he said these things with as straight a face as he could muster.

She laughed again. "It's called a *habit*, not a uniform. And it's a *rosary*, not baubles. My order allowed us to give up the habit—and the hanging rosaries, and the religious titles—fairly recently. Vatican II is changing a lot in the Church. As for my order, we proudly call ourselves the New Nuns. Our ministry is as it always has been, in social justice. That's why I know about Rosa Parks and so many of our other heroes."

"All I can say," Smit remarked, "is you're probably on the path to sainthood. All the time you spend taking care of

Sister Anna. Myself, I'm not religious at all, but I can see how it works for you. I admire that; envy it in some ways."

Lucy's eyes narrowed as she responded. It was the *stern correction look*: "My dear Smit. Caring for Anna is not about religion. It is about friendship. Religion first brought us together, but friendship has kept us together. There's a difference."

A sheepish look spreading across his face, Smit put up both hands as a sort of shield. "Sorry, sister. I didn't mean … well … I didn't mean it that way."

"Anyway," Williams broke in, what he's trying to say is that, we like you, see, and we notice how much you care for every patient here, especially Sister Anna. You're a rare bird, as the saying goes. They ought to have a hundred of you here. Anyway, whatever you need, you can lean on us."

"Yeah, just ask," Smit repeated.

"Thank you both. I will." She was taken by their immodesty, their depth of authenticity. *Who knows*, she thought, *maybe someday I will lean on them.*

The two men returned to swishing the floor. At the door to Ward 3 at the end of the hall, Lucy turned and looked back at them.

She wondered, *why on earth are they working here?*

Chapter 5

Mr. Tom Oakes, Director of Community Relations, had never published anything under his own name other than a letter to the editor in his college newspaper. Yet he remained a dreamer, imagining that one day, a blockbuster piece of his writing would launch a long and lucrative career as a successful writer. He would win awards, he would be reviewed in the best magazines, and he would never again write boring press releases about the rosy happenings at the Traverse City State Hospital. Even better, he would never again ghostwrite medical articles assigned to him by his superior, Dr. Alan Turner, M.D., whose name would be the only one to appear in the bylines.

That blockbuster piece never happened. Instead, life did. Married at thirty, life taught the hard lesson that he had to pay rent, buy food, and support a wife, with a *real* job with a guaranteed income. He and Lenore planned to buy a home, start a family, get a second car, and settle into the small but friendly northern Michigan community by the gorgeous bays off Lake Michigan. The years passed—and, for medical reasons that remained a mystery, no babies arrived, though they kept on trying. They did buy that house and second car, however. Lenore developed a social life in the neighborhood—mostly at her church, where she attended not one but two Sunday services, alone—and she landed a steady job in the admissions office at the community college.

After many attempts, they gave up trying to have children. When she had an affair with a married fellow—who also happened to be her dentist *and* a member of her church congregation—and when Tom's drinking and driving cost him a night in jail, a $100 fine, and probation, he and Lenore divorced. She packed up her Ford and drove away in a haze of blue smoke. She left him the house, the furniture, his books, and the "shitty excuse of a garden that he never could get to grow squat in anyway." That was five years ago, and he never saw her again.

Though he had failed at marriage, Tom still harbored a secret hope for success that a day would come when he would hit the big time—a novel, articles in *The New Yorker*, maybe even a Hollywood screenplay.

Unfortunately, what writers with initiative needed to have in order to do successful freelance work, he seemed to lack—like a keen eye for a fresh angle on a familiar topic, or discovery of a never-before-told story that would capture the minds and hearts of eager readers.

Then he met Lucy Greene in the hospital canteen one day back in late April, where they found themselves sitting next to one another at the counter for lunch. Lucy had let down her usual guard, mentioning "the accident that happened to Anna and me in the South," and "the subsequent events that led them to Traverse City today."

He seized the moment. His curiosity piqued, he asked, politely, "Could I learn more about what happened? What those events were? I'm thinking I could write an article. For a magazine."

She said it was difficult to talk about.

He apologized. "I don't mean to pry," he said, "but yours seems a story that others could learn from. And stories—why a good story can change a person's life. I'm always on the lookout for stories like that. Who knows, maybe it's not a good story, but then again, maybe it is. I don't even know your story other than what you just told me. But maybe it's time someone did. Maybe there would be some good in your telling your story. We could just start with a little conversation. We'll see if it works its way into an article. Will you think about it?"

She would give it some thought, she said. And she did, for many weeks. She was reluctant to tell anyone other than doctors and the intimate few what actually happened to Anna. She needed to protect Anna's privacy. And yet, there was a nagging thought in the back of her head that said the full story *should* be made public. That there was a time and place for telling the truth of one's life so that others hearing their story might, somehow, do some good in the world because of that story.

What she finally decided was that she would hear him out about what kind of "story" he had in mind. It was early June, the day after Mr. Frederick tried to escape, when he called, to ask again, would she consider an interview for "the story"? She gave him a qualified yes—she would see how comfortable she was once they got started.

"What you said, Mr. Oakes, that a good story can change a person's life—that makes sense to me. I grew up in an all-white community. But when I read *Invisible Man* in college, the world of race opened to me in a way that nothing had up to that point. Indeed, stories can bring about change. Maybe ours can too. We shall see."

On a cooler-than-normal June 19, Lucy entered Building

50 from a side door normally used by delivery people. She went up a flight of stairs to the wide hallway on the second floor. As she started down the hall toward Tom Oakes' office, a female patient approached bearing an envelope in one hand. As she walked, she glanced up and down the corridor, as if checking to see if anyone was watching. A matronly woman with long black hair parted in the middle and half hanging in her eyes, she wore a greenish shift under a well-worn brown wool sweater a couple sizes too large. Her thick eyeglasses tilted slightly to the right, begging for an adjustment. As she talked, she waved the envelope at Lucy as if it were a fan.

"This is for the FBI," she said. "I gotta get it off today 'cause it's getting worse all the time in here. Yesterday they took all my sheets away and the day before they put worms in my spaghetti when I wasn't paying attention. All my toothpaste too—gone. The FBI got to know what they do here! It ain't right, ain't right at all. I write them letters every week about it all. You should see what they did to Mrs. Glaussen. Took away her crutches and tossed them in the fire so she's gotta crawl all around on her hands and knees like some kinda critter or something. FBI's gotta do something."

She waved the letter above her head now, like a flag. Lucy looked around for a nurse or an attendant, but the hall was empty.

"I'm sorry ... I," Lucy muttered. "I don't know what I can do. Do you need help?"

"Yeah, I need help all right," the woman said. "I need 'em to give me back my sheets and my toothpaste and stop all their shenanigans. I need the FBI to answer my letters and get me the hell out of this stinkin' place. And Mrs.

Glaussen. Get her out too! But not that snooty Priscilla what's-her-face with all her servants and maids. Thinks she's so high and mighty. She deserves to be kept here forever. In chains, if I had my way. Not us, though. We're the good ones."

"Here!" She thrust the letter toward Lucy. "They won't let me go to the post office place anymore, so you just put this in a mailbox for me, okay? But not here, somewhere out of here where they won't see you. Can't trust a soul, you know. They're always watching, the buggers."

Lucy read the address line: *FBI, Head Quarters, Washington DC.* The return address read *Muriel Putney, Ward 1, Hell, Michigan.* The envelope had a 4-cent stamp on it.

Muriel grunted her way passed Lucy, stomped down the hall, and disappeared through the door that Lucy had just entered. Lucy put the letter in her purse and proceeded to Tom Oakes's office. Since Muriel had entrusted the letter to her, Lucy felt obliged to post it, which she would do later in the day. *A letter a week for who knows how long, and assuredly never a response?* Lucy thought, "Such determination!"

A few minutes later, she stood looking out Mr. Oakes' office window at the expanse of green they called "The Great Lawn," with Willow Lake, a pond actually, on the northeast side. Her hands locked behind her as she rocked from foot to foot, studying the scene before her. The trees had finally leafed out from a longer-than-usual northern Michigan winter. Enamored of birds since she was a child, she spied a pair of mourning doves on an adjoining ledge.

"If I believed in reincarnation," she mused aloud, "I

would come back as a mourning dove. Their colors are so unassuming, their tiny yellow eyes so friendly, and their call—not sad, as some people insist, but peaceful. To me, it's a spiritual bird. In Christianity, you know, the dove symbolizes peace. It symbolizes unfettered faith too. Peace and faith. It's a beautiful creature."

From his seat behind his desk, Tom Oakes stood. He craned his neck to see out the window. "Ah yes, the doves. People up here hunt doves, you know," he said.

Her reverie broken by his comment, she turned toward him. She smiled, perhaps the way a mourning dove might smile, if it could. Her eyes narrowed; it was the *meant-to-embarrass look* for saying something inappropriate or just plain stupid. What deeper truth she was getting at, he clearly missed. His next remark, intended to take some of the focus off his verbal infelicity, only underscored his unfortunate habit of being crass when he should have least intended it. Lenore never lost the opportunity to remind him of *this* shortcoming. Or any of his other shortcomings, for that matter.

"*I* don't hunt them," he said, "but people in these parts do, in the fall."

She sat down on a wooden chair opposite him; the smile faded. She shifted her gaze to the clutter on his desk. The moment passed.

"Okay, then. I'd really like to start from the beginning, if that's okay, and I'd like to record it, so I get the facts straight. If I have to write things down while we talk, I'll miss a lot. Then I'll just have my own faulty memory to rely on. My ex used to chide me for forgetting things." (Were Tom Oakes to tell *his own story*, it would have to include the many times Lenore had accused him of *deliberately* forgetting things. She said his "faulty memory, as you euphemistically claim," came from spite for her personally, or for their marriage—a claim that he denied, until the day he forgot her birthday because he was drunk and hanging out with the boys at Sleder's Tavern, watching the Detroit Lions game.)

"Please, Sister, just start anywhere you want." He switched on the recorder. She reached over and switched it off. A surprised look spread across his face.

"Before I start," she said, "let me say a few things that will help frame what I am about to share with you. I hope you will find a way to work these larger ideas into the story, because they are as important as the tiniest particulars of our journey. You see, Mr. Oakes, our journey to this point has been unusual, if not unique. It is not often that you hear of two women moving to an unfamiliar part of the country, away from family and friends, in order to support human rights. And yet, our order began centuries ago, in Europe, with women who founded hospitals for the indigent, homes for the penniless, and orphanages for the abandoned. They went quietly about their work, their own stories seldom known to the public. *Quiet saints*, Anna called them.[5]

---

5. The Sisters of St. Joseph (S.S.J.) began in France in 1650 by six women whose calling to follow God included serving the needs of the people in their community. Unlike other nuns who lived in cloister, these sisters lived and worked among the people. They came to America in 1830 to better the lives of deaf children in St. Louis. New communities were formed throughout the U.S. A founding community—Nazareth— was located in Kalamazoo, Michigan. The mission of the S.S.J. reads: "Responding to the unmet needs in our church and world, we serve in education, healthcare, pastoral and parish ministry, social work, spiritual care and faith development, and in other ministries that respond to spiritual, social and physical needs." These nuns were among the first to stop wear-

"But the times are changing. Perhaps the stories of women, sadly and too often untold stories, now *must* be made public. I have come to feel I *must* say things that *must* be said—especially about human rights in my small, and yet large, experiences. That, Mr. Oakes, is the covenant of the Sisters of St. Joseph, as it has been since the beginning of the order—speak truth, we believe, and our world will be the better for it."

He feigned a puzzled look, hoping to extract more from her. His expression did not escape her notice. She continued.

"Put another way, I have been made aware, for some time, that women's *real* stories—intensely personal, common, and hidden from public view but often filled with drama and passion nonetheless, seldom make it into the public eye, not their *real* stories anyway. What most people learn about girls and women in the newspapers and magazines are cute things—you see them on television and in movies and in glossy women's magazines. I grew up on them. Those are the women the culture wants us to see and hear about. But those are not real women doing significant work in the real world. Our journey, Anna's and mine, *is* one of real work in the real world. If you are capable of and willing to tell *that* story, then I will grant you permission."

He nodded in agreement. "Yes, I do understand what you expect. You can count on me to honor what you wish."

"All right, then, Mr. Oakes, I can share details of my story with you—*our* story, Anna and me—because, I've come to realize, that is what God expects of us—no matter how much discomfort that truth may arouse in us—that we share so we may help others."

---

ing habits in the 1960s. (https://www.csjoseph.org)

He squirmed. "Yes, Sister. I do understand that. I truly do."

She sat back, silent for a few moments, considering. She had misgivings about trusting this man, about whose character, not to mention whose writing abilities, she knew very little. What could he say that might alleviate her doubt?

She leaned toward him and narrowed her hazel eyes until lines showed up in the corners. It was her *thinking deeply look*.

"Good," she said. "But now, I must ask, why *are* you so interested? Your job is to write public relations pieces here. How we came to be here, our history, seems out of your realm."

"Well," he said, "truth be told, since you mentioned it, I aspire to write for the mass market. I've always had this crazy dream that I would become a famous—well, *somewhat* known—writer. And this job, well don't get me wrong, it's okay, it pays the mortgage and the alimony, but it's not all that exciting or interesting, to be frank. I don't really have free rein to write about things as I see them. I am responsible to the administration here. They write my paycheck and they have, shall we say, certain expectations."

"So, you believe your opportunity as a writer is still ahead of you, Mr. Oakes? Is that what I hear you saying?"

"You're right about that, Sister," he said, a degree of animation entering his voice.

"It's a noble dream, it's a vital dream," she said.

"I believe it is," he said, his voice rising. "Hell, I mean heck, there was a time when I believed I had a shot at being someone who gets paid by the word, someone that others look up to. But then, well, things began to unravel. In my life. Anyway, since my divorce, I'm sort of stuck. Actually,

I was pretty stuck *before* Lenore left. I just thought maybe writing an article that's engaging, that speaks to the times, well, it may just be my ticket to ... something more. Get it accepted into a major magazine. Gosh—that would be amazing, just amazing. I just need the first big break, is all. I just need ... something big."

Tom Oakes judiciously avoided any mention of how his drinking problem had nearly always gotten in the way of getting his ticket to *anything* better. Yet another point Lenore never neglected to make, especially when she gave the lawyer *her* side of things. But, then again, he knew of many famous writers who drank—*and* divorced—*so maybe there's a chance*, he thought, *in spite of that little problem.*

Little was his preferred understatement.

In spite of their differences, Lucy realized they had a connection, she and Tom Oakes. He was a dreamer, like she was, and he had a challenged past too. *His* past was of his *own* making, whereas *hers* was one of being in the wrong place at the wrong time.

She sensed in him the kinship of dreams thwarted.

But his drinking caused doubt about his reliability. She could tell by his reddish eyes, his constant disheveled appearance, his occasional slur. Was it occasional or chronic? While she felt sorry for Tom Oakes, his apparent drinking problem gave her pause about the whole process she was about to engage in. What if he took liberty with the facts? Could he be trusted?

And yet, he seemed an honest man, basically, not one to harm, not one to offend, intentionally anyway. She could clearly see that he *was* stuck. But so are lots of people, many of whom just need a hand sometimes. Who was she to judge? What did Matthew say? *Judge not that ye not be judged.* She had no interest in writing the story herself. It would be hard enough just to recall and relate the details. Pouring over them in draft after draft would only force her to relive that awful experience too many times.

She would help him, then, on the condition that whatever he wrote, she would approve it before he sent it anywhere. If it helped him along on his path toward becoming unstuck, so much the better. If it enfranchised the voices of women who try to bring about change, so much the better too. It was the right thing to do.

Chapter 6

T<small>OM</small> O<small>AKES</small> <small>HAD THE RECORDER RUNNING AGAIN.</small> H<small>E ALSO JOTTED</small> notes on a pad of paper.

"I was named Lucy after St. Lucia," she began. "Saint Lucia was the patron saint of the blind, because her eyes were plucked out when she was martyred. Lucia comes from the Latin word *lux*. *Lux* means light. I like to think that part of my mission in life is to bring things to light, or to bring light into people's lives."

"Well," Mr. Oakes remarked, missing the subtlety of her comment once again, "in my book, you are a bright light!" He laughed heartily. She dropped her eyes to the cross hanging from her neck as she turned it over in her hand; she paused until his laugh dwindled to a slight clearing of the throat.

She continued. She and Anna were both born in 1939 and grew up in Kalamazoo. They attended St. Theresa School, starting together in first grade. Father Pete was the assistant pastor at the time, and St. Theresa was his first parish after ordination. With his soft voice and knack for childish pranks, Father Pete was beloved by all the youngsters. As they moved through the grades, Lucy and Anna found their place among his favorites. Midway through sixth grade, they announced that they intended to become nuns. The two best friends wanted to become missionaries in exotic lands, just like the sisters they read about in religion class.

53

"Father Pete," Lucy said, "suggested that we join the Sisters of St. Joseph, the S.S.J., and go into their convent, right there in Kalamazoo, once we finished high school. After convent, we could go on to Nazareth College outside Kalamazoo, which just happened to have been founded by the Sisters of St. Joseph. It was all laid out before us, and our parents were just thrilled. So we did it all, just like he said."

She explained that the S.S.J. was among the religious orders of the late 50s and early 60s whose social activism anticipated the religious reforms of the Second Vatican Council. That revolutionary council opened the Catholic Church to changes that included dialogue with other religions; the use of English in the Mass instead of Latin; liberalizing of the liturgy; and acceptance of ordinary clothing instead of traditional regalia.[6]

After Lucy and Anna finished their one-year novitiate, they took their perpetual vows of poverty, chastity, and obedience. After convent, they attended Nazareth College, where they earned undergraduate degrees in three years.

Sister Anna's degree was in elementary education, which meant she would be expected to teach every subject, K

6. "In the 1960s, a number of Catholic sisters in the United States abandoned traditional apostolic works within Catholic institutions to experiment with new and often unprecedented kinds of apostolic works among non-Catholics. ... Calling themselves 'new nuns,' such sisters ... joined outreach ministries on public university campuses, counseled drug addicts in addiction recovery programs, assisted labor organizers working to unionize migrant farm workers, tutored adult residents of public housing projects to pass high school equivalency exams, to name just a few examples of these 'new works' (as sisters called them)"(Amy Koehlinger. *The New Nuns: Racial and Religious Reform in the 1960s* [Cambridge, MA: Harvard University Press, 2007], 2).

through 6. "She loved becoming a teacher," Lucy said. "Little kids kept her young at heart, she told me. She said her favorite class was recess because then she could join in the Red Rover and jump rope games, and she could screech like a six-year-old when she zoomed down the playground slide. No one loved children more than Anna."

More the intellectual, Sister Lucy majored in sociology and minored in linguistics. In her linguistics course work, she became particularly interested in a new field called sociolinguistics, which was the study of how language is used in society. She was fascinated to learn how understanding people's use of language illuminates gender, race, culture, class, and interpersonal relations. Sociolinguistics made her a more attentive listener and a more deliberate observer of human interactions. She felt sure that her sociology and linguistics background would prove invaluable. Her plan was to use her degree to better humanity in the secular world, perhaps as a guidance counselor, policy analyst, or even a lawyer.

"The world floats on a sea of talk," she said, "Understanding how that talk works seemed to me to be a supreme investment in understanding people—and power."

Anna and Lucy remained the best of friends whose faith bestowed upon them a strength of character and determination to do right in the world. As Sisters of St. Joseph, they embodied a time-honored tradition going back to the seventeenth century, a tradition that, in America, included nuns serving as nurses in the American Civil War, becoming fierce opponents of the death penalty, and providing care for the sick and infirm. Social justice and non-violent protest had always been the political cornerstones of the order.

While the two women shared the same religious and

political beliefs, they had very different personalities. Where Anna was outgoing and gregarious, Lucy tended toward inward reflection. Where Anna never missed an opportunity to express her opinion—even before thinking of what she would say—Lucy took in all manner of information before offering a thoughtfully considered perspective. Anna, the carefree life of the party even in the stoic halls of the convent; Lucy, the organizer of the party, the one who made lists and planned. Anna, doer; Lucy, thinker.

Sister Anna never hesitated to offer her opinion that, "Lucy is the stronger one; she's a pillar; she's the one I lean on. I'm not sure I ever would have made it through convent were it not for her. She has a faith that knows no depth. I admire her beyond belief."

At the same time, Lucy would say of her friend, "Anna is *my* strength. She's always getting me to be more spontaneous. She would say, 'Don't think about it anymore; let's just get going,' and I would say, 'Wait. Count to fifty. Sleep on it. Life is long. Give it time.'"

When they finished college in the spring of 1961, Lucy and Anna were not certain just what they were to do, though they both felt called to support the growing civil rights movement in the South.

"God called us," she explained to Mr. Oakes, "and that was that. Unfortunately, God didn't guarantee a source of income." Anna figured the fastest way to assure employment was to teach school. Lucy wasn't prepared to take a teaching position, but she suspected she could talk her way into some legitimate job in a Catholic school.

"We figured we would spend our weekdays with children

in classrooms, but then evenings and weekends, we could support the movement locally. You know, food banks, protests, marches, sit-ins.

"So, we made some calls to a few parish schools in Mississippi and Alabama, and found out that they were hiring in the Negro Catholic School System in Montgomery. We were interviewed on the phone and offered jobs on the spot. God answered our prayers! And so, we packed up my Chevy and headed south. Anna sang kids' songs all the way to Indianapolis. I was pretty sick of 'Wheels on the Bus' and 'If You're Happy and You Know It,' but life was stretching long and golden before us, and her songs just made the trip even more precious."

In August 1961, the two arrived in Montgomery, one of those flashpoints in the south where the civil rights movement first gained momentum with the Montgomery Bus Boycott in the mid-50s. In keeping with the historical mission of the S.S.J., Lucy and Anna integrated themselves into the Negro community in Montgomery by applying their teaching skills at St. Martin DePorres School. Lucy served as a reading resource aide while Sister Anna had her own second grade classroom. They were paid starting salaries. They got by through frugal living, and they found daily renewal through Anna's upbeat *We may* aphorisms: "We may have holes in the soles of our shoes," she was fond of saying, "but the fresh air keeps our socks from smelling." For Anna, life was always about seeing the glass as half full: "We may have a flat tire, but the other three work just fine!"

"It helped to have taken a vow of poverty," Lucy said, chuckling. "In our religious training, we learned how to live on little and that made us want for naught. Except for popsicles, with which we both rewarded ourselves, in abundance, as often as we could."

Beloved by their Negro students for their kindness and cheery dispositions, the sisters quickly found the meaningfulness they sought when they had joined the order years before. What they did throughout the week *mattered*—to their pupils, to their pupils' families, and to themselves. What they did on weekends mattered too: they volunteered at a food bank and they participated in marches.

"Our lives were good," Lucy said, "and we were confident that we were doing the right things. So we volunteered to take part in a Freedom Ride ... and then ... everything changed."

Tom sat up straighter. "Changed? How so?"

Lucy stood, walked back to the window. A mourning dove perched on the concrete windowsill outside. It craned its neck and stared in the window.

Her back to Tom Oakes, she spoke. "Mr. Oakes, I'm afraid we will have to continue this conversation at another time. I ... hope you can understand ... I *will* tell you about what happened next, but just not now. It's ... difficult. I hope you can understand."

She turned to look at him. Tears welled up in her eyes.

He turned off the recorder.

"Of course," he said. "Whenever it's comfortable for you. There's no hurry."

"Thank you. Now I must go. Please, don't get up. I will be fine."

She closed the door behind herself. Wiping sweat from

his brow, he hunched over his pad of paper and began sum-
marizing his notes.

Damn! he wrote. *This is the story I've been waiting for!
This could sell!*

Chapter 7

June 21. Tom Oakes sat at his desk. The headache he had treated with aspirin since getting up that morning had eased enough for him to think more clearly about the work ahead of him that day. He swore he would not have whiskey and pretzels for dinner again tonight. He promised that he would cook up a square meal and eat it *before* pouring his first drink of the evening. That, of course, would exclude the drinks he depended on regularly throughout the day. He had divided his drinking routines into three groups—mornings (light), afternoons (less light), and evening (unpredictable and dependent on circumstances).

Did *he* think he drank too much? Lenore said that was why she left him. He said he drank *because of* her—but when she finally admitted having an affair with that dentist, divorce court was inevitable. For Tom, drinking *too much* was a relative question, relative to how much he liked the taste of whiskey and relative to how much he needed in order to deal with the stress of life in general, divorce notwithstanding. The reason he sucked on Neccos or Smith Brothers Cough Drops all the time was to cover up the smell of whiskey that otherwise would have followed him everywhere.

That said, since he had become a bachelor again five years ago, he had a modest but sufficient income, even with the alimony payments, and employment that didn't ask much of him. His job was not exactly a thinking man's job.

In the monthly hospital newsletter (*The Hospital Organ*) he produced on a ditto machine, he wrote as he was directed—ceremonial events at the institution; anecdotal accounts of patients' acts of kindness in the community or community acts of kindness for the patients; historical pieces on some nurse or doctor who gave their all to the institution.[7] Some of these pieces he revised and sent to the local paper, which, when they appeared in print, reinforced the image of good relations between the asylum and the town. The occasional murder, suicide, assault, or theft at the asylum would never be mentioned.

Then there were the notes Dr. Turner would send him for a longer piece he wanted to appear in, say, the Detroit or Chicago dailies. Things that made the hospital look good, like patients who beat the odds and returned to their homes "cured." Or a historical piece on a dedicated nurse who worked tirelessly to save the life of a young tuberculosis victim, only to have the poor nurse contract tuberculosis herself and die, in an ironic twist of fate. Tom liked ironic twists.

Occasionally, Dr. Turner directed him to write up a more serious article for one of the medical journals. Dr. Turner would provide some notes and Tom would compose a draft. Dr. Turner's name went on as author, while

---

7. "[As for] material that appear[s] in the house organ, [there is] 'local news.' This includes reports about recent institutional ceremonies, as well as reference to 'personal' events, such as birthdays, promotions, trips, and … deaths. This content is of a highly congratulatory or condolence-offering character, presumably expressing for the whole institution its sympathetic concern for the lives of the individual members" (Erving Goffman, *Asylums: Essays on the Social Situation of Mental Patients and Other Inmates.* (New Brunswick: Aldine Transaction, 1961 and 2007).

Tom's went on as assistant to the author, if it was mentioned at all, which was seldom the case.

So, there he was, a pack of Neccos on his desk, when an asylum courier dropped off a mailer sent over from Dr. Turner. Tom glanced through the typed cover note:

Tom,

I'm thinking about a piece for the Journal of Psychiatry, *not a research article, per se, but more of a commentary on a promising approach to treating mental illness with pharmaceutical intervention.*

I'm thinking the introduction would highlight a patient who arrived here (I have some notes on him below) a year ago with severe schizophrenia (pseudonym JB) and who, after medical intervention, is now able to be released. The body of the article will review a new pharmacological regimen for schizophrenia that we ourselves have pioneered here at the hospital. This drug (Progrol) is fairly new, but no longer considered by some to be experimental. Our focus in on the frequency of the recommended dosage, which is more intense than what the pharmacological industry advises. I'd like the tone to be 98% objective, like "this is to inform you that this new drug, Progrol, and this new procedure, etc.," and then work your charms on that message to underscore that there are serious minds at work here, cutting-edge things going on. Our work with Progrol is but one example. In other words, temper the zeal in this one because the journal will want the piece to sound scientific; it should ring of calm certainty with just a hint of excitement (the 2%).

I will add a cover letter that suggests they consider the

article as a commentary, and put it at the front of the journal, like an editorial. Then we won't be held to the stricter standards required of an authentic scientific article. More journalistic, less academic. Though many readers will give it scientific credibility just because it appears in the Journal of Psychiatry.

Here are my notes and some informational materials on Progol. I'd like to get this cranked out in the next week or so.

Tom sat back in his swivel chair and thumbed through the pages of handwritten notes Dr. Turner had provided. It was another wonder drug article, pretty much the same as the others he'd ghostwritten for his boss. He reached into the bottom drawer of his desk and pulled out a flask of whiskey. He poured a shot into his half-full coffee cup and swirled it around.

He remembered his undergraduate days when he would ghostwrite term papers for football players. They'd supply a handful of ideas, maybe even rough notes, and he would fashion an essay. He'd make it sound like the guy knew what he was talking about; throw in a few references; add a few academic turns of phrase, like "It seems to this writer that" and "When considered through the lens of history"; and put it all in proper grammar, making liberal use of such locutions as "with which" and "as it were." For a few extra dollars, he would put in a few sentences connected by semicolons. Those never failed to impress.

He got so good at writing term papers that he could turn out the short ones out in a couple of hours and the longish ones on a Saturday. He ran a good underground business and made a lot of friends in the athletic department. And enough money to pay the next semester's tuition and buy a round of beers for his friends on a Saturday night out.

So, it was no surprise that Tom Oakes could ghostwrite for Dr. Turner and not complain about it. He had used his God-given skills honed in college and applied them to this job. That little industry he had going back in college was one that could have gotten him in big trouble had he been found out. Not so with this one: Here he was considered a legitimate collaborator whose role in the article was acknowledged. Occasionally. At college, he was underground. Here he was professional. Sort of.

He put a piece of white paper into his IBM Selectric and wrote back to Dr. Turner, expressing his enthusiasm for the project and his likely timetable for getting a draft to him by week's end. He stuck the note in an interoffice envelope and dropped it in the mailbox down the hall. He glanced at his watch. Where had the morning gone? It was already time for a morning stroll around the grounds for some fresh air.

He stopped at the canteen for a chocolate donut and take-out coffee, made his way over to the little cluster of tree stumps beside Men's Cottage 24. There he sat sipping coffee and munching the donut when Sister Lucy emerged from the front door of the men's infirmary. She slowly stepped down the wide stairwell and picked up her bicycle from the tree where she had leaned it. She turned in the direction of where Tom Oakes sat. She pedaled toward him. He waved her over when she approached Blue Drive. Smiling and waving back, she crossed the street.

A car sped by, sounded its horn. She turned to look. The driver waved at her and at Tom, but Lucy didn't recognize him. She wheeled her bike across the grass and lay it down on its side.

"Who was that?" she asked.

"Dr. Turner," Tom said. "Nice car, eh? He just got it last week."

She watched as the shiny new car made its way around the corner and onto Silver Drive. "Yes ... it ... is," she said, slowly.

Tom rose, unfolded a handkerchief, and dusted off one of the large wooden stumps.

"Hello, Sister, care to have a seat? I still have half a chocolate donut I'm willing to share."

She sat down, stretched her legs out before her.

"Yes on the seat, Mr. Oakes. No thank you on the donut."

"Suit yourself. Nice to see you again. What brings you to the men's infirmary today?"

"My work. I try to make it to the men's and women's infirmaries at least twice a week. To see who needs comfort, or magazines, fruit, or just someone to hold their hand. Sometimes a patient asks for Father Pete to bring communion to them, so then I'm the messenger if he cannot take it. Sometimes I pray with a patient. It's all part of the mission here, the work."

Tom turned to her, his interest in "the work" starting to pique. "You know, Sister, I would really like to write up the piece about you and Sister Anna. Are you any more able to continue the interview we started?"

Lucy didn't respond. She had a troubled look when she said she had other, more pressing things on her mind.

"What sort of pressing things?"

"It's Sister Anna. Until recently, she was causing quite a stir in her ward. Losing self-control and then having to be restrained. I felt so helpless. So, I agreed to trying a new medication. At first, I was hopeful about the drug. Skeptical, but hopeful. She has suffered so much, I just had to try something. But it makes her sleep most of the day, or she just sits and stares at the television when she *is* awake. I can't get a rise out of her, no matter what I try. This Progrol just puts her in a drowsy state. But if they take it away, they say the headaches and oppositional behaviors will return. It's a lose-lose situation right now and I don't know what to do."

Tom sensed the contradiction. "Well," he said, "it sounds like the medication does work. She doesn't get the headaches or the behaviors when she's on it, right?"

"That's the point. We have to choose between her having this unbelievable pain but being conscious, versus her not having the pain because she's almost unconscious."

"Wait. I'm sorry," Tom Oakes said. "Did you say Progrol? Is that what they're giving her?"

"Yes. Why?"

"For headaches?"

"Yes, but not normal headaches. These are like migraines. Worse."

Tom scratched his temple. "I didn't know she was schizophrenic."

"No one ever said she was schizophrenic. Did someone tell you that?"

"Well, I may be wrong," Tom said. "But Dr. Turner told me about a new drug that's used to treat schizophrenia, and I swear he called it Progrol. No, I'm sure of it. I remember seeing that name in the notes."

"Notes?"

"For an article he's—we're—writing. For a medical journal. I've ghostwritten articles like this one for him. For newspapers, magazines, and medical periodicals that go to other doctors and hospital administrators. He's considered quite an authority, you know. For this article, he's developed a new regimen for administering that very medication. He wants to share this development with the medical community. He says that Progrol is used to treat a wide range of conditions, including severe headaches, and the rest. But when I read about Progrol in the materials, I recall that it was targeted toward reducing hallucinations and delusions associated with schizophrenia.

Lucy stared at him, or rather, through him. Thinking.

"That was never discussed with me," she said. "This specific treatment for schizophrenia, it was never mentioned."

Whoa, thought Tom Oakes. *I'd best be careful here.*

He said, "Heck. On second thought, maybe I'm wrong about that medication. I'll have to check. You know, I'm no doctor, so I ought not talk about what I really don't know. I'm just the ghostwriter—you know, don't dangle the infinitives, make sure there's subject-verb agreement in those longish sentences he prefers, that sort of thing. Basically, he gives me the core ideas and what to say about them, and I put the right words in the right order." Sister Lucy sat quietly, taking in what sounded like deliberate equivocation: *I don't make the news, I just report it.* But she was puzzled—and troubled by what she heard. Why would Dr. Turner prescribe a medication that was expressly used to treat schizophrenia? Heaven forbid that he was experimenting with the drug on Anna. No, she couldn't believe something like that. There must be a logical reason.

She didn't share any of these thoughts with Tom Oakes. But she did intend to get to the truth, and she had an inkling how that might happen.

She said, "I think it's time we continued that conversation. About our history."

"Great," he said, surprised at her sudden eagerness.

"But there's one thing I need from you," she said, "in exchange for my telling you the rest of our story."

He cocked his head in surprise. "Oh?"

"I'll tell you what that is when we get together."

They arranged to meet in his office as soon as she finished visiting the women's infirmary. Tom Oakes ate the last piece of his donut, brushed the crumbs off his lap and headed back to his office, where he waited for Sister Lucy.

Chapter 8

"I BELIEVE I LEFT OFF WITH THE FREEDOM RIDERS," LUCY SAID.[8]

"You did," he said, switching on the recorder. "Please, continue."

In mid-October, they had taken a bus to Plainfield, a small town about a hundred miles from their home in Montgomery. There they joined a group of blacks and whites who were to travel back to Montgomery on a chartered Trailways. The Freedom Riders intended to challenge local laws that enforced racial segregation in bus seating. The Freedom Riders' strategy was to have one interracial pair sit in a front seat, while one Negro rider would sit in an adjoining front seat normally reserved for white customers. Sister Anna volunteered to sit next to a Negro man on a seat in the front of the bus. Sister Lucy joined other riders sitting toward the middle and back of the bus.

The bus was attacked at the Plainfield bus station by a white mob. It was unsuccessfully firebombed, and a tire was slashed, but the driver managed to get the bus a few

---

8. Freedom Riders were groups of white and African-American civil rights activists who participated in Freedom Rides, bus trips through the American South in 1961 to protest segregated bus terminals. Freedom Riders tried to use "whites-only" restrooms and lunch counters at bus stations in Alabama, South Carolina and other Southern states. The groups were confronted by arresting police officers—as well as horrific violence from white protestors—along their routes, but also drew international attention to their cause (Accessed November 15, 2019, https://www.history.com/topics/black-history/freedom-rides).

miles out of town before they were set upon again. On a remote stretch of rural road, a caravan of cars loaded with angry white men forced the bus to pull over. In minutes, the mob, many holding bats, chains, and canes, surrounded the bus, shouting obscenities and jeers. They forced their way in by prying open the front door. Up and down the aisle they paced, slapping one person here, spitting on another there, swinging their weapons wildly in the air. Pandemonium erupted as passengers were pulled from their seats and beaten, especially whites, who were seen as traitors to the white race.

Sister Lucy suffered bruises to her arms and legs, and a small laceration behind her left ear where her attacker hit her with a chain. Once the carnage began, she fell to the floor, crawled under a seat, and put her hands over her head to protect herself.

She lost track of Sister Anna.

"I remember calling for Anna, but there was so much screaming, so many people hurt, my voice was drowned out in the melee. I feared getting up and getting beaten again. I just called and called, but she didn't answer."

Unlike the last time she sat with Tom telling her story, now she was calm, as if she had rehearsed the entire scenario, which she had many times—for the FBI, the doctors and nurses at the hospital in Montgomery, the sisters in the Michigan convent, her parents, and Sister Anna's family.

Eyes closed, she told about the next part slowly, as if it were a movie. Her speech moved at a cadence that resembled frame-by-frame viewing.

"I ... we ... tumbled ... out ... of the bus ... and ... discovered that Anna had been dragged from the bus and beaten."

Fifty yards from the bus, Anna was unconscious, battered from head to toe, and bleeding from blows to her temple and the top of her skull. Someone covered her with a blanket and others carried her into one of the ambulances that showed up, eventually. All the way to the hospital, tears streaming and mixing in with blood on her own face, Lucy cradled Anna's head in her hands as she rocked her and sang "Ave Maria."

Slowly, painfully, it all came out. Lucy learned the particulars of what happened from Anna, hours later from her hospital bed, where Anna could barely manage a whisper. Two men had dragged her to a cluster of tall bushes some distance from the bus. One tore off her skirt while the other towered over her, the butt of a baseball bat pressed into her neck. They had chains and canes too.

"They beat me with the bat," Anna muttered, "And they hurt me, here," pointing to her groin. She could not bring herself to say "raped."

"She was violated," Lucy said. "By both men, one after the other. Anna told me, later, that she was conscious during the assault, but she pretended to be unconscious. She was terrified that they would kill her if she resisted. *Don't fight me, bitch, or I'll cut your goddam throat*, she repeated, as if in a dream.

"All the while she lay there in the bushes," she told me, "the worst part was hearing them laugh as they talked about killing her. One said that they should kill her 'to teach the niggers a lesson about minglin' with white women.'"

Lucy's eyes welled up and her voice trailed off, as she massaged the cross she held in her fingers.

"She would have been better off unconscious," she said. "At least then she wouldn't remember. Now she will never forget."

"I knew then that she would never be all right. Even if she recovered from the physical wounds, I feared the psychological ones would prevail. My life—our lives—would never be the same. That I knew for certain."

Tom Oakes shook his head; disbelief clashed with anguish.

He asked, "Did she suffer brain damage?"

"The doctors thought so," said Lucy. "But she had suffered so much, mentally and emotionally, that they said it would be difficult to separate brain damage from trauma. In the end, how can you separate her brain from her spirit? Her physical injuries were severe, but she suffered mental injuries that were more severe. Perhaps it's best to say that what those men did destroyed her *mind*—so talking about brain and spirit seems useless."

Lucy turned toward the window and stared in silence as her last words lingered in the air between them. Then she turned sideways to look directly into Tom Oakes' eyes.

"Our lives changed irreversibly that day," she said. "Our faith was tested, but I can only speak for myself when I say *my* faith passed the test. I had always been told that God works in mysterious ways, that even the worst tragedies can have purpose. I clung to that belief, that faith that some call *blind*. I wish I could say as much for Anna. Her faith in God had always been as strong as mine, and we both leaned on that through thick and thin. But then, one day a few weeks after the attack, she told me that God had forsaken her. That's what Jesus said on the cross, you know, at his most vulnerable moment. Then she said that God had taken away her words."

"What a strange thing to ... " Tom started to say, but stopped mid-sentence.

Lucy's eyes fixed on her hands folded demurely in her lap. She smoothed the wrinkles in her blue skirt. She adjusted the yellow silk scarf she wore around her neck. She stared at the floor.

She told how Anna never again spoke more than a muted monosyllable at a time. Occasionally, she would pull Lucy's ear close to her mouth as she would attempt to say things in a slight whisper. Lucy struggled to make sense of what Anna would say to her at those times. It was as if she *had* to say something, but she just couldn't get it out.

"She seems to be engaged in a great war within herself, between letting out her anguish through talking about it and keeping it sealed inside no matter how great the pain."

Here at the hospital, Lucy explained, when others are near, Anna will stare, wide-eyed, as if something terrible could happen at any moment. A slammed door, a loud voice, any intrusive noise or motion, will frighten her. There are sudden outbursts too. If someone drops a tray full of dishes in the dining hall, Anna could spring up and run to a corner, hands pressing around her head as if to protect herself. There, she'll shiver and whimper until nurses calm her down with caresses and soothing words. If the normal bickering of two women on the ward escalates into angry shouts and accusations, Anna will often fall to the floor, curl into a fetal position and cup her hands over her ears to block out their voices.

"Sometimes she'll scream to block out the others' shouts.

There's a violence in her mind that she cannot escape from," Lucy said. "There was a time when she had faith, when she would thank God for His gifts to her. I can't tell if she prays any longer. Who can peer into the heart of a broken human being? I'm convinced that the evil she experienced that day destroyed her utterly. She just ... gave up."

Tom Oakes sat there shaking his head. He said nothing. He couldn't even take notes.

Lucy continued.

Often, she would find Anna sitting perfectly still, eyes closed, hands shaking—as if the Plainfield attack were playing over and over in her mind. The headaches and behavior outbursts at the hospital even occurred without provocation. Did they indicate brain damage or trauma? Like the doctors in Montgomery, the hospital doctors here could not be sure which was which. Eventually, it really didn't matter, though Dr. Turner was of the medical opinion what she suffered was, in fact, trauma, not brain damage. That's why he believed a chemical solution would benefit her. Dr. Gordon, who saw Anna daily on the floor and knew her better than any doctor there, would not comment on a diagnosis; he kept his opinion to himself as he deferred to the medical view held by his superior, Dr. Turner.

Listening intently, Tom wondered to himself how a benevolent God could allow such brutality to befall such innocence. It was yet one more reason he had become a non-believer long ago. *It's a godless world we live in*, he used to say to Lenore, whenever she complained that he never went with her to church anymore. *How could I worship a god who could allow the Black Plague, the Holocaust, or the bombing of Hiroshima and Nagasaki?* His religious skepticism, which became outright atheism once Lenore moved out, was yet one more reason why she left him. Aside from his drinking and his lack of investment in the marriage itself, his rejection of her religious piety (betrayed by her infidelity anyway) finally drove her away.

"We spent two weeks in a Montgomery hospital," she said, "until it became clear there was nothing they could do once the physical scars had begun to heal, and the broken bones were casted. Then, in November, I moved Anna back to the convent in Kalamazoo. Doctors at Sparrow Hospital took over her care on an outpatient basis.

"We stayed in Kalamazoo for a year and a half, at the convent. Everyone tried to help her regain her mental stability, but that proved too difficult to manage without professional help. Anna needed the support of medical professionals and a community where she would be cared for around the clock. Returning to her parents' home was out of the question because her parents were now in their 70s and not in good health themselves. After meeting with the family attorney, it was suggested that I assume the role of guardian for Anna.

"Of course, I agreed. And now, being her guardian has become my mission."

But becoming her guardian did not solve the problem of finding a suitable home for her friend—who was now her *ward*. She called St. Theresa's, her old parish, to ask Father Pete's advice. He was no longer at the parish, she was told. He'd been transferred to Traverse City, where the bishop had assigned him to be the assistant to Father Fred, the chaplain at the state hospital there.

In the spring of 1963, Lucy got Father Pete on the phone and told him their story. Through a long phone conversation, she learned that he and Father Fred had convinced the hospital administration that a chapel to serve *every* faith tradition was vital for Father Fred to continue his ecumenical ministry to *all* patients—Catholic, Protestant, Jewish, or atheist—and to link the hospital population with the community surrounding it. His intent was to bring together the patient population and the townspeople in common worship. With that grand vision, the new All Faiths Chapel was approved for construction, and Father Pete's work as assistant chaplain grew proportionally. It was clear that he and Father Fred would need help.

"'You happened along at just the right time,' Father Pete told me. 'God must have sent you my way! Bring Sister Anna here,' he said. 'The hospital is overpopulated and has a waiting list, but I'll see what I can do for two of my favorite students.'

"Father Pete gave me hope," Lucy said, "when I was beginning to lose hope."

"The problem is merely an economic one," Father Pete told her. "We just need money to support a part-time assistant-to-the-chaplain position. We need a small miracle, and I know just the person to work it."

A man of great empathy and immeasurable kindness, Father Pete pulled a few strings with Mrs. Dorman, administrative assistant to the hospital finance director. With a well-earned reputation for colorful language and administrative cunning, Mrs. Dorman said she would like nothing better than to oblige Father Pete, and it would not be conditional, but if "he could find his way to consign my annoying and self-serving sister-in-law RoseMarie to a cloistered nunnery somewhere in New Guinea, I would much appreciate it."

Father Pete agreed to take her request "under consideration, no promises made." She agreed to "cook the books" and get the finance director to sign off.

Within a day, Mrs. Dorman called Father Pete back to give the good news: Money would be forthcoming from the operating budget for a part-time assistant to the resident chaplain. Don't ask how. Then she added, "Though I was hoping to be saying sayonara to my grotty sister-in-law by Christmas, if you catch my drift, Padre."

And so, in April of 1963, Lucy drove Anna north to the Traverse City State Hospital, where her dear friend would be admitted and she herself would move close by. She rented an apartment on Pine Street, and she visited her friend daily—reading children's stories aloud to her; cutting up Milky Way bars into small, sharable pieces; and strolling arm in arm outdoors for fresh air. Mostly, however, they just sat side by side, holding hands, and watching the television in the sitting room, or listening to classical music coming from the phonograph the nurses had set up on the ward.

It was hardly the life either could have imagined just two years earlier, when they had driven south from Kalamazoo—heads high, degrees in hand, determined gaits—and started the next chapter in the book of their lives.

Sister Lucy (both priests insisted on calling her by her religious name) began her hospital ministry with secretarial office work and outreach to the patients. It was a perfect arrangement for her: She could earn a small wage and have the time to care personally for Sister Anna. By May of 1963, their lives had settled into a familiar routine, where Lucy worked in the chapel office, tended to Anna, and ministered to the needs of other patients.

"So now you have it all, Mr. Oakes."

Tom Oakes turned off the tape recorder and sat back in his chair, hands behind his head. Lucy rose and pulled her yellow scarf out from around her neck. The late day's sun began streaming into the office, casting a golden hue over everything.

"That, Mr. Oakes, is our story. I hope you can make something interesting out of it. I told you that I believe in truth—and telling the truth about one's experiences. What happened to us, especially Anna, can happen to anyone who fights for justice. Some might say we were in the wrong place at the wrong time. But that existential thought would only serve to denigrate *why* we were there. It would ignore the significance of what we were doing. My only hope now is that if others know our experience, in the long run, it may matter. I must believe that. Those men will probably never be prosecuted, but someday, somehow, justice will prevail. Others will be harmed, even killed, before ignorance and intolerance are beaten back or legislated out of existence. At first, I resisted going public with our story, for Anna's sake, her privacy, you know. But I have come to see that publishing this story, if it should come to that, is in itself an act of resistance. It is right staring down the face of wrong. You should be proud to be a part of this act, Mr. Oakes. I hope you see that."

He smiled. "I do. And I'll do my best, Sister."

She stared, nodding, eyes narrowed as she studied him silently. It was her Trust look.

"Good. Then we understand each other. Now then, please, just *Lucy*. *Sister* Lucy in the story if you wish, but here, just Lucy. Actually, as I think about it, please do not use our real names. You can use *Sister* but make up other surnames. It won't affect the story, and it will still guarantee Anna some measure of privacy."

"Will do."

"Thank you, Mr. Oakes."

"Please, *Tom*. Now then, you mentioned that there was something you needed from me?"

"Yes."

Lucy explained that she was troubled by a couple of things Tom had said to her. One, was about how Progrol is supposed to be used to treat schizophrenia, and how puzzled he was that Dr. Turner recommended it for Anna's condition. Two, Tom's revelation that he would ghostwrite an article with Dr. Turner touting the benefits of Progrol, and yet he seemed to equivocate when she asked about the drug being used with Anna.

"There is some incongruity there that I can't put my finger on," she said.

"Then," she continued, "Dr. Turner's dress—the watch, the gold cuff-links, the expensive shoes—seem incongruent with the typical salary an asylum administrator must be paid. I have seen no other doctors or administrators so lavishly dressed; and now, I see he drives a fancy new car."

"I'm ... not sure ... what you're getting at." A tentative cadence to his words.

She hesitated, thinking about what was brewing in her mind. "Well, I'm going to trust you with something, Tom. I think I can trust you, can't I?" A slight tilt of the head as the Trust look returned.

Tom Oakes was struck by Lucy's candor. And he was taken by the fact that his new friend—and confidante of sorts—would enlist his trust. It gave him a rare sense of honor. Lenore had tossed his honor in the trash can, and his drinking did nothing to help restore any honor for any reason. Thus, he was, in an odd way, smitten by Lucy's request for his trust.

"You can trust me 100%. I'd swear on a Bible. But truth be told, I'm an atheist so that wouldn't work very well, would it?" he laughed.

"I'll just take your word," she said, "We are only as good as our word."

Lucy proceeded to lay out a scenario that she had only an inkling of at this point. She intended to find connections between a number of things that she had encountered thus far at the asylum.

"And those are?"

"Until I work this out in my own head," she said, "suffice it to say that I would like to connect some dots— between the broad use of drugs as a first-line therapy; the faith in medicine as a *scientific* remedy for human ailments; pharmaceutical industry investments in its own products; and patients' civil rights. To be honest, I've never thought about *patients'* civil rights. I never even knew someone who had been committed to a mental institution."

"Few people do," he said. "Don't be hard on yourself, Sister ... Lucy. You just never had any contact with, you know, people like these. Sounds like your mission, as you call it, has broadened."

"Indeed, it has. But now that Anna is here, and now that a medical doctor is giving her a medication that, apparently, should only be used for schizophrenia, I think Anna and her guardian have the right to the truth, whatever that truth may be. I just can't shake this feeling that there is something not quite right going on.

"In my religious order," she continued, "we believe that where truth is lacking, injustice is lurking."

Tom regretted mentioning his doubts about the use of Progrol: He did not want to cast any aspersions on Dr. Turner, a man who could have him fired at the drop of a hat. But at the same time, he felt an allegiance to Lucy— because she valued *him* for something she saw in him as a fellow human being. Lucy and he had fashioned a human connection, one that he had not felt since long ago when he felt essentially happy.

"I need you," Lucy said, "to help me get to the bottom of this ... this doubt I have. I'm not sure just what help I need, but I think you are one person who knows more than he lets on about what happens behind the scenes here. I know others, and I'll ask for their help too. My education with the S.S.J., my study at college, and my experience in Alabama, they've all taught me that small instances of injustice portend larger patterns of injustice. Speaking out against injustice is my work, *our* work, Anna's and mine. She cannot speak, and so I must speak for her."

"You think there's injustice here? At the hospital? Oh my."

"I don't know. I just ... I have this feeling that I can't shake."

Her words about patient civil rights set Tom Oakes back on his heels. Lucy had awakened in him a feeling of self-worth that once stirred deep in his gut. For too long he had lived a life bereft of that vital sense of commitment to something—anything—meaningful. What he felt now was an intimation of something bigger than himself. Just an intimation, but enough to convince him that here, in this small woman's huge heart, in her determination to connect the dots, she had awakened in him a sense of purpose lost long ago. He had no idea what she intended to do or what she wanted to find out. It was all too vague, and he was cautious. He did not want to get caught up in some civil rights business. He was too old for that, too dependent on his own security.

But, on the other hand ...

He was conflicted.

He muttered, "Well ... I ... well, sure, whatever, you know, whatever you need."

With that, he said, "I'm willing to help you figure things out, whatever those things are—to put your mind at ease, 'cause there's really not anything here that would qualify as injustice that I know of," he said. "But, sure, I'll help if you need it."

What Tom Oakes didn't say, what was clearly apparent in Lucy's proposal, was that she was bartering with him: Her willingness to let him write her story in exchange for his willingness to do some fact-finding, or whatever it was she had in mind. His strong hope was that she would find nothing amiss, nothing that would qualify as injustice or wrongdoing, nothing that would draw him into controversy, or worse, conflict with his superiors.

They both rose; they shook hands. She thanked him and showed herself out the door. She had work to do.

Chapter 9

Every first week in July, Traverse City welcomed caravans of tourists from downstate driving north in station wagons loaded to the hilt with kids, coolers, and beach toys—to escape the heat and humidity of the lower part of the state and from Ohio, Indiana, and Illinois. They were all headed "up north," and the first week in July marked the beginning of the busiest time of year in the city—the annual National Cherry Festival.

Begun in 1925 as the Blessing of the Blossoms Festival, it attracted thousands of visitors who arrived in May to see the stunning cherry blossoms up and down the Old Mission Peninsula and throughout Benzie, Leelanau, Grand Traverse, and Antrim counties. In 1931, the festival was renamed the National Cherry Festival, and over the years, it moved from May to June and finally settled into the first week of July to coincide with the Independence Day holiday.

The 1963 Cherry Festival parade down Front Street featured over fifty floats, five marching bands, hundreds of decorated cars, tractors and trucks, and kids riding colorfully decorated bicycles. Mary Kardes was selected as the Cherry Queen, and 100 patients from the Traverse City State Hospital were brought into town to see the parade as a special reward for their hard work in cleaning up city beaches as the townsfolk prepared for the crowds arriving for the week-long festivities.

These patients had their own viewing area reserved just for them as a gift from the city—right in front of Milliken's Department Store on the corner of Front and Cass.

Sister Anna was not among those who tidied up the beaches, so Lucy walked her over to enjoy the colorful parade. She wanted Anna up and moving for exercise in the sun and open air as much as possible. It was never easy, as Anna had begun acting more and more like the ancients in her ward. But this Fourth of July day was sunny and warm, and Anna had been promised her favorite cherry Popsicle if she'd walk all the way to Front Street and all the way back. She eagerly agreed.

Anna watched the parade with the same passive attention that she gave everything these days—watching without reacting, staring indiscriminately, flinching at the sound of firecrackers. Lucy hoped that seeing the Knights of Columbus marching past would spark Anna's memory of when the Knights marched in parades in her Kalamazoo days, but she remained dispassionate when they marched by in their regal uniforms and plumed hats. On their way back to the hospital, they stopped by Oleson's Grocery, farther west on Front Street, where Lucy bought two cherry Popsicles. On a bench in front of the store, she broke one Popsicle in two, and placed Anna's half delicately in her hand. She licked hers slowly, savoring the sweet syrupy frozenness.

"Mmm," Anna said, a slight smile crossing her lips.

"Mmm," echoed her friend. "I love it when you love something so much," Lucy said, grateful there was still a glimmer of the true Anna she missed, grateful also for the Popsicles and for a few hours in the sunshine and festivities. Within minutes, they finished both Popsicles. Lucy coaxed Anna over to Oleson's big front window to show her the red rings around both of their mouths. Anna grinned, and then leaned over to kiss Lucy's cheek.

They made their way back to the asylum grounds by way of Elmwood Street. Just as they entered the grounds, they stopped suddenly. Mr. Frederick was running toward them, again wearing only his boxer shorts, T-shirt, and black oxfords. Trailing him by about one hundred yards was a group of white-uniformed attendants and two campus security guards. At one hundred yards, they spread out strategically to prevent him from veering off in either direction when they knew they would finally catch up to him.

As he sped past the two women, he let out a loud cackle followed by a whoop and the words "STOP SCREAM-ING AT ME, ARTHUR! I DIDN'T DO NOTHIN' WRONG!"[9] He whooshed past them, leaped across Elm-wood Street, and disappeared into the bush-thick entrance to a wooded walk affectionately known as "Lover's Lane." The posse separated and took different routes, some behind him, others into the woods at various locations that would likely intercept him at some point. A security car raced down Eleventh Street to block any possible escape where Lover's Lane ended at a stand of tall pines behind the Employee Building.

Anna and Lucy followed all the commotion, but then

---

9. "Schizophrenia is a serious mental disorder in which people interpret reality abnormally. Schizophrenia may result in some combination of hallucinations, delusions, and extremely disordered thinking and behavior that impairs daily functioning and can be disabling" (Mayo Clinic, Accessed December 16, 2019, https://www.mayoclinic.org/diseases-conditions/schizophrenia/symptoms-causes/syc-20354443).

continued on their way once the excitement trailed off beyond their route. Lucy took Anna back to Ward 3 for her afternoon rest. Whatever Mr. Frederick's fate was to become that day Lucy had no idea. She suspected that he had managed to avoid taking his daily meds that morning, and she felt certain that when they got him back to his ward, he would be tranquillized. She made a mental note that Mr. Frederick's story was one she would want to know more about—it may be yet one more dot to connect.

Once out on the grounds again, Lucy strolled in the warm July sun. Behind the warehouse, she came to the Weaving Shop, where she saw a bench beneath a huge oak tree. She approached the tree and spied a plaque about six feet from the base. It read: "English Oak, brought over from Dorset County, England, 1910."

Dr. Munson, she remembered, *first medical superintendent here, brought back trees from his wide travels. Wonderful that they are identified by where they came from.*

She turned when she heard her name called.

"Lucy Greene!" said one male voice. "Hi, Lucy Greene!" came the second voice. Two men emerged from the Weaving Shop. One carried a paper bag.

"Why, Georgie and Harold! How nice to see you again! I was just taking a walk and I found myself here and wondered if you would be working today. It's a holiday, you know."

"Oh yes, we know," spoke up Harold. "But we had some weavings to finish up so here we are at our job."

Georgie broke in. "B-b-but listen, Lucy Greene. We m-made something for you. We k-k-kept it here in the sh-shop but then when Harold saw you c-c-coming toward the shop, we got it to g-g-g-give you. Here." He handed her the bag.

They stood together like two school chums, arms around one another's shoulders, broad smiles stretched across their faces. Georgie's glasses continually slipped down his nose and he dutifully pushed them up again each time with a gnarled finger. Gleeful anticipation was in both their expressions.

Lucy opened the bag. It was a soft hand-woven scarf. Four feet long with frilly edges. Light blue with a diamond pattern running the center length. Lucy held it up to her face.

"It's so soft! And so, so beautiful! I don't know what to say. Thank you so much."

Georgie giggled and puffed out his chest, while Harold swung around as if in a one-man twirling dance.

"Whoo-hoo, Georgie! I told you she'd love it. We were going to make you a table runner, but then I thought why not a scarf for when the weather turns cool in the fall."

"Yeah. Th-th-that's what you said, all r-r-right. A-and it looks much better on her than a t-t-t-table runner!" With that they all three broke into laughter. Lucy came up to first one and then the other and planted a big kiss on each cheek.

"You two are my artists of life. My dear Georgie and Harold. How can I ever thank you enough?"

Harold spoke up. "You can't, Lucy Greene. But that kiss was worth a million bucks. Why, I can't remember the last time anyone's kissed me. How about you, Georgie?"

"I-I'll never forget it," he said. "It was 1937. My cousin Mary B-B-Beth, New Year's Eve party at my Uncle

R-R-Robert's. Midnight and all the b-b-bells ringing and guns going off outside. Somebody switched off the lights. And there was my c-c-c-cousin smelling like Uncle R-R-Robert's spiked punch. She wrapped herself around me like a g-g-grapevine and g-grabbed the back of my head with b-b-both hands and pulled me d-d-down to her level and kissed me, right on the lips. That k-k-k-kiss must've lasted a full minute. I had to c-c-come up for air a few times. G-G-G-Good thing the lights stayed off or Uncle R-R-Robert would've trained his sh-sh- shotgun on *me* instead of the s-s-stars outside."

He winked at Harold. Harold winked back.

"No sir," he continued, "I'll n-never forget that last k-k-kiss."

Harold broke his friend's reverie: "Yeah, but now it's no longer the *last* kiss, thanks to you, Lucy Greene."

The two men went back into the shop and Lucy started on her way back home.

How sad, she thought, *that a person could go without a kiss for as long as 26 years. How trivial—and how important—one tiny act of love like a simple kiss on the cheek can be.*

Then she chuckled. *And he had to come up for air!*

Chapter 10

WEEKS LATER, THE CHERRY FESTIVAL CROWDS LONG GONE, AND THE town returned to "normal" July tourism, Lucy sat with Head Nurse Nancy Brownell in Dill's Café on Union Street. Their time for "a good conversation" had finally come. Nancy wore her nurse's whites while Lucy sported a green summer frock full of small white polka dots.

Dill's was a favorite spot among city-dwellers and visitors alike—great food at great prices and waitresses who called their patrons "Darlin'" and "Honey." Dill's had been serving "the best coffee in town" since 1938, and its dinner specials featured fresh meat loaf "from Maxbauer's Meat Market just a few doors down," and "fresh, farm vegetables brought in daily."

They sat in a corner booth where they dunked donuts in cups of coffee that the waitress never let go below half full. A bell from the kitchen rang every time an order was ready.

"There has to be something better than doping her up for so many hours every day," Lucy remarked, stirring milk into her coffee. "She's been on that medication for nearly two months now, and I can't see any benefits other than that she's not a bother to nurses when her anxiety gets out of control."

"I know, it's hard on you," Nancy said. "It's hard on the nurses too. They're the ones closest to the residents. They're trained to care for them as if they were their own family. Giving them drugs that only seem to sedate them really

89

bothers the nurses. Not all, but most of them. Most would rather have lively patients, even if they *are* obstreperous at times. I worry that some patients on some medications lose their identities. That's what my nurses say too. Especially on the wards where so many of the younger women get daily meds, even though they just suffer from depression or anxiety—the ones who are not generally disorderly or who are only mildly bothersome. We've always been able to help them be somewhat stable. But when their medications sedate them? That little core of who they really are disappears."

"Exactly," said Lucy, "That's what I wanted to talk to you about, privately."

Nancy took a long sip of coffee as she studied her young friend. "You're one of the smartest women I've known, and I admire you. I so appreciate your commitment to your principles and your commitment to caring for Anna. Somehow, I sense an intersection between those two commitments has you here today. Am I close?"

"Yes, you are."

"What's on your mind, then?"

The waitress returned with a full pot of coffee, topped off their cups and wiped a few drips off the table that had spilled. They waited until she left.

Lucy began, "I'm thinking that the civil rights experiences that Anna and I had, they changed my way of thinking about systems of oppression. And about the power that is vested in people considered *authorities*. I'm thinking of that familiar saying—that money corrupts as much as power corrupts. Right now, I have so much on my mind,

I'm pretty scattered in my thinking. I'm not usually like that, but this past year, well, it's been hard. So hard."

Nancy reached across the table and took Lucy's hand. "Let it out, dear. I'll just listen. You can trust me." She enveloped her friend's hands in her own.

"Just let it out," she repeated.

Lucy gave a sigh of relief. "Thank you, so much. I don't want to waste your time, taking off work like this, but like I said, I'm not sure how all these thoughts connect. See, the way my mind works is, ideas seem to float around like they're in search of a theory that will weave them all together. Where are these thoughts, these inklings, leading me? I'm not sure, but I know I need information—and comrades who are willing to help me figure some things out. I'm sorry to be so vague. I just, I don't know—I just need to make sense of it all."

Nancy leaned against the table, withdrew her hands from Lucy's. Their eyes settled on one another for a long, silent moment.

"If information is all you seek," Nancy began, "sure, I'll help as much as I can." Then she sat back against the back of the booth. Her face lit up in a comforting smile, her eyes twinkled as she said, "It's funny, how things come 'round again."

It was a cryptic comment that puzzled Lucy. It showed in her face.

"I see you're perplexed," Nancy continued, a slight laugh. "Let me explain. For me, this is history repeating itself. It's an eerie coincidence. But a good one. So, do you remember, the day when we met by Ward 3, when I nearly ran you over with my arms full of papers?"

"I do."

"Good. Do you remember I mentioned Henry Merchartt, a fellow who was at the hospital nearly ten years ago?"

"That, too, and I've wanted to ask you about him. Oh, and the conference you mentioned, the one about some new medicine being introduced. Dr. Turner, you said, was running it but you didn't want to go. I remember you were upset about that."

"Oh, that. Yes, well. Not much to say about that other than what I've heard many times before—new product coming on the market, very excited about the trials so far, expected to curb ... what was it? Oh, perseverative behaviors from the mild sort to obsessive-compulsive. That was it."

"Perseverative?"

"Patients who can't seem to get their mind off one topic or another. Or repetitive behaviors, like compulsively washing their hands."

"I see," Lucy said, "but why were you so upset?"

"I was worried. That this new drug will be overused, like so many others have been. That it will be prescribed for what I might consider *acceptable* repetitive behaviors, the kinds of things we nurses have always successfully dealt with through kindness and understanding. But now, given the overall effect of the medication, the side effects, it's more complicated. That's where things get very difficult. For me, it's a moral issue."

Lucy played devil's advocate. "I mean, if a pill could be the cure, why not?"

Nancy nodded, smiled, not in a condescending way, but

more to acknowledge she understood devil's advocacy quite well.

"Just hold on to that thought," she said, "because my response to it is fairly complicated. First, let me tell you about Henry Merchartt.

"He was, shall we say, idealistic and highly ethical, impulsive but courageous, and he cared so much about the wellbeing of patients. Really cared. He was here completing an internship for his degree back east, and he was greatly affected by the events of the time that brought about the closing of our farm program here. It was a very difficult period for patients who lost the right to work in the fields or anywhere on the grounds. It was a difficult time for all of us who've committed our lives to what this institution has always stood for—humane ways of treating our patients, natural ways. For us, *therapy* has always meant that beauty is therapy, art is therapy, work is therapy, and social life is therapy. Like the rest of us, Henry saw first-hand how the closing of the farm program ended our work-is-therapy philosophy. Patients lost dignity and personal worth. They had stolen from them the only source of pride and accomplishment that mattered to them. Their hearts and spirits were broken, as were the hearts and spirits of the nurses, doctors, and staff who cared for them. It was a dark time in our history."

"I got wind of this from Father Pete," said Lucy, "when I was corresponding with him about bringing Anna here. How painful that time must have been."

"Well, it was, but not for some of those in positions of authority, here and at the state level—people who were influenced by power and money and politics to make

decisions that were devastating for so many here. Henry
worked hard behind the scenes to try to prevent the inevitable. He failed because he himself was powerless, and
because his time here came to an end. He had to go back
to complete his degree. Which he did. Then he went on to
begin a wonderful academic career at a university in Iowa.
We keep in touch. His passion for righteousness, and his
zeal for humane patient care had a lasting effect on so many
here—staff and patients alike."

"It sounds like Henry meant a lot to you."

"He did. Henry had this wide-ranging curiosity; it was
infectious, actually. He made me realize that I lacked, how
shall I put it, historical perspective. He inspired me to learn
more about the history of patient care in institutionalized
America. He had a contagious exuberance for history and
philosophy, for going deep into understanding how things
work—or don't work—in a big system like this. After he
left, I convinced myself that I needed to have knowledge of
the past in order to understand the present. What's remarkable to me, is that I see in you the same qualities of temper-
ament, determination, and courage that I saw in Henry. In
so many ways, your own principles inspire me too."

"So that's what comes around, as you said?"

"Yes. And, as it was with Henry, your doubts about
medicating patients, that touches a sympathetic nerve in
me. Just as it was with Henry and the decimation of the
farm program, issues pertaining to medicating patients are
both practical and philosophical. That is to say, I can be
practical and just give patients what the doctors prescribe.

"But, philosophically, I have to ask such questions as:
Should we medicate? Why should we medicate? And, is
some treatment other than, or in addition to, medication

to be preferred? My nurses, by and large, don't ask such questions. They simply look to me for direction. So, you see, I feel a sharpening of the conflict between my beliefs about medicines and my role as head nurse. I have a lot to balance, you see. I have position here; people who depend on me have many people who depend on them. I have to maintain an equilibrium between my role as administrator and my personal beliefs about patient care. For the good of the nurses and our patients. Do you understand what I'm saying?"

"I do," Lucy said. "You're saying your work, quote unquote, is complicated and behind the scenes. Like Henry Merchartt, you have unsettling questions, correct?"

"That is exactly right, my dear—as do you. But enough about me. None of what I've said means I cannot help support you in whatever your quest is destined to become."

Lucy felt relief. Nancy would help, from backstage, so to speak. And that was fine with her. The first thing she needed was to know more about how the philosophy of humanistic care at this asylum had evolved into what she now perceived to be a philosophy of chemical care.

She asked Nancy if she knew much about the methods of patient care that Henry Merchartt researched, the methods that made the Traverse City State Hospital famous, she said. How did they come to be?

"Something tells me," Lucy said, "that I, too, should have some knowledge of the historical depth if I am to understand the present."

Nancy laughed. "Oh, that is so Churchillian of you, Lucy."

"Churchillian?"

"Probably before your time, dear, but Winston Churchill

said in a speech after the war that those who fail to learn from history are doomed to repeat it. Something like that, though I learned later, from Henry, that he stole the quote from a philosopher named George Santayana."

Lucy perked up in her seat, eyes widened. "How does a head nurse come to know so much about philosophy?"

Nancy laughed again. "My father, he was a self-made philosopher. He was a voracious reader in philosophy when he wasn't practicing medicine. Our dinner table had nightly lectures on philosophy, though he called them *discussions*. I remember how my mother would roll her eyes and mutter something about 'fifty more years,' and shake her head as if to say, 'What's the use?'"

"You loved your father."

"Very much. He was the best. Is. He's retired now and living in the West. But let's get back to your question about history. I can tell you a few things that might matter, what I have learned through my personal study of patient care. Would that be helpful?"

Lucy said yes, of course it would be. She took out her notebook to jot down notes while Nancy talked.

"When it comes to institutional care for those who suffer from mental illness," she began, "there has always been a tug of war between moral and medical—or scientific—models."

Nancy started with the seventeenth century, when English scientists and philosophers believed that what separated men from animals was the capacity to reason. "Mad people, having lost their capacity for reason, were thus considered brutes and treated accordingly, the way one would treat animals in that day—'discipline, threats, fetters, and blows,' one writer said, were the only therapies considered effective. Mad people needed to be physically weakened, then broken; they should cower before those who knew what is best for them. This was the prevailing philosophy of patient care. Uniformly designed to rob patients of their strength, the methods of patient care induced debilitating vomiting, allowed near-starvation diets, and temporarily drowned a person—all in the name of science."

"Oh my," said Lucy, writing feverishly. "The scientific *authorities*!"

Nancy continued. "Whether this brand of medicine could cure mental illness or not, is another matter altogether. But the key thing was—is—the public perception that *science can cure*, if by cure they only meant a poor victim was too weak or too scared or too incapacitated to resist. Think of the folly of bloodletting. So yes, dear, the doctors *were* the authorities, and they were to be accorded the respect one would give, at the time, to men of science."

"Oh my," said Lucy, "A *man of science*! I've heard that very phrase used here, by a doctor describing himself!"

"That seems to be a consistent theme in this little history," Nancy commented, "and the authorities are always *men* of science, so add gender to your theory."

She continued. Belief in the power of science to solve the problems of mental illness extended from Europe to the United States, where medicine was widely considered a *scientific* enterprise. Yet, at the same time, another philosophy was becoming popular, and that was what would come to be called a *moral model*.[10] The Quakers had a lot to do

---

10. "Benjamin Rush [social reformer and signer of the Declaration of Independence, (1746-1813)], in his writings and in his hospital practices, had actually synthesized two disparate influences from Europe. The medical treatments he advised—the bleedings, the blisterings, the psychological terror—were the stuff of medical science. His counsel that the

with it, because their religious views said that no man is a wild beast, that people could recover from mental illness via their own internal powers supported by humane care, rather than through external, often violent means. From a Quaker perspective, people could change by God's grace, because they were essentially good themselves, but perhaps had lost their way. And so, asylums were designed to bring out this good in people—kind treatment by nurses and doctors, engaging activities to stimulate the mind, beauty in all its forms to satisfy the spirit and fill the heart. It was, in a word, *moral* treatment.

Lucy stopped writing notes. She couldn't get enough of this history lesson. The tension between the medical and moral models was beginning to connect some dots for her. It gave historical depth to what she saw as scientific versus naturalistic approaches to patient care.

"You can guess how things evolved out of the moral treatment philosophy," Nancy continued. "Fresh air, flowerbeds, natural beauty, art, sunshine, games, education, rewards for good behavior—and the virtual absence of punitive measures. All the things that the Traverse City State Hospital had cultivated since its beginning in the 1880s, starting with the Kirkbride design of Building 50; continuing on with the cottage system (smaller buildings connote greater, more intimate care for the individuals

---

mentally ill should be treated with great kindness reflected reformist practices, known as moral treatment, that had arisen in France and among Quakers in England (Robert Whitaker, *Mad in America: Bad Science, Mad Medicine, and the Enduring Mistreatment of the Mentally Ill* [New York: Basic Books, 2002] 20).

living there); and the famous farm program—a vital source of pride and personal transformation."

"Tell me more about the Kirkbride design," Lucy said. "I heard that name mentioned when I toured the Kalamazoo State Hospital. I notice how much sunlight fills the halls of Building 50. It's wonderful to have that much natural light."

"Sunshine and fresh air truly make a difference in our patients' wellbeing," Nancy said. "The first medical superintendent of the asylum, back in the 1880s, was Dr. James Decker Munson. He believed sunlight itself was therapeutic, and so he insisted that the design of Building 50 be done on the Kirkbride Plan, whereby every patient's room had access to natural light and fresh ventilation. The building stretched out like a giant bird in flight, in a linear plan that had "wings" extending from the center, where administrative offices were housed.

"Dr. Kirkbride, superintendent of the Philadelphia Hospital for the Insane in the mid-nineteenth century, believed that putting patients in a pleasant, if not cheerful environment, had a healing effect on them. In keeping with this philosophy, the interior of Kirkbride-designed buildings should boast large pots of flowers and green plants, works of art, and comfortably furnished rooms and parlors. Outside the buildings, one should find cultivated landscapes full of lush trees, ornamental bushes, and wide lawns. Dr. Munson himself brought back from his travels nearly 70 varieties of trees, which he used to create the arboretum on the Great Lawn. He ordered that flower beds be planted that carried robust blooms six months a year. In general, landscaping was designed to bring about pastoral comfort when patients gaze out their windows or walk the grounds. All in the name of a moral philosophy for treating mental illness.

"Having an office in Building 50," Nancy said, "means that I live and breathe the legacy of Dr. Thomas Kirkbride every day."

Reflective, Lucy said, "This takes me back to college, when I studied art. I loved the American Romantic painters and their reverence for the natural world. I think of those paintings by Thomas Cole and the Hudson River School—you know, pastoral scenes with vast amounts of sunlight streaming through lovely cumulus clouds. Those artists saw God in the heavens peeking through at us."

Nancy leaned back in the booth. "Well then, you can begin to see the connection between art and natural beauty as a treatment mode. God in His heavens, all's right with the world—that's the moral model."

"It's deeply religious, isn't it?"

Nancy laughed. "I can see that. But it's as much philosophical as it is religious. Either way, it amounts to the same thing—the same thinking about patient care. But let me continue with this short history.

"At the time of Kirkbride, and then later, Dr. Munson, some people tried to wed the moral model with the medical model by injecting medical treatments into moral regimens, like sedating patients with morphine and opium while allowing the natural world into their living quarters and environment. Even punitive measures could be interpreted as medical procedures—in a twisted logic: If they caused a change in the patient's behavior, that's a good thing. Actually, in some asylums, punitive measures had never been abandoned, and so they returned with a powerful ally—the doctors who persisted in their beliefs that science, not religion or philosophy, was essential to patient care.

"Some even said that moral treatments constituted the *art* of healing, while medical treatments constituted the *science* of healing. At the turn of this century, madness, as they called it, was seen as a biological phenomenon, a condition that must be treated by medical means."

"Funny, how science always seems to win out over art," Lucy said.

Stirring her coffee, Nancy said, "It does seem that way, doesn't it, dear? But in this case, people like Dr. Munson persisted, and institutions like our hospital thrived— because the moral model of healing actually got results— and because he and subsequent superintendents resisted the medical model. That's what Henry Merchartt discovered, and what we nurses all knew—*still* know. Unfortunately, while we nurses see our *art* as the most essential element to healing, most of the doctors in charge see *science* as most essential—and those doctors rule the day."

They sat silent for a few moments, reflecting on the way of their world.

Lucy screwed up her face, puzzled. "What I don't understand," she said, "is this. You're a nurse; you, too, had medical training. In the sciences I presume—chemistry, anatomy, physiology, etcetera—and yet you seem to fall on the side of art, not science."

Nancy shrugged her shoulders, said, "I do, and I don't. That's why I said pharmaceutical approaches are complicated. See, I live in both worlds. I revere science and all the good it has brought to humankind, especially in medicine. Medicine has brought great things to civilization. Look at morphine, sulfa, penicillin, the polio vaccine, even some of the drugs used to treat schizophrenia. How can I not celebrate the wonderous effects of such medicines?

"At the same time, as a nurse, I am also trained in the ministry of healing, to use your familiar term. As a woman, that ministry is bred in me, I feel. Call it the maternal instinct, whatever fits. It is what gives nurses an emotional bond with our patients. But that bond does not have to be at odds with science. Our hospital has always tried to find balance. We have tried to treat patients with the respect they deserve as human beings. But we have also invested in dubious scientific approaches, like lobotomies and electroshock, as they have come into fashion and then gone out. In fact, do you know about Dr. Jack Ferguson? He was a doctor here at our hospital, up until a couple of years ago."

"Never heard of him."

"There's a book about him. Written by someone who greatly admired him. It's called *A Man Against Insanity*. It came out five or six years ago. About his experiences here at the Traverse City State Hospital. Jack was a fierce advocate for combining medication with love. He was a controversial figure here. I knew him well. He once said to me, 'The nurses treat all their patients as if they were their little sisters.' Jack was … an amazing doctor."

"I don't know that book," Lucy said. "It sounds like I should, though."

"Well, if you're interested in any of what we're discussing, you should read it. But, you know, I have so few people here with whom I can be as open and honest as I am with you, so if you can't get a copy, I'll give you mine. But I would just as soon tell you about it."

Nancy glanced at her wristwatch, opened her purse, and removed a brown wallet.

Lucy put up an open hand as a stop sign. "No," she said. "My treat. The least I can do for this free seminar is take care of the bill. I'm looking forward to learning about Dr. Jack Ferguson in part two. Check your calendar, please, and let me know when we can meet again. Soon. And, thank you so much, Nancy. This really has me thinking."

Nancy smiled, "That's a date, my dear. And now, I have to get back to my work." She rose, in unison with Lucy and reached out to shake her hand.

Lucy stayed at Dill's a while longer. She sat and thought. In her notebook, she made notes on her new "research project." She now had a team—Nancy, Tom Oakes, perhaps Smit and Williams—as she leaned into the uncertainty of where her research might lead her.

She strongly suspected something was awry with the whole business of medicating patients. *It is a commercial enterprise*, she wrote. *Pharmaceutical companies, whose very livelihood depends on drug sales, have extraordinary amounts of money involved, and their investment will only grow as more drugs are developed and marketed.* She would ask Smith and Williams to help her better understand the role of the drug companies; those fellows had connections at the University of Michigan who may be able to help with getting information.

She shared Nancy's feelings about the use and misuse of medications to treat mental challenges—that the *intent* of medications was sound, but the *use* of medications bordered on *over*use, if not *mis*use. She doubted the claims that the new drugs were miracle cures, though they *did* have benefits. She would have to find out more about the benefits, who profits, and for what reasons. Her skeptical mind suspected that the pharmaceutical companies and their spokesmen profited more than did the patients.

In the long view of history, she reflected, reverence for scientific cures was responsible for surges in curative treatments followed by backward steps if not wholesale abandonment of those same treatments. That's what happened to "therapies" that nearly drowned people (hydrotherapy) or that shocked them into catatonic states (electroshock). On the treatment spectrum from popular to defunct, mental patients were occasionally the beneficiaries, most often victims. Worse, as long as those patients were housed in state institutions, they had no legal rights.

Lucy sat back in her chair, her head spinning as a new connection emerged: Those who suffered from mental illness were the brothers and sisters of those who suffered from racial discrimination—both were victims, both had few if any advocates, both were caught up in a complicated struggle for basic human rights. Her instincts for discerning injustice, coupled with her calling to serve justice, forced the inevitable question:

Was God, once again, calling on her to act?

Chapter 11

Lucy stood with Doctors Turner and Gordon in the hall outside Ward 3. Lucy had asked them to meet her before rounds in Ward 3 to discuss discontinuing Progrol for Anna.

Two months, she felt, was enough time to know that this medication was having no effect on Anna other than to sedate her. Lucy was grateful that Anna had suffered none of the more obvious side effects Dr. Turner said might occur—joint pain and sensitivity to light, for instance. But a full regimen of natural treatment approaches had not yet been tried, and Lucy would not be satisfied until all options had been exhausted.

Dr. Turner was reluctant to take Anna off Progrol. He argued that the medication reduced her fits of anxiety and relieved her traumatic memories. "In short," he commented, "it is not perfect, but we must admit that Progrol *does* work.

"I follow the literature on psychotropic medications closely," he said. "Every medication used at this hospital has undergone scientific trials by prominent researchers, and the results are reported in the medical research journals.[11] It is too early in the drug trials to know just *how*

---

11. A substantial number of the so-called medical scientific papers that are published on behalf of the drugs are written within the confines of the pharmaceutical houses concerned. Frequently the physician involved merely makes the observations and his data, which sometimes are sketchy and uncritical, are submitted to a medical writer employed by the compa-

some medications work," he said. "We only know that they *do* work, and after all, isn't that what's best for the patient? To be relieved of as many symptoms as possible? It's the humane thing to do, don't you agree?"

Lucy did agree that relieving symptoms was humane, but she thought Anna's trauma could be better treated, over time, through alternative therapeutic approaches, such as emotional support from nurses (who were trained and willing to do just that, she pointed out), increased outdoor activity, hobbies, art, music, "...anything that heals the spirit," she said. "Her spirit has been broken. Progrol doesn't heal spirit. Up to now," she noted, "Progrol has had little effect other than to transport Anna into a semi-conscious state, and since she's half asleep most of the time, obstreperous behaviors beyond her control are absent. It is definitely *not* a cure."

Lucy repeated, "She's hardly a problem if she's asleep all the time."

She didn't go so far as to ask if Progrol, like other medications used on the ward, had the same effect on other patients. *I can understand*, she thought, *if exasperated staff*

---

ny. The writer prepares the article which is returned to the physician who makes the overt effort to submit it for publication. The article is frequently sent to one of the journals which looks to the pharmaceutical company for advertising and rarely is publication refused. The particular journal is of little interest inasmuch as the primary concern is to have the article published any place in order to make reprints available. There is a rather remarkable attitude prevalent that if a paper is published then its contents become authoritative, even though before publication the same concerns may have been considered nonsense (Pfizer physician Haskell Weinstein, *Administered Drug Prices*, Report #448, by the Senate Subcommittee on Antitrust and Monopoly [Washington DC: U. S. Government Printing Office], June 27, 1961, reprinted as an appendix, 477).

want them to be still, even catatonic, because that's better than their being hostile, or oppositional, or childish. Not the nurses, according to what Nancy Brownwell had told her; the nurses were trained to work *with* patients' eccentricities: "The ministry of healing," as Nancy put it, "is their specialty." Lucy was careful to not bring up the question about Progrol's apparent target disorder—schizophrenia—and the fact that that was not Anna's diagnosis. There would be time for that to come out, eventually, as the dots connected.

Maybe on the most disturbed wards, she thought, *strong sedatives could be justified. But in the other wards and cottages? For patients who did not pose dangers to themselves or others? That seems to be different.*

Dr. Gordon was a kindly man with a long career at the hospital but little experience deciding upon and administering medications. Down the line in the medical chain of command, he toed the line in agreeing with Dr. Turner: "We really don't want to see Anna moved to the Disturbed Women's Ward," he cautioned. There was an air of false camaraderie in his choice of the collective "we," she noticed. It could have meant just the two doctors; or it could have included Lucy, as part of Anna's care team. If that were the way to interpret his words, it implied that she, Lucy, would be held responsible if Anna got worse again off Progrol.

Dr. Gordon sensed her dilemma when he cast the decision to move Anna as the *last* choice Anna's team would want to make: "It may not be a safe place for you to put your friend, but things may reach a point where choices must be made, regardless of objections."

Again, his use of the passive "choices must be made" troubled her. Without actually saying it, all three knew that doctors would make that choice even if she objected.

But to avoid a power struggle, they tiptoed around that central fact. As legal guardian, Lucy had the right to make certain medical decisions, as long as they did not expressly go against the medical opinions of at least two physicians or psychiatrists. She declined to pursue the topic. She understood the ultimate authority doctors had in making decisions *for* patients, as well as what little power patients or their guardians had themselves. Her guardianship papers from the court did not address her legal authority in medical matters. Institutionalized people existed in a legal limbo *because they were institutionalized.* There she was, once again, coming up against *systemic* injustice. There was a time, she reminded herself, when people with black or brown skin had restricted rights *because their skin was not white.* Decisions that affected their very wellbeing had to be made *for* them, not *with* them. It was no different in the mental institutions.

Still, Lucy knew from previous interactions with both doctors, that standing firm while offering plausible alternatives could dissuade them from going against her wishes. An awkward silence ensued as a nurse pushing a supplies cart caused them to step aside so she could enter the ward. Feeling the impasse, Lucy's face took on a resolute look as she stared at one and then the other. It was her *stand-my-ground* look. Dr. Turner deflected the tension by scribbling notes in a spiral notebook. Dr. Gordon rocked back and forth on his heels, hands clasped behind his back, waiting.

Discomfort edging toward opposition filled the space that enveloped them.

Lucy broke the impasse. She proposed a trial period, whereby Anna would not be given any medication other than aspirin for headaches. No time frame would be put on this trial, but Lucy (and nurses) would triple their efforts to provide alternative treatments. Lucy would provide more one-on-one time with Anna—painting with watercolors, listening to classical music in the library, wading at the "patients' beach" on West Bay, and reading Anna's favorite books aloud to her. When Lucy couldn't be there for Anna, Nurse Bennett would take over. Anna would never be far from a caring source of healing.

Both doctors agreed. "Nothing to lose," Dr. Turner remarked, "so we'll see." Dr. Gordon mumbled something that sounded like "hasten to agree."

Lucy thanked them for their willingness, shook hands, and entered Anna's ward as the two doctors hurried down the hall to continue rounds.

On August 15, Anna was taken off Progrol.

At first, Lucy was encouraged by the way Anna seemed to come around. Indeed, there were moments when Anna's natural spirit shined through. When she would reach over to a nurse seated beside her and put her hand in the nurse's palm. When she would beckon Lucy to bend over her so Anna could plant a small kiss on her forehead. At these times, she radiated a gentle wordless smile that said, "I'm still here. I love you." Then her eyes would close tight, and her face would grimace. In either state, Lucy observed a person alternatively happy or suffering.

Though there was some hope, Anna was, by and large, still not well. Then she began getting worse.

Lucy's hope dwindled as Anna's days off Progrol became weeks. Anna's headaches increased in frequency and intensity, to the point where she had begun hitting herself in the side of her head or banging her head on her bed board until attendants or nurses could come to her aid. Sleep disturbances too, in the form of vivid dreams, whereby she would shout out in the night and flail arms and legs until patients on the ward became disturbed. Even agitating events on the ward involving other women caused her to have panic attacks. Anna simply could not find a peaceful center that would last more than a few minutes.

Doctor Gordon suggested a return to Progrol, but with Dr. Turner on a long trip out west, Lucy prevailed upon him to delay any such decision until Dr. Turner returned.

Lucy felt it was a conundrum: She couldn't support a medical approach that didn't actually bring about a better quality of life, but she couldn't bear to see Anna struggle so much.

She herself struggled, spiritually. She prayed for Anna day and night, but at the same time, she wanted to curse the men whose violent attack caused this suffering. Her faith said she had to forgive them, but her daily experiences with Anna made forgiveness nearly impossible. She started praying for *herself*—that she would be able to maintain the personal strength that she knew in her heart Christ expected of her. It would have been easy for her to ask the same question non-believers ask, "How could a merciful God allow this to happen?"

One Saturday when Lucy was feeling especially discouraged, she brought that nagging sentiment to Father Pete.

"God's mystery confounds all of us," Father Pete counseled her, "and the human condition is such that we have no choice but to accept that evil, like good, exists. Jesus never said ours would be a perfect world. What he did say is that God is perfect, and humans are not. Evil exists because we are not perfect. Our faith demands that we love in spite of the presence of evil. Our strength lies in our love.

"It is not a sin to doubt," he said, "but it *is* a sin to hate. Love your enemies, Jesus advised, for whatever reason they have become your enemies. In the end, love will win out." The priest's words reminded Lucy of what Dr. King had said at a speech in Montgomery—that hate for hate only intensifies the existence of hate and evil in the universe. Though she believed in love as the ultimate solution, neither Father Pete's nor Dr. King's words were able to heal the hole in her heart that only grew as Anna's condition worsened.

She increased the time she spent trying to rehabilitate Anna through natural means. Time became a precious commodity, and she went home exhausted most days. Reluctantly, Father Pete asked her to put in even more time at work because Father Fred was moving ahead with his proposed project to build a stand-alone chapel, a church home for people of all faiths at the hospital. It would be called All Faiths Chapel. Father Fred's long view was to make All Faiths a community church, where patients would worship alongside people from Traverse City proper. It was a radical idea but one that would prove, eventually, to break down historical barriers between hospital residents and city dwellers. He envisioned that the chapel would hold services for Catholics, Protestants, and Jews.

She could hardly say no to the two priests, and so she increased her workload, putting in extra hours when she was done with Anna for the day and before going home. Once home, she could barely manage a can of soup for dinner before collapsing into bed. She stopped reading. She stopped writing letters to family and fellow sisters downstate. She was burning her candle at both ends, the only hope for relief being that Anna would somehow improve. Her life had become one of sacrifice as, bit by bit, she surrendered more and more of herself to her calling.

Given the load, she was unable to pursue her research project. *One step at a time,* she told herself. *First, we get Anna on the right track, then there will be time for the project.*

Twice, Nancy Brownell invited her for lunch, but Lucy begged off. Weekly, Williams or Smit passed her in the halls or on the grounds and greeted her with something like, "Whatever you need, Sister, whenever you need it." Tom Oakes called one day to say he had completed a draft of the article and could she come by to take a look at it? She put him off, too, saying she was so busy, could it wait for a few weeks until she had some room to breathe?

Some relief came one weekend in late September when three nuns from the Kalamazoo convent drove up for the day. The visitors had been mentors to Anna and Lucy during their convent training. They were the ones who had introduced the two young sisters to community activism practices, and involved them in anti-poverty initiatives in southwest Michigan. They were dear friends whose mentoring inspired the two of them "to go forth and change the world."

Their visit came at just the right time for Lucy to get a break from the daily grind of work and patient care. Lucy gave them a walking tour of the asylum grounds, elated to spend time with old friends with whom she had deep and affectionate bonds. The tour ended in Ward 3, where they visited with Anna in her room. Anna showed no recognition, though she did allow each nun to give hugs and forehead kisses.

The visitors took Anna and Lucy on a "road trip" to the giant sand dunes west of Glen Arbor in Leelanau County. On the westernmost side, the dunes rose more than 400 feet above the shores of Lake Michigan. Years later, these same dunes would become a protected national lakeshore, but in 1963, they were just wide-open spaces, free for anyone to climb up and tumble down. The easternmost side of the dunes was a popular tourist destination because the climb was a manageable less-than-two-hundred feet.

Lucy sat with Anna at the foot of one dune as their friends attempted, unsuccessfully, to reach the top. Coming down, they laughed and fell, rolled and sat, until finally, they arrived at the feet of Anna and Lucy—sand in hair, sand in shoes, sand clinging to their sweaters and skirts. Lucy roared with laughter. Anna smiled.

On their way back to the hospital, they stopped in tiny Glen Arbor for a late lunch at Art's Tavern. Sister Katharine Mary and Anna had tall root beer floats, while Sisters Geniece and Theresa cajoled Lucy into imbibing one of Art's draft beers. Mugs raised high over their hamburgers and French fries, they toasted to old times, to everyone's health, and to Pope John XXIII, who, through the Vatican II Council, said "it was time to open the windows of the church and let in some fresh air."

Feeling happier than she had in months, Lucy proposed a second toast.

"A toast," she said, "for the Sisters of St. Joseph. Fresh air yesterday! Our own cars and checkbooks today! Tomorrow, ordination of women!" A chorus of hearty cheers went up as glass mugs clinked one another and then, one by one, made their way over to clink Anna's root beer float where she sat, befuddled but amused.

The nuns left that evening for the three-hour drive back downstate. Alone at home, as the gaiety of the day receded, Lucy became melancholic as she reflected on their visit. While she loved seeing her former teachers and friends, she was saddened by the realization that, up here in northern Michigan, she was isolated from the religious, activist community that she once believed would sustain her for life. There were, of course, other sisters in Traverse City who belonged to other orders, like the Dominicans who taught in the Catholic schools, or the Carmelites who lived in cloister. But they were not of her ilk. What Lucy missed were the S.S.J. nuns who shared her passion for human rights, and who themselves were activists in so many communities. She longed for the solace of their camaraderie, and she yearned for their courageous tenacity in the face of struggle. She realized that she had depended too much on Anna for these comforts of the spirit.

Their visit awakened in Lucy the distressing thought that *this was it*. That she could be living this life of isolated toil for a very long time. That this demanding, almost round-the-clock regimen may have no end date. She wondered if she could fulfill her promise to Anna to stick it out. She thought, *what do people do when they suspect that the life they have committed themselves to may not be the life they can actually live*? Convent life, college education, and raw experience had not prepared her for that gray area of life, where moral obligation intersects with existential purpose, where one is forced to ask, "What *am* I doing?"

But now, that is exactly where she found herself.

This feeling was different than the one she'd confessed to Father Pete. That one was about doubting God's mercy and forgiving one's enemies. This was about doubting one's own strength to carry on.

Admitting vulnerability in the face of loss, she prayed for resilience to Saint Brigid of Ireland, the patron saint of healers.

Chapter 12

One morning in early October, Nancy Brownell appeared suddenly at Lucy's tiny desk in the chaplain's office. She had been alerted to an event involving Anna that morning in the women's dining hall. She pulled up a folding chair and sat next to Lucy, grasped Lucy's hand in her own, and reviewed what Dr. Turner had reported to her in a phone call.

Sitting opposite Anna at breakfast (before meds were distributed so patients could take them on a full stomach,) a young female patient known to have fits of anger accused her of taking all the syrup in the syrup cruet. Anna just stared back at her, then cast her innocent eyes down, shaking her head from side to side. The young woman leaned across the table, grabbed Anna by her hair, shouted a string of expletives, and yanked her halfway across the table.

Anna broke free. Then her panic attack began. She threw plates of food at the woman, grabbed handfuls of food from others' plates nearby and tossed them at the attacker. In an adrenalin-fueled moment, she herself reached across the table, grabbed the woman by her blouse and tried to pull *her* across the table. Chaos broke loose as other patients joined in the melee, some thinking it was great fun, others taking the side of one or the other adversary.

Attendants scrambled to subdue and separate the fighting women, pulling off one at a time and handing them off to nurses, who removed patients back to their wards.

It took a few moments for additional attendants to make their way to Anna and her opponent, who continued to pull and tug at one another from either side of the table. Once they were separated, attendants were able to restrain both women with bear hugs.

Anna and her opponent were each escorted out of the dining hall. Anna was taken back to Ward 3, where Dr. Gordon gave her Miltown, a powerful tranquilizer. Within minutes, she had calmed down. Then she slept.

Once Anna was tranquil, Dr. Gordon called Dr. Turner. They conferred on the phone, revisiting their previous opinion that Ward 3 may be better off with Anna transferred out. Protocol demanded that the head nurse be informed, and she was. Nancy Brownell was granted time to speak with Lucy before any decisions were made.

"I know you want to rush to Anna's side to comfort her," Nancy said, "but she's been sedated with a powerful tranquilizer, so she's not going to know you're even there. Wait a while, please. Let me show you something before you do anything. This is not a time for rash moves. We must be even more thoughtful about what happens to Anna now."

Lucy agreed, and she confided to Nancy her most recent concern about Anna.

"I fear that there's something the doctors aren't seeing," she said. "Anna is getting worse. Her spells are more pronounced, and her muscle tone is greatly reduced in spite of my efforts to have her exercise more. I can't prove it, but I even think her eyesight is declining; she squints and doesn't seem to recognize familiar faces. These just don't seem like symptoms of trauma or anxiety. There's something strange that's happened to her in just the last few weeks."

Nancy took it all in, nodding empathetically.

"Let me look into that," she said. "I don't recall seeing anything on her chart but give me some time. For now, I would like to talk with you about Hall 5."

"Hall 5?"

"The Women's Most Disturbed Ward. I want you to see it, because that is likely where the doctors will decide to put Anna. Until now, they have been conciliatory, but *they* will decide, not you and not me. They have that power. We can't let that happen, my dear. I am not the one to counter their decision; I don't have that authority. But you must see that ward before you fight against it."

The Women's Most Disturbed Ward was located on the third floor, north side. By the time Nancy and Lucy entered, the women there had been given their morning medications, so it was considered a "safe" time to tour.[12]

"Smile and say hello as much as you can," counseled Nancy. "These are women who, in spite of being heavily medicated, may have an outburst if they think ill of you. One never knows. That's why we have male attendants on

---

12. "[It] was true that the severely mentally disturbed could have a much better life when on the medications. For those who worked with the severely disturbed and chronically incarcerated patients, particularly with the most violent ones, medications were a blessing, a true boon from on high. At one time or another, attendants on the back wards of hospitals had all struggled to apply physical restraints or to push an 'upset' patient into a padded room. Staff members had been frightened often and harmed occasionally. Medications did seem to those who remembered incidents in that past a godsend, literally lifesavers in managing patients" (George Paulson, M. D., *Closing the Asylums? Causes and Consequences of the Deinstitutionalization Movement* [Jefferson, NC: McFarland & Company, Inc., 2012], 107).

the ward. The nurses could never defend themselves or fully restrain a patient, if needed."

They strolled slowly through the ward, smiling and greeting emotionally dulled women sitting in chairs that lined the walls, some asleep, others gazing about themselves at nothing in particular. Not one woman was dressed in day clothes; all wore green nightgowns, some with old robes covering their sleeping clothes.

A woman who looked to be in her 20s sat on the floor, her back against a wall, picking a scab on her cheek; blood ran down her face; she ran the back of her hand over the blood stream and then sat staring at her red hand. She looked up at the nurse and nun as they passed, eyes half open, blinking. She wiped the bloody hand on her gown.

A television playing a daytime soap opera flickered in one corner, the sound turned off. There was no sign that anyone had completed any essential daily hygiene, though one woman, who appeared to be in her late teens, sat in front of another, older woman in her 40s, who slowly brushed the younger one's long brown hair. When Nancy and Lucy passed them, the older woman looked up and asked, "Want your hair brushed? Want to go with me on a date? Want to go pee with me?"

Nancy took Lucy's hand and hurried her along without comment.

"Piss off," rang out from behind them.

One woman seated in a cushioned chair put out both hands and asked Lucy for a cigarette.

Nancy spoke for Lucy. "I am so sorry, Mrs. Gilmore. We don't have any cigarettes today, but I'll make a note to get you some. Will that be all right?"

The patient spit on the floor. "Shit," was all she could muster.

"Chocolate cake. I need cake," said a woman, stringy-haired and red-eyed, who walked with some determination right up to them. "Some cake, lady," she announced, "Gimme some fuckin' chocolate cake." She stood her ground in front of them, blocking their way. Behind her, from the other end of the hall, a burly male attendant made his way toward them.

"Let's go, Hansen," he said, coming up from behind and pulling the woman aside. "Let the nurses pass."

"That short one with the red hair all curled up, she ain't no nurse," said Hansen. "I know that tall one is, not that short one. That short one who won't give cigs or cake, I'd like to give her what's up, so high and mighty she is!"

"All right, Hansen, that's enough," said the attendant, "We're going to have a little quiet time, you and me." He took her firmly by the arm and led her past the two visitors. Lucy watched them as they made their way down the hall.

"He'll take her to a padded isolation room," Nancy said. "Until we leave. It's better that way."

Their tour took all of five minutes. What Lucy learned in that time was that, in the Women's Very Disturbed Ward, the capacity for violence—verbal abuse and intimidation at the very least—exceeded greatly what might happen on the other wards, where outright intimidation was the exception rather than the norm.

Here, though, the mood seemed charged with tension. Some women were housed here because they had assaulted others; some had attempted suicide. She thought it was very possible that Anna could be hurt before any attendant could get to her in time to protect her. Or it could happen behind a closed door. Although patients were given strong medications that normally made them sedate, many of them had learned to "tongue" their meds and then spit them out secretly. They would then pretend to be placid, so they could see an opportunity to make life miserable for others.

"Anna wouldn't last an hour there," Lucy said as the two of them descended the stairs on their way to Ward 3.

"That is why I wanted you to see it."

Lucy started to say something but then halted mid-sentence. They both stopped walking and turned to face one another. Nancy took both of Lucy's hands in hers.

"Lucy," she said, "what I have to say, you won't like."

Lucy stared deep into the nurse's eyes. Recognition. "I think I know what you're about to say. It's about Progrol, isn't it?"

"Yes."

"You think Anna should be put back on Progrol, don't you?"

"Considering the alternative, and not having the authority to ... yes, it would be better. She'll die in there."

"It seems I have no choice then. I could move her to another institution, I suppose. But we both have so much here—familiarity, the supports, my work. A move would be too hard on her. I can only hope God will guide me and protect her from further harm."

Nancy squeezed Lucy's hands. "Let me handle this, my dear. I will speak with the doctors. I'll recommend that the dosage be minimal. Maybe that will make a difference. Let's be hopeful."

Chapter 13

LUCY WAS HEADED TO DR. TURNER'S OFFICE. SHE WOULD SPEAK DIRECTLY with him about Anna. She would argue for no return to Progrol: She had a persuasive alternative that might just work. If it didn't, she would, as a fallback position, agree to a milder dose. She hoped Nancy Brownell had gotten to him by now with her recommendation for a reduced-strength dose. That would make things easier when she spoke with him.

Just a few feet before she reached his office door, she was accosted by Muriel Putney, a patient whom she hadn't seen since their encounter in July when Lucy mailed a letter for her to the FBI.

Muriel came at her like a strong westerly wind, waving a white envelope in her hand. She wore eyeglasses that leaned toward men's rather than women's fashion—thick and rounded bifocals, black plastic on the top half, gold rim on the bottom.

With Muriel, there was never a greeting or announced reason for what she had to say. She just started in where her last thought left off.

"I had to pilfer stamps, you know, trade 'em for packs of gum that come in the care packages the church ladies bring," she began. "Anyway, here it all is, just like I said last week. They been especially rough on me lately. Maybe they got drift of the letters, I don't know. They put me out in the cold to sleep on the grass all night when it was raining cats and dogs. For no reason, mind you. Then they hid my stuff—*again*—all of it, up in the attic where they keep them chickens and pigeons and whatnot. No food either for three days, just scummy broth with bugs in it. I had the runs so bad from the broth but none of 'em gave me any medicine or nothin'. It's all here."

She held her eyeglasses firmly in place with one hand as she brandished the envelope with the other. She waved the envelope in the air between Lucy and herself as if she were fanning the ceiling.

"And Mrs. Glaussen, what they did to her, that's all here too. Put her in the hydrobath for two weeks nonstop. She turned into an old wilted raisin, not that she had very good skin to begin with. Took away her brown shoes and put some broken glass in her bed. She got all cut up and then they put her in the hospital, said she was a danger to herself. The FBI, they're gonna shit bricks when they hear about all that."

The envelope stopped in midair and held its own for a few seconds; then it was propelled into Lucy's midsection with a mighty "HERE! Get this one in the mail before Mrs. Glaussen up and up dies and I get the plague. They'll stop at nothin', those bastards."

She turned on one heel and made her way back down the hall. At the exit door, she turned back to look at Lucy.

"When the FBI comes," she said, "I'm gonna have a big party. You can come too 'cause you're on my side, lady. But not that pain-in-the-ass Gladys Ann from the UP. She's nothin' but a party pooper on a good day, which ain't many, lemme tell you."

Muriel waved; Lucy waved back.

Lucy glanced at the envelope. Like the last one she

mailed, it too was addressed to the FBI in Washington, return address *Muriel Putney, Ward 1, Hell, Michigan.*

Lucy slid the envelope into her purse; it would be mailed later that day. She pushed open the door that had DR. TURNER, ASSISTANT MEDICAL SUPERINTENDENT, written in bold black letters. She announced to a prim secretary named Shiela that she did not have an appointment, but that she needed to talk with Dr. Turner on an urgent matter. Sheila's eyebrows rose half an inch as she sensed something amiss. She pushed a button on an intercom and said "a Lucy Greene" needed to talk with him.

"She says it's urgent," Shiela said, referring to Lucy in the third person, as if to indicate that there may or may not be anything urgent, but only that the person standing before her *claimed* urgency.

"Send her in" came back, loud and clear. Shiela nodded toward the inner door; Lucy made her way herself.

She pushed open the door and slowly took in the interior of Dr. Turner's office. Elegantly furnished with an enormous, dark wood desk with four carved gargoyles as legs; tall, polished bookcases stocked with what appeared to be medical books all neatly lined up like soldiers at attention; and plush cushioned chairs with legs sporting the same gargoyle faces. The office spoke of order and gentility bordering on splendor.

She told him she knew about what had happened with Anna at breakfast and she expressed concern that he may again be considering transferring Anna to the Women's Most Disturbed Ward. He said, yes, that was where his thinking was going. Then he said he had received a call from Nurse Brownell recommending Anna be placed on a lower dose of medication.

"But I think that would be a mistake," he said.

Lucy was disappointed. She would have to press him with her persuasive strategy.

She responded, "With all due respect for your medical understanding of patients' behaviors, the fracas in the dining room was started by another patient, not Anna. And, actually, it was a good sign that Anna had enough sense to defend herself before the other woman hurt her." Lucy did not agree that a *panic attack* was evident; in fact, she thought it was clear evidence that Anna had improved enough to have sufficient clarity of mind to protect herself.

"She was a victim, not a perpetrator," she said. By design, Lucy did not mention that she had toured the Women's Most Disturbed Ward. She omitted that detail in part to protect Nancy Brownell, and in part to make the case against *any* transfer, to any other ward, at this time.

"I'm sorry this happened," she said, "because Anna *is* making progress, I believe. We have to allow more time for less intrusive treatments to work.

"Who knows," she added, "it may very well be that, as new medicines come on the market, there may very well be one that is just right for Anna. So, time is our friend here, don't you agree, Dr. Turner?"

Lucy was deliberate in the rhetorical game she was playing: Appeal to his vanity as a man of science; acknowledge that a medication may well be just the ticket, *some day*; and use time in two ways—time for Anna to improve, and time for the discovery of a magic pill that might treat extreme trauma or might address possible brain damage. Appealing to his vanity was expedient; holding out for a new wonder drug was a long shot.

Dr. Turner agreed that Anna had been the victim and she had likely experienced a fight or flight response. Staff had not seen this kind of disruptive behavior from her in months—because, he agreed, she appeared to be making progress. (Lucy noted the tentativeness in the way he chose to say *appeared*.) Then he said he was pleased to hear that Lucy hoped a new medication might be on the horizon.

"Still," he argued, "it is my professional opinion that your friend will be best served if she were to be placed on Progrol again. It is the best alternative to moving her." His tone was peremptory: There would be only two choices. His use of friend distanced himself from Anna as *his* patient.

Lucy caught it all.

She was afraid things would come to this, again. She, on the side of natural means of treating Anna; he, on the side of science-proven means. Though they had been down this familiar road before, she felt it was different now. This time, Lucy had become more broadly suspicious of the use of medications as a treatment approach; and she had had more time to know more people at the asylum whom she might call on, if needed, in her struggle to care for Anna. Among those people would be Dr. Turner's own boss, Dr. Anderson, Chief Medical Superintendent at the hospital.

Cautiously, Lucy played the only card she had left up her sleeve. "I wonder if other doctors would agree with your recommendation? Dr. Anderson, for example, whom I had the pleasure of meeting just last week."

Dr. Turner eyes moved around the room as he considered what Lucy was intimating. Would she actually go over his head to the hospital's chief medical superintendent? If she did, what would that mean? He couldn't imagine that his boss would ever side with a lay person against the recommendation of his assistant medical superintendent. Besides, and he doubted Lucy knew this, Dr. Anderson, as a matter of policy and principle, resisted, if not outright refused, to be dragged into the particulars of medical treatment for individual patients.

Dr. Anderson represented the hospital to the trustees, the legislature and other hospitals through his travels, meetings, and correspondence. He often compared his job to that of a university president—very important meetings, working lunches and dinners at restaurants, trips downstate and out of state, and hours on the phone with others *at his level.* Like a university president, who would never get involved responding to the complaints of students or the routine gripes of faculty members, he preferred to "stay above all that." He gave Dr. Turner free rein in his domain, unchecked, as a convenience to himself.

Lucy was ignorant of these boundaries, he felt certain. Her remark about talking with Dr. Anderson must have been an idle thought, nothing more. But he could not be certain, and so he felt a slight bit of intimidation.

If Lucy *did* go over his head, and *if* she were successful in making her case to the chief medical superintendent, Dr. Turner might lose some of that blind trust he had worked so hard to build. His credibility might take a small blow, and he did not want that to happen. That would be a slippery slope in the event that, one day, other patient advocates upset the balance of power he felt he needed to protect. In maintaining his grip on all medical decisions, he had too much at stake.

On the other hand, and more personally, he would not

tolerate threat, even implied threat. Especially from a woman. *It may be*, he thought, *that going over my head hasn't even occurred to her. So why be concerned prematurely? No, he was in charge of treatment plans for all patients, no matter what opinions anyone may hold. Who knows, one day, there may be more Sister Lucys poking their noses into the professional decision-making of the men who run the institution! Now, wouldn't that be a sad state of affairs?*

"Dr. Anderson? Oh, I'm so glad you finally got to meet him. Great man, great man for our institution. Of course, you can consult with him, but you should know that he defers all medical decisions to me, so I doubt he would be interested in giving his opinion. You could try, of course, but frankly, I think you would be wasting your time. But let's try your idea before we make any hard decisions. Let's see, once again, what time can do, as you suggest."

With that, he agreed to delay a decision that Anna be returned to a regimen of Progrol. Give it a week, perhaps two. If there were any more incidents, or if Anna became problematic in other ways, she would be put back on Progrol—or moved.

Lucy was pleased. She would pray harder for Anna's stability. Or for divine intervention.

Lucy left Dr. Turner's office relieved. She went in search of the head nurse to share the good news. Nancy was back in her modest office fidgeting with a new typewriter ribbon when Lucy arrived to share her conversation with Dr. Turner. She had prevented Anna's transfer to the Women's Most Disturbed Ward for now and she had gained a week or two to see if Anna would stabilize. She thanked Nancy for helping her see more clearly her alternatives, and she was a bit more hopeful that things may just turn around in the coming weeks.

Nancy placed the typewriter ribbon aside. "We could go downtown and celebrate your little victory with a cocktail," she said, "but it's only eleven in the morning, so that's probably not a great idea. Still, I do want to finish what we began talking about weeks ago, 'the second half of the seminar,' I think you called it."

"Oh yes, I do too."

"Well then, dear, why don't we just talk here and have some tea? Given what you've learned this morning, and given your interaction with Dr. Turner, this seems a most opportune time. You do know, don't you, that as assistant medical superintendent at this hospital, it is Dr. Turner's job to oversee medicinal decisions."

"Yes, I do."

"As such, he is the most direct link between the pharmaceutical industry and the patients. If there are any medicines on the market that may be considered as a treatment option, he is the one to approve them for use here at the hospital. Now, just tuck that in the back of your mind as I tell you about Dr. Jack Ferguson. Were you able to read that book about him, *A Man Against Insanity*?"[13]

---

13. Jack Ferguson, M. D., came to the Traverse City State Hospital in 1954, with the intent to perform hundreds of lobotomies. He never performed any. Instead, he set out to experiment with various drug therapy treatment protocols that combined medications with loving patient care. "It isn't the new medicines alone," said Jack. "They aren't much. They only start up a mental awakening. By themselves they can't carry the patients along. The nurse attendants have got to pour in the confidence—they've got to wipe out the fear ... The nurse attendants treat all their patients as if they were their little sisters" (Paul De Kruif, *A Man Against Insanity* [New York: Grove Press, Inc.], 1957).

Lucy sighed, "I hardly have time to read the newspaper, not to mention a book."

"Then I'll just summarize for you what I think is relevant to you and Sister Anna. And permit me to frame what I am about to say in terms of four lessons. Lesson one has to do with the limitation of medications currently on the market."

Based on his personal experiences with new medications on the market in the mid-1950s (for a time, he himself was addicted to barbiturates, but he overcame the addiction), Dr. Jack Ferguson became a staunch believer in the "new medicines" that were coming on the market.

Jack secured a position as a staff doctor at the Traverse City State Hospital in 1954. At the time, Thorazine, and then Serpasil, were hailed by their makers as the new "miracle drugs," and Jack quickly became their major promoter. He experimented with these medications on patients, with some successes and many failures, until he came to discover that, in treating depression, a combination of Serpasil and a new drug, Ritalin, genuinely helped them out of their woes.

He became famous in psychiatric circles and in the medical field generally, appearing at conferences where he made large claims for the efficacy of the Serpasil-Ritalin treatment regimen. Of course, the drug companies loved him. If they showered him with gifts, no one knew, but they did find in Jack Ferguson a master marketer up here at the northern Michigan asylum. By 1956, he had a good following of believers in the medical field, and he had a string of VIP's coming here to see firsthand what they had been hearing about.

"To Jack's credit," Nancy said, "he cautioned against

believing *solely* in medicines as *the* treatment plan. I remember him saying that it wasn't the medicines alone that mattered. They had to be balanced with tender, loving care. He saw how our nurses treated each patient with gentle dignity, as if each woman were a fragile auntie, each man a beloved uncle. There is a line in the book about him that I committed to memory. It was that 'the mightiest pill still needs love to make it stick.'"

Lucy sat back, raised her eyes to the ceiling, and gazed about the room. "What I hear you describing, is a mid-50s version of the tension between the medical model and the moral model that you talked about the last time we met. Except here there's no conflict between the two. They are in balance. Dr. Ferguson advocated for balance."

Nancy's affirmative nod reinforced Lucy's thought. "Exactly," she said. "In theory, it's a smart balance. But in practice, it presupposes that all the right medications are now available to treat most patients' maladies. But they aren't. It's too early in the development of medications for medicine to be able to say, 'This one is for X, this one for Y,' and so on."

"Someday," Lucy said, "that would be the case, we hope."

"Yes, we hope, *some* day. For *physical* ailments, there are many effective medications, and more that are in development. But for *mental* disorders, medical treatment is much slower, because mental disorders are not physiological. You can't just put, say, depression under a microscope or x-ray it to find the cause or the cure. Mental disorders are far more complicated.

"What scares me the most," Nancy said, "is that the medications we *do* have for mental illness are being used to treat more than what they were intended to address. Though they were intended primarily to treat X—schizophrenia, for example—they are widely used to treat X *and* Y *and* Z, etcetera. The day may come, and I hope it will, when a broad range of medicines will have been developed to pinpoint treatment, but that is not where things stand today. Today we have Prolixin, Haldol, and a few others. Progrol is a new one.

"On to the second lesson : *All medications have side effects*, some worse than others. Some, in fact, are horrible."

"Whew," Lucy sighed. "I can begin to understand why the patients eschew their medications, why they say they make them into zombies. The sedative effect is profound. Look what happened to Anna. She was nearly a vegetable."

"I know," said Nancy. "She was lucky, in a way, because she did not suffer the side effects we nurses see in other patients."

"I need to know more about these side effects."

Nancy cleared her throat. "Yes, you do. But you will learn more about side effects as you spend time on the wards, so we needn't dwell much on this point now. I suspect you already have made some observations, correct ?"

"Yes, I have. Of Anna and others on her ward, as well as patients on other wards. But nothing systematic, nothing that I've gleaned directly from patients themselves, though I would like to do that."

"That would be important, Lucy, first-hand observations. You've made a fine start, however. Now then, on to the third point."

"You're the teacher," Lucy said. "I'm the student."

"Oh, Lucy. I'm sorry if you feel I'm lecturing you—as if you were one of my nurses in training."

Lucy waved a stop-signal hand. "No, no. I'm loving all this education. I've been so tied up in caring for Anna, that I nearly abandoned my research project. No, please, continue. This is bringing me back to purpose, and I desperately need purpose. *Desperately.*"

Nancy continued. "Okay, then. The third lesson has to do with doctors and prescribed medications. It is another history lesson: doctors were only granted the sole right to dispense medicine in 1951, by the Durham-Humphrey Act. That was federal legislation co-sponsored by senators who were pharmacists before entering politics."

"Humphrey? Senator Humphrey? From Minnesota?"

"The very same. He actually was a pharmacist before he entered politics. His co-sponsor was Carl Durham; he was also a former pharmacist. That act, which President Truman signed into law, differentiated between *over-the-counter* medications like aspirin and laxatives, which anyone could buy—and *prescription* medications, which the law established could only be purchased with a doctor's written authorization."

Lucy scrunched up her nose. "Okay? So ... ?"

Nancy sat back. "Well now, think about it, Lucy. Since 1951, who alone has had the power to decide who gets what medications for serious medical and psychological conditions? Who are now the gatekeepers for medications?"

Lucy's eyes widened. "The doctors. Of course."

"And that would include psychiatrists, wouldn't it?" Nancy asked her student.

"I suppose it would. I'm starting to see the big picture," Lucy said. "So, if doctors are the gatekeepers for which medications get prescribed and which ones don't, that gives them discretion."

"Yes ... and?"

"Let me see. And, so, those who manufacture and market medicines have strong incentive to make sure that doctors and psychiatrists not only know *their* pharmaceutical products but also make sure, somehow, that *their* products are preferred over competitors' products."

"In theory?"

"Yes, in theory.

"Some-*how*?"

"Ahh. I get it," Lucy said. "So—*how*, then, might a pharmaceutical company influence doctors to dispense *their* preferred product over others' products? They run a business, and the business of business—is making money!"

Nancy continued. "Correct. So, if doctors believe a medication is really effective, they go around telling the world about it, which I understand. But the problem is that they are susceptible to making claims that aren't necessarily supported by the research, much of which, in my opinion, is unreliable and invalid. Like many of us, doctors have long days with too many patients. Most have little time to do the research needed to verify the claims of new medicines, so they rely on others' recommendations."

"Ah," Lucy said, "like Dr. Turner?"

"It is best that I not comment on that," Nancy said, continuing. "Doctors are under pressure to, as the Hippocratic Oath says, 'either help, or do not harm the patient.' In that spirit, doctors desperately want to help, preferably cure their patients. The pharmaceutical industry—and it *is* an industry—looks for ways to harness that spirit, so they don't mind if their claims are overstated. Maybe they give doctors gifts from time to time. Little perks for some doctors, bigger ones for more valued doctors. Jack Ferguson was given all the drugs he wanted by one company, and guess what, he became a spokesman for that drug—and, by default, for the drug maker."

Nancy now leaned over the edge of her desk, her eyes trained on Lucy's.

"That is lesson four: Making money."

Lucy shook her head as if to clear her mind of all that was piling up there.

"These four lessons have really got me thinking," she said. "Now I see that my research project has to connect the four."

"Yes, you do," Nancy said. Then, "I think you have a very interesting research project. Please remember that all that we have discussed is strictly between the two of us. Nurses nurse; doctors treat. Nurses do not challenge doctors. That is just the way things are and always have been. Besides, I could be fired for suggesting anything that might smack of challenging the wisdom, dare I say, the ethics of my colleagues."

"I never heard you say a word," Lucy beamed. "This is *my* research project."

"Good."

Lucy stirred uncomfortably. "Nancy, what I'm about to say is not about your old colleague Jack Ferguson. But it's historical fact that where money is involved, there is potential for corruption. The *potential*, that's a fact. Money and politics have always been involved in civil rights injustices and exploitation of those living in poverty. That was one of the lessons I took away from our time in the South."

Nancy nodded. "Then you know first-hand why *potential*

is a key word," she continued. "I am not suggesting that there is corruption here, at our institution, but only that the potential is there, if you know what I mean."

"I do," said Lucy. "I don't think you're saying there is corruption here. I understand all that only as theory."

"All right, then," Nancy said, "let's continue with this theory. Some people might think that patients at mental hospitals are the guinea pigs for the pharmaceutical industry. Let's remember that patients are a captive audience, with no legal rights, and no people to advocate for their best interests. You, of course, are a noble exception! But the others here, they can be experimented upon with new drugs that, by and large, don't get extensive trials before they are released. If some of the drugs succeed in keeping patients quiet or serene, the hope looms large that those patients, now calm and no longer a bother to their caregivers, may even be released and returned to their homes."

Nancy pulled out a handkerchief from her desk drawer and dabbed at one eye. Her gaze thoughtful, her cadence slow and even, she continued. "I'm sorry," she said. "I know patients who have been released, sent back to their hometowns cured, quote unquote. Only to lack medical and emotional supports. Lost in a world that no longer has a place for them. Families who find it impossible to cope with their illnesses. Jobs that they can no longer perform. Simple tasks that they cannot accomplish. I can hear their crying voices, I can see their grief-stricken faces. And I am deeply saddened that, in releasing them, we failed them. For everyone who found a way to be successful out there, nine more were returned. The asylum is their only hope, ironic as that may sound."

She dabbed at her other eye as she continued.

"People in state government want to believe in miracle cures because fewer patients in state hospitals reduces the enormous costs associated with more costly, time-and-re-source-intensive moral treatment models. That is why, in the eyes of our legislators, our hospital has come to be considered so expensive. You know, we had an extraordinarily successful farm program, one that gave us a surplus of income, enough of a surplus to not need much money from the state. We could *afford* to treat patients with love and tenderness then, though it was expensive in terms of paying staff to do their work. What did the state care, as long as we were holding our own and expecting little financial support from it?

But when the state put a stop to our independent income stream, we were forced to rely solely on appropriations from the government, and, as institutional costs began to seriously impact state budgets, the politicians began to take the long view based on economics: State hospitals had to be slimmed down, patients had to be cared for in the least costly ways, or sent home, preferably *cured*—or at least *believed* to have been cured. That is why the miracle drugs are so essential to this grand plan of sending patients back to their communities, supposedly restored to health. They are the monetary path to one day boarding up the asylums.

"It was always about money," Nancy said, "not about genuine, thoughtful care. And those, my dear, are the four lessons from today's seminar.

Lucy said, "The tension between the moral and the medical models, that lens seems to illuminate *everything*. For you, it must be impossible to avoid the conflicts, in your daily work, I mean. Practically, not philosophically."

Nancy placed her handkerchief on the desk before her,

folding it over as she spoke. "Moral treatment approaches are my life, you see, and I can get easily discouraged when, as head nurse, I must maintain an equilibrium, and an upbeat attitude lest I fail to provide the stable leadership my nurses deserve. God forbid that I should ever join the ranks of those who believe that medication is the *only* treatment. But, as you know, powerful people here and in government believe that to be scientific fact. I fear that is the rising tide and I fear what it will bring."

The phone rang. Nancy answered. She asked the caller to wait a moment. She put her hand over the receiver and whispered, "I need to take this. But I have to say one more thing."

Lucy put up her palms to indicate she understood time was up. She half rose and then looked to Nancy for the one more thing.

"I know you'll be diligent in your research, and I know you will discover much more that will bolster your commitment to truth—and justice. I just ask that you keep patient care in the front of your mind, that you consider whatever the future may bring through the lens of the *quality* of patient care. If this asylum is to close one day, let us do all we can to ensure that patients receive the care they need and deserve. That is their right."

Lucy rose, walked around to Nancy's side of the desk, leaned over, and kissed her on the forehead. She said, "Thank you for your time and your wise counsel." Nancy blushed.

Lucy headed down the long hall toward the west exit door. She stopped before a captivating portrait of Dr. Munson, the founder of the asylum, and she turned fully toward it. His kindly eyes gazed down at her, and that visage gave her pause, this man who lived and breathed the moral treatment model, whose entire career was based on treating patients with dignity and respect, love and understanding, long before the rise of the pharmaceutical industry. *What would Dr. Munson have done*, Lucy pondered, *had he been chief medical superintendent still today?*

She stared up at him, recalling what Nancy had said about Dr. Turner: "If there are any medicines on the market that may be considered as a treatment option, *he* is the one to approve them. Now, just tuck that in the back of your mind."

Chapter 14

THE ORANGE-AND YELLOW-LEAFED TREES OF EARLY OCTOBER TRANS-
formed into the leafless-branched trees swaying in the
chilly northerly winds of late October. Lucy struggled
through each day, her life one constant shuttle from the
chaplain's office to Ward 3 and the other wards as she made
her humanitarian rounds of comfort. Almost daily, she
would pass Smit or Williams in the halls or on the grounds,
but seldom was she able to share more than a brief greeting,
or more likely, a wave from a distance.

Smit took notice and so did Williams: Lucy's face
showed weight loss, and the way she carried herself registered fatigue.

"Girl needs some fun," Williams observed.

"She's going to run herself ragged," said Smit. "We need
to intercept."

"We need a plan," said Williams.

Saturday morning, Smit called to invite her to join a group
who were going roller skating in the basement of the Michigan Theater on Front Street. Smit had corralled two of the
younger nurses, one with a boyfriend and one with a fiancé,
to go to the Moonlight Gardens Roller Rink that evening.

"I see you around," he said, "and you look so tired and
overworked. You deserve some fun. F-U-N! And who else
to have fun with than Williams and me and a couple of

friendly nurses and their beaus. Come on, Sister Lucy, think of a night on the town as therapy. It's the preferred treatment option."

He would not take no for an answer; he and Williams would pick her up in Smit's "singularly ancient auto" for her well-deserved evening out. There was not a little hint of pleading in his voice. He was firm. Lucy agreed to go.

Smit's ancient auto turned out to be a swamp-green '55 Plymouth station wagon with rusted out rocker panels, a radio antenna bent 45 degrees halfway up, and one white-walled tire among four. Two nurses were already in the back seat when the car pulled up to the front of Lucy's house. Williams gave up his seat in the front to Lucy and hopped in the back with Betty Neilson and Sandy Hughes, first shift nurses from one of the women's cottages.

At 6:30, the Plymouth pulled up in front of the Michigan Theater, where, below the theater, lay the Moonlight Gardens Roller Rink. Loudspeakers blasted popular tunes from the top 40 and colored lights flashed on and off over the wooden floor. They found the rest of their party (two men in their twenties) seated and lacing up on the periphery of the skating area.

Nurse Betty Nielson from Women's Cottage 35 (geriatric women) introduced her boyfriend, Roy, a blond-haired, suntanned house painter whose arms bore white paint speckles from work earlier that day. Nurse Sandy Hughes, also from Cottage 35 introduced her fiancé, Billy Jackson, a Coast Guard Chief Warrant Officer from the Traverse City station. Billy was a huge bulk of a man, crew-cut hair, a chest that testified to years of weight training, arms that bulged with muscle, and soft brown eyes that belied his otherwise steeled physical stature.

Smit introduced Lucy as Sister Lucy Greene, patient advocate and assistant to the hospital chaplains. That introduction earned him a nudge in the ribs.

"Lucy, everyone—please, just Lucy," she corrected.

Billy rose from the bench to shake Lucy's hand.

"I never knew nuns roller skated," he said. "All the nuns in the school I went to—

Saint Pat's—never seemed to be out of the convent except for being in the school where my friends and I did our best to terrorize them!"

"Well, Billy," Lucy laughed, "what you didn't know didn't hurt you. School kids think all we do in our free time is pray. But the truth is, when we're not trying to tame little Billies like you, we ski, listen to music, dance, and—get ready—play poker."

Billy stood up straighter with these last words.

"Well, I'll be darned. I never knew any of that." Then, "Poker? In the convent?"

"In the convent," Lucy said with a smile, "but I've never been on roller skates in my life," her voice rising as Leslie Gore's "It's My Party" belted out over the speakers. "So, let's see how all this goes."

She decided it was not the time to mention, that back in her Kalamazoo convent days, she had acquired a minor reputation as a crackerjack poker player whose ability to bluff was considered "a gift from God—or the devil," depending.

Once out on the floor and semi-confident, the group sailed around and whooped and hollered like teenagers. Lucy had the time of her life, falling more than anyone, and laughing like she'd never laughed in her life, when Williams "danced" her around the rink to Martha and the Vandellas' "Heat Wave."

By nine o'clock, they were exhausted. Back on the benches, Williams suggested beers and burgers at a local spot. Smit put in a vote for the Little Bohemia Grille farther down on Front Street, "because they have the best olive burgers in the state." Williams put forth the U and I Lounge just down the block, where the beer was cheaper, the burgers greasier, and the dance floor bigger than the one at Little Bo's—"just in case our feet get spirited," he added, "though there is one little problem regardless of where we go."

Smit shook his head, said, "Come on, Williams, that was months ago. Besides, there's seven of us now, not two."

Nurse Hughes spoke up. "What?" she said to Williams.

Smit spoke for his friend. "We were at the U & I a couple of months ago, the two of us. And a couple of guys didn't like it that Williams was in there. Because he's, you know, not a white guy like everyone else in this town. They made some trouble, and we, well, we decided to leave rather than, you know … "

"Than get our butts beat," added Williams, turning to Lucy. "Sorry for my language, but you more than anyone would know what we were up against."

"Racism raises its ugly head in the least expected places," Lucy remarked. "No surprise that it should exist here out here in the provinces."[14]

Billy waved his hands and shook his head from side to

_____

14. "While the racism of the South had rattled my nerves, racism in the North would bruise my soul" (Barbara Reynolds, writing in *The Washington Post*, March 6, 2015, about her experiences in the Civil Rights Movement in the 1960s. Accessed February 1, 2020, https://www.washingtonpost.com/posteverything/wp/2015/03/06/i-fought-for-voting-rights-in-1965-racism-in-the-north-hurt-me-as-much-as-racism-in-the-south/).

side. "In the Guard, we have a name for people who cause trouble for people because of their skin color. We call 'em honkies. My Negro Coasties taught me that one."

"All right," broke in Smit. "Let's just go down to the U & I. We'll be fine." But in the back of his head, he thought, Saturday night, well into the drinking hours, in a busy downtown bar in very white Traverse City. He was relieved that Chief Warrant Officer Billy Jackson would be with them.

The U & I Lounge was longer than it was wide, typical of most ground-level establishments on Front Street. They came in from the street entrance and were greeted by loud music from the juke box opposite the mahogany bar where every stool was occupied and where the bartender moved back and forth serving drinks and taking in cash. Nurse Neilson and Roy eyed an open table toward the back of the place and beckoned the others to follow. The group began to weave their way between the backs of patrons sitting on bar stools and the crowded tables opposite the bar. Smit and Williams were last in the entourage.

A couple of men turned on their stools to eye the group as they drifted toward the empty tables in the rear. Their eyes followed Williams, and they turned 180 degrees as he approached. One had slicked-down curly black hair and the other had brown hair combed straight back. Both were dressed in workmen's denim overalls and T-shirts. They'd been drinking since work ended hours earlier, eyes reddened and speech slurred.

Slicked-hair remarked, loud enough for Williams to

hear, that "niggers ain't welcome here." Williams ignored them, proceeding past, staring straight ahead, saying nothing.

Smit, however, stopped in front of the two drunks and faced them, his legs hip distance apart. Hands at his side, he stared directly into one pair of eyes and then the other. His smile was confident, his own eyes narrowed as his head scanned from one man to the other. In a calm voice, he asked them to say that again. Then he sensed someone standing behind him. He glanced over his shoulder to see Billy Jackson standing there, his head cocked so as to hear what the bar drunks had to say. Smit turned back to face the two men at the bar.

One of the drunks began to rise from his stool, his hand clutching a glass mug half full of beer. That's when Billy spoke, over Smit's shoulder.

"Is there a problem, here? Do you gentlemen have a problem with my Negro friend there? Is this something we need to discuss in the parking lot?" He stepped from behind Smit and stood next to him, facing the men at the bar. He pointed toward the rear door and said, "Parking lot, out that door, to my discussion area."

Black-hair pulled on his buddy's sleeve, jerked his head to signal he should sit back down.

"Hey, no problem, man," he said. "We're just shootin' the shit, here, just mindin' our own business."

"Shit, Ernie, I ain't afraid of this asshole," said his accomplice, now half seated on the edge of his stool—and fuming.

Hand still on the sleeve, Ernie said, "Shut up, Larry. That's beer talkin'. Just shut the hell up."

Smit spoke. For his own personal pride, he wanted to

reclaim that moment weeks ago when two other drunks' racist slurs forced him and Williams to leave. He wanted redemption.

"'Cause if there was to be a problem," Smit said, "the cadaver dogs will find your worthless butts in the parking lot tomorrow morning."

Both drunks turned to face the mirror on the wall behind the bar. Larry took another swig and stared down at his mug; Ernie glanced up at the mirror behind the bar where he could see Smit and Billy standing behind him in the reflection. Loud enough for Smit and Billy to hear, he turned slightly toward the two men waiting behind him.

"Like I said, no problem, man."

"All right, then," Smit said. He and Billy stared for a few long seconds and then strolled down past the bar to join their friends at their table.

All that was said came from Billy Jackson, with a jerk of his thumb back toward the bar: "Honkies. Seen one, seen 'em all. Punks. Someday, I hope, fellows like them will be history."

The U & I Lounge speakers blasted out popular tunes, especially Motown. They drank beer, ate giant cheeseburgers and hot fries smothered in ketchup—and they forgot about racing from desk job to ward rounds, calming down frantic patients, changing bed pans, painting houses, training Coasties, and facing prejudiced drunks.

After her second beer, Lucy got up slowly from her chair, announced that it was "recreation time in the ward," pulled Williams up from his chair, and danced the Twist on the dance floor. After which, Williams taught her the Hitchhiker, Smit taught her the Loco Motion, and the two nurses showed everyone the Hully Gully. It was the most fun Lucy had had since—she couldn't remember, it'd been so long since she'd let loose.

When Elvis's "Only Fools Rush In" played, Billy grabbed his fiancé's hand and shuffled off to the dance floor, where they clung to one another. Roy went over to the juke box with a handful of quarters to select the next tunes. Betty Nielsen was invited to dance by a shortish guy in a trimmed goatee who lisped but who made her laugh when he promised to stand on his tiptoes unless she wanted to move around on her knees; off they went. Williams said he needed the john, so that left only Smit and Lucy. He reached over and put out his hand real formal-like. She stood up and curtseyed like they were in a grade school pageant.

As Elvis crooned the first chorus—"and I can't help falling in love with you"—Smit's right hand pressed firmly into Lucy's waist in the rear, pulling her close to him, and he raised her arm closer to their shoulders at a 90-degree angle. She let his arm rest there on her lower back while Elvis sang the second chorus. Then she pushed back to create some modest space, and she pulled her right arm back out to a more proper 135-degree angle.

She stared up at him, with a cock of the head and a smile that said *I understand*—and eyes that said *but, sorry*.

Neither uttered a word, but the moment hung in the air between them as the song ended.

The menacing drunks at the bar were long gone by the time the hospital friends called it a night. Sandy went off with Billy in his car while Roy took Betty back to her nurses' quarters in his. In Smit's station wagon, Lucy sat in the back while Smit and Williams, in the front, rolled down the car windows to let in the frigid air. They all sang along to "Surfin' Safari" on the radio. Smit pulled over in front of her flat. He put the gear in neutral and opened his door just as Lucy opened her rear door. Williams fiddled with the radio, searching for another song.

"I'll walk you up to the door," Smit said, "just, you know, to be safe."

Lucy laughed. "Safe from what?"

She walked to the front steps, he followed.

"Oh, escaped convicts, an unhinged hoodlum from the UP, some crazed predator hiding in the forsythias. You never know."

A goodnight kiss was what he actually had on his mind.

Lucy burst into laughter. "Oh, Smit. You are such a gentleman. But please, get yourself and Williams home while you can still drive. I go home every night, in the dark, alone. I'm sure I'll be just fine." Then she went over to the bushes in front of the porch and said to them, "Hello? Any escapees or hoodlums hiding in there? Anyone a crazed predator? No? Good."

She looked back toward the car, where Smit stood looking at her.

"All clear, Captain!" she shouted.

In the darkness, no one could see Smit's sheepish look as he tumbled back into the car and sat behind the wheel.

When Lucy reached the front door, she turned to wave at her friends. "Thank you both for a wonderful evening," she shouted to the car. "It was just what I needed!"

Once inside, she leaned her back against the door, grasped the cross that hung from her neck, and recalled how wonderful she felt slow dancing with Smit and how thoughtful he was in offering to walk her to her door. The feeling lingered as she undressed for bed, brushed her teeth, said her prayers, and still tipsy, fell into a deep sleep for the first time in months.

Chapter 15

Lucy's night out on the town provided a much-needed break from the tedious responsibilities that made up this chapter in her life. Would it *ever* change? She could not predict. That would depend on Anna. But a mere two days following her therapeutic adventure with roller skating and dancing, change began.

She had just finished her rye toast and coffee, and she was listening to the local news on the radio when a phone call from Nurse Bennett in Ward 3 interrupted her breakfast. There had been another incident in the dining hall, this one involving a female patient at whom Anna began screaming for no apparent reason. In Nurse Bennett's opinion, something, somehow, just clicked the wrong way, and Sister Anna exploded. Dishes thrown, food smeared on faces, some hair pulling—until attendants were able to separate the two. Anna was returned to her room, cleaned up, and given a tranquilizer per Dr. Turner's orders. She was now stable (sleeping) and would be that way for five or six hours, at least. Doctor's orders were that she would be given a full dose of Progrol daily until further notice. "No reason for you to hurry over," said Nurse Bennett. "My shift runs until four, and I'm keeping close tabs on her, poor sweet soul. I ... I just feel so bad. I really hoped it would work out. You know, stopping the medicine and all. I love all my patients and I want them all to be better. But Sister Anna, she's special. You're special. I know you didn't

want her to be on that medicine but now she is, again. I …
just … worry about her—*and* you."

Lucy could tell Nurse Bennett was beginning to choke
up and so she thanked her for the call and her comforting
words.

"And don't you fret about the medicine," Lucy said, "I
knew Dr. Turner might decide to start her on that regimen
again. We *did* discuss that possibility. There's no need for
distress."

Lucy would not argue: this time it *was* different. This
time, Anna was the perpetrator, not the victim, though *why*
she erupted was a mystery.

She poured herself more coffee, thinking. Would Anna
ever recover enough health to come to some degree of independence, some day? That would give hope. That would
allow Lucy to plan her own future. If it were true, as Father
Pete always reminded her, that God works in mysterious
ways as we journey through life, then Lucy could easily see
that her being at the Traverse City State Hospital was just
one more stop on her journey as a Sister of St. Joseph.

This was the religious conviction that buoyed her in
challenging times: she may not know *why* things happened,
they happened for a reason known only to God. Believing
that, without questioning it, was the traditional version of
faith, pure and simple. She called it Faith I. She recalled
a line from St. Paul's letter to the Romans: "Be joyful in
hope, patient in affliction, faithful in prayer." Practically
speaking, "having faith" means being passive, for one's duty
to God demands acceptance. In the secular world of hospitals and treatment plans and doctors, it means accepting
the authority of medical professionals.

But there was another version of faith that Lucy also coveted: Faith II, as she called it.

In her mind, faith was still a source of strength, but also a way of recognizing and enduring the challenges of uncertainty. She could still be "joyful in hope, patient in affliction, faithful in prayer," but she could also act upon personal convictions even when those convictions came into conflict with others' convictions. Faith II meant that no one, including doctors, could have absolute certainty in human affairs, especially when it came to medical matters. It meant that her role in life's journey was to become an active agent in the search for deeper understanding, not a passive acceptor. It meant that instead of praying for a miracle, she was to actively apply her mind and spirit *toward* grappling with the complexities of human frailty.

For Lucy, faith alternated between these two versions. If she could do nothing to prevent Dr. Turner from implementing his medical decision, she had no choice but to accept it. But she could also advocate for alternatives to that treatment plan, as she had before. And as she would again, at the right time and place.

A week after Anna started on Progrol again, on that brisk last day in October, Lucy drove from her home to the hospital. She passed broad front porches where carved pumpkins stared at her in their ghoulish visages—eyes round, triangular, square; mouths with a tooth or row of teeth fiendishly grinning at her. She wondered, *what would this day of tricks, treats, and general revelry be like at the hospital?*

She had heard from nurses what Halloween used to be,

how excited the patients would become at the thought of costumes, games, treats—and tricks of all sorts. Halloween was a day of unpredictable gaiety. Staff would show up for their shifts in various costumes, or at the very least, they would wear masks. Most patients knew that Halloween fell on this day, and many dressed up in their own home-made costumes to mark the event. A visitor to the grounds would see male patients wearing dresses and female patients wearing men's trousers, shirts, and ties. Others wore hobo garb (with red handkerchief bags hanging from long branches carried on their shoulders, just as they had seen depicted in movies), or they donned masks purchased in town, such that devils, angels, clowns, vampires, a variety of Frankensteins, and a handful of witches roamed the halls and grounds, growling and snarling at one another when passing.

In the cottages and wards, Halloween parties featured 2500 donuts made in the asylum bakery; real apple cider made from 20 bushels of apples that had been crushed, pressed, and fermented weeks earlier in the General Kitchen; and 1500 "mummy dogs" (hot dogs dressed in dough strips to resemble bandages, with a singular "eye" made by making a gouge with the finger and placing a raisin in the hole). Depending on the cottage or ward, Halloween games ranged from Bobbing for Apples to Freeze Dance and Make the Zombie Laugh.

Caution was exercised for those patients for whom the ghostly imagery and trappings of death and dying were alarming, if not downright nightmarish. These patients were protected from the parties, according to their wishes, some preferring to view the eerie goings-on from a safe distance. Other patients, for whom one day was no different from another, were oblivious of the controlled mayhem on the floors and grounds.

But those days were long gone. By 1963, the Halloween animation that once filled the campus had dwindled to a shadow of its earlier form. Donuts and cider were still the traditional "treats," available all day long in the wards and cottages, and a few patients still dressed up in costumes or donned scary masks to work their favorite "tricks" on one another, but their numbers were few compared to even five years earlier. The spirit of Halloween had all but disappeared in the new era of wonder drugs: Most patients could not care less about gaiety and trickery.

Lucy spent the morning organizing some files for Father Fred, who was preparing a presentation to the diocese on his vision for the ministry of the new chapel once it was built in the coming year. Convincing the bishop that All Faiths Chapel would be an interdenominational church would be a challenge, but his determination to have a chapel that would serve the range of religious beliefs at the hospital would not deter him. *All Faiths* seemed the perfect name. Securing the bishop's enthusiastic support meant the project could go forward without delay.

She arrived at Ward 3 shortly after the patients had finished lunch. Dr. Gordon was escorting two ladies out of the ward when Lucy entered. He paused, both of his arms firmly wrapped in the arms of the two women. Both looked around him and gave one another fierce looks.

"Frog eyes!" said one.

"Dog breath!" said the other.

"Now ladies, hold your compliments in front of Sister Lucy here. Please. Sister Lucy, Ann Mary here and Mrs.

Wilensky are having a bit of a disagreement, about what, I haven't the faintest idea, and so I'm talking them out to the great lawn for a game of miniature golf. Winner of the game wins the dispute, if it's even remembered by that time. Isn't that right, ladies?

"I'll cream your ass."

"I'll wipe you out."

"Oh my" was all Lucy could muster. "Golf?"

"Therapeutic golf, to be precise. Somehow that game can soothe a savage breast, in a manner of speaking. You know, many deals have been struck on a golf course. Partnerships have been formed; treaties have been struck; even adversaries have overcome their differences. It has a way of deflecting even the most contemptuous inclinations. Who knows how the world would be different if Pilate had had a golf course to adjourn to when he presided at the trial of Jesus?"

"Get bent!"

"Stuff it!"

"Well," Dr. Gordon continued as he made his way with his captives down the hall, "you have a pleasant day, Sister Lucy."

She stopped by Alice's room first, as she always did, to check on her. Still wearing her green nightgown and wool slippers, Alice lay motionless on her bed, her back to the door. Lucy came in quietly, moved around the bed so Alice could see her. Alice glanced up; her eyes half rolled back in her head; saliva dripped from her mouth. Crumbs from something she had eaten lay scattered about her head—the remains of crackers, it appeared.

Lucy brushed the crumbs off the sheet and into the palm of one hand as she caressed the shoulder of the old woman with the other hand. It was past that time in the day when she could expect Alice to speak to her, that time before she had been given her daily meds. Lucy pushed aside some strands of gray hair from the woman's cheek and placed them behind her ear. Alice stared at the wall, silent.

There is no one in there, thought Lucy. *Where there was once a woman suffering from dementia, a woman whose existence, however limited, consisted of believing she had a family nearby and a baby to care for, now there was nothing but time passing, unmarked by the hands of a clock or the anticipation of events.*

"You are a beautiful mommy and a wonderful friend," she whispered in the prone woman's ear. "And I love you, and I know you love me too. May God bless you."

Lucy stepped back into the hallway. She recognized the sound of the applause meter and Jack Bailey's voice as a television in the corner broadcast the game show *Queen for a Day*. Two women sat on stiff chairs in front of the monitor, one tearing a newspaper into tiny shreds that she dropped into a metal basket while the other pointed up to the screen and shouted, "The fat one, she's gonna win, 'cause she's got a sick kid."

Lucy sat with Anna most of the afternoon and evening on this Halloween, taking her to dinner in the women's wing and offering her a donut and cup of cider or dessert. Anna's face brightened when she heard Mrs. Rayburn poke her head in her room to shout, "Happy Halloween," and when a handful of revelers belted out "Screaming Ball at Dracula Hall" outside her window. Of her own volition, Anna rose from her bed to look down at the costumed group gathered on the sidewalk.

Anna cocked her ear to the window in order to hear the singing. Lucy stood next to her and pointed down at the singers, saying, "Look, Anna. Look at their colorful costumes."

But Anna didn't look down at the group. She stood there, her ear pressed to the window. Lucy came around and stood in front of her friend as she placed her hands on Anna's face and looked directly into her eyes. "You can't see them, can you, dear heart? The singers down there in their costumes."

Anna shook her head slightly from side to side. The revelers were only one story down, so close that it would have been possible for Anna to make out some faces. Tears rolled from Anna's eyes as she wrapped her arms around Lucy and placed her head on Lucy's shoulder.

"I ... can't ... see ... you," she said, her voice trembling. "I ... can't ... see."

They held one another for long moments. Silence. Lucy took both of Anna's hands in her own as she stepped back and said softly, "You suffer silently. You want to cause no burden, not to me, not to the nurses. You are an angel."

"Mmm," Anna mumbled.

"But even angels have vision problems. So now we must get to the bottom of this."

A doctor showed up in five minutes. With his little pen flashlight, he examined Anna as she lay on her bed. She did not flinch when he put the light on bright, nor did her eyes follow as he waved the scope from side to side.

"Hmm," he mumbled to himself. Lucy stood, alert,

expecting he would say something to her, but he didn't. She had gotten used to the way doctors kept information to themselves when stumped. *He could have explained the curious hmm,* she thought to herself. *After all, I'm not a stranger here.* It didn't matter to her if it was the *hmm* of puzzlement or the *hmm* of surprise. She was not one to be left standing there uninformed. Still, she waited.

He turned to her and said Dr. Turner needed to examine Anna. Nothing more was said as he left the room to call from the nurse's station.

Dr. Turner conducted the same tests with his own ophthalmoscope. Then he felt around the sides of Anna's temples and the back of her neck. Lucy sat on a chair in the corner of her room, her fingers twitching nervously, her feet changing position every few seconds. *What is he looking for?* Like the previous doctor, he kept things to himself.

Dr. Gordon showed up, fresh from the miniature golf course. He peered down at Anna, watching as Dr. Turner took a pulse.

"Normal," Lucy heard Dr. Turner say.

Then he nodded Dr. Gordon toward the hall, and both doctors passed by her chair and left the room, closing the door behind themselves.

In the hall, they spoke in soft whispers. Only Dr. Turner returned to the room. More tests were in order. In the morning Anna would be transferred to Munson Hospital on the adjacent campus, where they had state-of-the-art x-ray equipment. Munson Hospital had the best specialists in all of northern Michigan.

Another long silence forced her to ask the obvious: "Well then, Dr. Turner, this seems very unusual. We've had no indications that her vision was threatened. Why didn't someone notice something on rounds? She kept the problem to herself, yes, but … still. I would like to know, what is your thinking?"

He hunched over a bit, hand rubbing his closely shaven cheek. He glanced out the window as the revelers struck up another song. He took out his small notebook and scribbled something down. All in silence. His reticence had made her nervous, almost as if she had asked something inappropriate, as if she did not have a right to know his thinking. Sociolinguistic thoughts raced through her mind: *Could it be that he's challenged by what he cannot explain? Is it hard for him to admit to her, a mere woman, the limits of his knowledge? Or worse, that his medical staff missed some warning signs?*

Finally, he spoke. "Well, her vision *is* challenged, but I predict it's only a temporary condition brought on by the headaches. And, even though she hasn't had severe headaches lately, they can cause ocular spasms and narrowing of blood vessels leading to the eyes. This could be the result of the, ah, unfortunate event that brought her here. The technical term is amaurosis fugax. It's also known as episodic blindness, but that normally only occurs in one eye, not two. That's what is so unusual. In her case, that is. Both eyes."

Lucy knew that he knew she didn't know what amaurosis fugax was, or how long temporary blindness might last. She was tempted to ask what he meant by *temporary*: Was it temporary like the common cold, or temporary like the cold war?

She responded with the most pressing question on her mind.

"Could this be caused by the Progrol she was taking? Could that have set in motion a slow progress toward loss of vision? Maybe there *were* warning signs?"

Dr. Turner's own eyes widened, and his voice rose. His tone was defensive.

"Absolutely not," he said. "Progrol has been tested thoroughly. The research has clearly demonstrated its safety. Never has there been a side effect associated with vision. Never."

Lucy avoided his stare. He had been too quick to respond. *Never* had been too repetitious. It was a put-that-thought-out-of-your-mind brand of *Never*.

Too quick, she thought to herself, *curious*.

In the eerie silent interval following Lucy's question and Dr. Turner's response, Dr. Gordon came back in the room. His presence broke the impasse.

"Why don't I just call over to Munson now and get things rolling?" he said. "We should be able to get Anna there first thing in the morning."

Lucy spent the night in Anna's room, curled up with a blanket and dozing occasionally on a cushioned chair brought to her by the night nurse. In the morning, an ambulance arrived to take Anna over to Munson, even though the hospital was only two blocks away. Lucy followed in her car. Once Anna was admitted and comfortably settled in her hospital room, Lucy was urged to go home and get some rest. The tests would stretch over days, not hours, and she would be alerted immediately if there were any news or if she were needed. Assured that Anna would be well cared for by *those* nurses, Lucy drove home. She was exhausted.

As she pulled up in front of her house, she saw Smit's station wagon parked across the street. The chill of early morning had given way to a warm front moving in. The temperature had risen to 50 degrees and the sun shone through the leafless trees.

Smit sat on the top stair of her porch. He wore his asylum whites under a blue nylon parka. A red stocking hat covered his head. Surprised to see him sitting there, Lucy waved as she closed her car door and walked up to the porch stairs, where she stood, arms akimbo.

"Smit? What are you doing here?"

"I heard about Sister Anna and I ... well, I just was wondering how you're doing. I know she's at Munson for some tests, so I called over there and they told me you were going home, and so I took an early lunch. I have something very healthy to cheer you up."

He pulled a paper sack from behind his back and handed it to her.

"Chocolate doughnuts. Fresh today from the canteen." He handed the bag to Lucy. "Here. Try one."

"Oh, Smit. You're so kind. What would I do without you thinking about me all the time?"

"Well, I don't think about you *all* the time. Sometimes I have other things on my mind." Then he scooted over and invited her to sit down, saying, "Anyway, I have something that'll interest you. Have a seat—and a doughnut, Sister."

She sat next to him on the steps, stretched her legs out in front of her and let out a big yawn. She munched on a doughnut. Could he be brief? She was very tired.

"I'll try," he began. "It's about that research project—you know, the one you're doing, the one you asked us to help you with?"

She nodded.

"Okay, then. I received this letter yesterday, from my faculty advisor from the U of M, Professor Higgins.

"I told you about him a while ago," Smit said. "Political science department, specialty in Indochina history but a generalist on current political events. He's very connected to other scholars at other schools, and he has a close colleague at Georgetown, in DC. So apparently, he told this colleague about how his two students (Williams and I) figured out how to avoid the draft by going to work at a mental hospital."

He looked sideways at Lucy. "Something I never told you about. How Williams and I ended up here. We have a deferment as long as we work here."

"I always wondered," she said.

"I figured you did," he said. "Anyway, with Dr. Higgins and this other professor, a Dr. Jamison, it was all just a friendly exchange of information and points of view, like what academics do when they talk at conferences. Wait, back up. I hope you don't mind, but, in an earlier letter, I did tell him about you and your experiences in the South and how you came to be here. Just the barest of details. No names, no personal information. Sorry I didn't ask your permission, but I did that only because he's written articles on civil rights, human rights, a lot of things that I thought connected with your *mission*, I think you called it. I was just fishing for anything that might help you with your research project."

Lucy interrupted him. Her fatigue was working on her

patience. "Where is this going, Smit? I've had a long night. I don't mind that you told your professor about me, so don't worry. Go on, please."

He pulled out the Higgins letter and unfolded it.

"Professor H says that President Kennedy is expected to sign into law some new legislation.

"It's called *The Mental Retardation Facilities and Community Mental Health Centers Construction Act of 1963*, the *Community Mental Health Centers Act* for short.[15] This legislation, has been in the works for a long time and it comes about as part of the president's *Bold New Approach* to mental health care."

"I didn't know about this," Lucy said.

"I didn't either. But Professor H gives some context for Kennedy's interest in the issue. "See, Kennedy's sister, Rose Marie, suffered from a mental condition that was made much worse when she underwent a lobotomy some years ago. She was committed to a mental hospital somewhere in the Midwest—Wisconsin, maybe Minnesota; the family kept it all pretty secret. But his experience with mental

---

15. "In 1963, President John F. Kennedy passed the pivotal Community Mental Health Centers Act (CMHCA), which provided grants to states allowing for the establishment of community-based outpatient mental health centers. The legislation was meant to phase out institutionalism and reduce federal mental health costs" (Heather Artushin, "A Cathedral of Care: The Traverse City State Hospital," [*Chronicle*, Historical Society of Michigan, Winter, 2017] 14-17).

"Fewer than half of the envisioned 1,500 community mental health centers were ever built—about 650. In addition, federal funds were provided only for their construction, not for maintaining their staff, and the states were generally not prepared to provide funds to run the centers at the levels needed" (Anne Harrington, *Mind Fixers: Psychiatry's Troubled Search for the Biology of Mental Illness* [New York: W. W. Norton & Company, 2019] 11).

illness in his own family and Rose Marie's institutionaliza-
tion made the president especially sensitive to the issues."

"I see. So, what else is in the letter?" she asked.

"Plenty," he said. "The intent of this new law was to
create a national network of community mental health
centers that would eventually replace large state hospitals.
They would resemble clinics for people to drop in, get help
for medications, see a counselor, etcetera. It's pretty vague
in the legislation, Professor H says. More the big ideas than
many specifics."

Smit read directly from the photocopy of a piece of the
legislation that his professor had included in the letter:
"*State hospitals, the decrepit and costly anchors of mental health
in the country, were to be supplanted by community mental health
centers.*" Then he paraphrased again. These centers, along
with the emergency rooms of regular hospitals, would
become the front line treatment facilities in the war on
mental illness. Professor H's read on all this is good theory
and smart politics, but the reality will come when mental
patients are actually cared for properly outside of institutions. In fact, he wonders, if so many mental hospitals
can't provide adequate care in the very structures that were
designed for quality care, how will anything be different if
everything is decentralized? He even goes so far as to suggest that mental patients ought to have legal representation,
or at the very least, personal advocates. Now, does that part
sound familiar?"

Lucy took it all in thoughtfully, the wheels in her mind
beginning to turn in spite of the cloud of exhaustion. She
was reminded of the last thing Nancy Brownell urged just
weeks ago, that Lucy consider whatever the future may
bring through the lens of the quality of patient care. "If this

asylum is to close one day," Nancy had said, "let us do all we can to ensure that patients receive the care they need and deserve. That is their right."

"There is one more thing from the letter," Smit said. "But first, an aside. Professor H, he has that rare, wide-ranging vision that makes him a learned mind. In his classes, he was always giving students a law or a pending legal case and then inviting us to investigate how the law would actually work in society. Like *Brown vs. Board of Education*. It was supposed to desegregate schools, but all it did was cause white people to start moving to the suburbs and leave inner city schools all black and subject to inevitable decline.

"Okay, so stay with me, Lucy. This will be a long chain of dots.

"Dot one: civil rights. Dot two: Professor H believed the American Civil Rights Movement was related to the growing conflict in Southeast Asia. The 1954 Geneva Accords that divided North and South Vietnam when the French pulled out of southeast Asia, were supposed to keep communism in the north and democracy in the south. But Professor H suggested that was a solution to the wrong problem. What the world powers didn't recognize was that the situation in Vietnam was a war of independence from *any* colonial power, first from the French and now from the U.S. He thought the U.S. was going to make the same mistake the French made. At the end of the letter, he wrote that his friend at Georgetown had learned that the Joint Chiefs are asking for thousands more troops to send over there. The U.S. thinks it's preventing communism from spreading, but the truth is that the U.S. is just another colonial power trying to control another country's historical struggle to maintain its cultural identity in its own way.

Professor H refers to this as a struggle for nation's rights. That's dot two.

"Dot three? Patient rights in a mental institution. Summary? Human rights."

Smit folded up the letter and stuffed it back into his shirt pocket. He went down the stairs and then turned to look back at Lucy.

"Interesting," she said, "the interconnectivity of human rights."

"Exactly. The exploitation. The injustices. The ignorance of history. I knew you'd see the bigger picture that Professor H paints," he said. "It's all related—civil rights in the south, nation's rights in Viet Nam, patients' rights in institutions like this one. What you said about your mission in life really stuck with me, Sister. With Williams too. He and I talk about these things a lot. For you it was the rights of Negroes and now it's the rights of mental patients. For Williams, it's civil rights too, of course. But for us as young draft-age males, we, too, can easily become the victims of politicians' fears and ideologies. I'm not sure what to call our rights, Williams and me and a few thousand other guys, but we do have the right to refuse to hurt or kill people we have no beef with. It took me a while, but now I see how it's all connected. Funny how I never gave a thought to the rights of people institutionalized until I landed here and began to see things firsthand. For me, the big picture is that no one has the right to colonize others."

Lucy beckoned him back. "Come, sit here again, Smit," she invited. "I want to ask you about something we talked about, that day on the grounds when we sat by the warehouse. Do you remember what we talked about?"

"Sure," he said, up the stairs and sitting next to her again.

The engine of a car starting up on the street drowned out their voices momentarily. He waited until the driver stopped revving the engine.

"We talked about a lot of things," he said.

She reminded him that she had asked if he and Williams were willing to share with her things they saw or heard on the grounds and in the wards and cottages.

"*Odd things*, I think you said, Lucy. What we might see or hear that might cause you to question the civil rights of patients."

"That's it."

"Yes, I remember that, and I told Williams about it, and we both started carrying little notebooks to write down anything that strikes us as curious—things that seem out of place.

"I can speak for Williams on this too," he continued, "because he's as much eyes and ears as I am, and we compare notes."

Lucy took a deep breath, still fighting off fatigue but driven to know more about the side effects of medications now that Anna's vision had been affected, and now that she suspected Progrol to be the cause. Without going into her conversation with Dr. Turner on that topic, she asked if he and Williams had gathered any observations on the side effects of medications given to patients.

"Not really," Smit said. "We see side effects every day, they are so common. No need to write anything down. I didn't think that was something odd. It's just a way of being here."

Lucy asked him, could he elaborate? But Smit now had his sleeve pulled up to check his watch.

"Williams and I can tell you all you need to know about

side effects, but right now, I'm way past my little hiatus from work and need to get back. But tell you what, when it comes to side effects, rather than *me* telling you what *we* see, why don't you just go talk to the sources themselves? Find a couple of patients who can tell you firsthand what it's like to be taking some of these drugs. Get it directly from the horses' mouths. That'll be ten times better than Williams or me describing things. The patients can tell you better than I can. Try old Mr. Frederick, for one, in whatever cottage he's in now. He's the most outspoken about taking medications; runs away every chance he gets just to avoid it. Get him in the morning before they force him to take his meds. He'll level with you. And try one of the ladies on Sister Anna's ward, one of those elderly ladies who're getting drugged just because she's old and losing it."

He glanced again at his watch, muttered, "I have to go," and then started out in a half run to his car. The green Plymouth roared down the street, a plume of exhaust following.

Chapter 16

THE FIRST TWO WEEKS OF NOVEMBER HAD LUCY SHUTTLING BACK AND
forth to the hospital, where Anna had undergone a battery
of tests and examinations. Dr. Caulkins, an ophthalmologist, oversaw Anna's case. On November 14, Anna was
ready to be returned to the ward.

The doctor met Lucy outside Anna's room when she
arrived to take her home. A tall, angular man wearing a
white hospital coat complete with stethoscope dangling
from a large side pocket, he spoke fast, and he glanced at his
wristwatch once or twice, as if to signal that a busy doctor
has much to do. Which was probably true but in poor taste
to demonstrate it so crudely.

"As you were likely briefed by a nurse on the phone," he
said, "Anna's acute traumatic brain damage that she suffered in a previous *incident*, resulted in a rare eye disorder
called microaneurysm."

With a too-loud voice, he assured Lucy that the condition could be treated with cold compresses, eyedrops, and
rest. "Ninety percent of the time full vision is restored," he
said. "The treatment could take weeks but the daily care
she will get in Ward 3 would be more than sufficient for
her recovery. And, rest assured, she *will* recover." Smiling,
he rocked back on his heels and dug his hands into his coat
pockets. "That's really all I have to say, unless you have
questions, Miss."

At first, Lucy was elated with this news. But the doctor's

manner of delivering it—the way he spoke fast, the way he exuded confidence in stating his medical opinion—just gave rise to more questions for her. Why, Lucy wondered, had he attributed Anna's condition to what *he already knew* from Dr. Turner—that Anna had suffered brain damage? Why didn't he bring up the possibility that a medication—Progrol—might have had something to do with it? Perhaps a side effect that didn't quite make it into the medical journal review? Or that Dr. Turner chose to ignore?

She said, "I do have a question. What else could have caused this?"

He visibly winced. "Well, Miss, uh ... "

"Greene."

"Miss Greene. She suffered blunt trauma to the head at one time, and ... and that often takes a while for latent effects to show up. It's rare, but not uncommon, to take that long. In this case, I think it's most likely. But you shouldn't worry, your friend will surely recover soon with the right home treatment approach. I've already sent over my notes to Doctors Turner and Gordon. They'll know just what to have the nurses do. Don't you worry."

She gave him that *I'm-not-worried-I'm-just-wondering-and-by-the-way-don't-patronize-me* look that created an awkward silence. He checked his wristwatch again and then fidgeted with the dangling stethoscope.

"Doctors Turner and Gordon are colleagues of mine," the ophthalmologist explained, looking past her, for her question and her stare were starting to make him uneasy. "They will be able to oversee her recovery. There's no worry," he added, "no worry at all."

She smiled. "It's not that I'm worried," she said. "It's just that your tests can only determine the diagnosis, not the cause, with any degree of absolute certainty. So let's say the cause were to be repeated in the future, like something dangerous she does with her eye or with a medication's side effect, say, then diagnosis without knowing causation for certain would not prevent the same thing from happening again, would it?"

He cleared his throat. "It's a valid point, Miss Greene. But in this case, we doctors can be fairly certain that what happened to her months or years ago is the most likely cause."

A call came over the intercom asking him to take a phone call. He excused himself and went over to the nurse's station to take it.

Lucy stood there thinking.

She ignored the linguistic fact that "we doctors" excluded her. She remained convinced that the "we doctors" had arrived at the most *available* reason, not necessarily the most *likely* reason.

Questions swirled through her mind.

Do doctors do this regularly? she wondered. *Do they latch onto the first available possible cause—just because it occurred recently or just because "the research" says it often causes this condition?*

Perhaps Anna had had another underlying condition, something cardiovascular, or neurological. Perhaps their battery of tests was unable to find *any* underlying condition. If that were the current limitation in the state of medicine, then why didn't he just say so? Or did pride enter into this whole thing? Had he been so quick to ascribe causation because he wanted to appear all-wise? Did he even know that Anna had been taking Progrol? Or had that fact been withheld because it *really may have* contributed to her condition? And, if that fact had been withheld, why?

But let's turn the tables, she thought: If he *had* known about her taking Progrol, and did *not* know about the trauma she had suffered, would he have speculated that it was the medication that had caused her to lose her sight? Would Progrol have become the first available possible cause? If he didn't know she was taking Progrol, why didn't he?

The ophthalmologist said he was a "colleague" to Doctors Turner and Gordon. Was that code for the old boy network? Was the ophthalmologist somehow in collusion with the whole wonder drugs phenomenon sweeping the nation? Would attributing Anna's vision problem to Progrol violate some spoken or unspoken mores among "we doctors?"

What the ophthalmologist had said—and had not said—gave her a glimmer of insight into possible connections between medications, the medical profession, and diagnostic procedures. *There's something here*, she thought, *more dots. But now is not the time nor the place.* She let it go for now.

Dr. Caulkins came back from his call. He apologized but said he had an emergency to get to in the ER. He said Anna's release papers were being drawn up and she could go home within the hour. He reached out and shook her hand. She thanked him for taking time with her. It was all very cordial.

Lucy secured Anna's release and drove her back to Ward 3. On the way, they stopped by Oleson's Grocery and picked up orange popsicles, which they ate while sitting in the car in front of Building 50. They both had orange lips when they entered the ward. The nurses and awake patients cheered and clapped when she and Anna came in. Lucy escorted Anna to her room, where a large bouquet of late fall goldenrod and purple mums greeted them. Lucy guided Anna's hands to the flowers and described them to her.

"From your dear friends," she whispered as Anna lay down, fully clothed, to rest—a slight smile breaking across her face.

Lucy's work for the chaplainry increased. Longer hours every day as Father Fred's plans for the new All Faiths Chapel advanced to soliciting contributions from the wide range of counties that constituted the northern Michigan diocese. Every parish in the diocese had families with a loved one in the state hospital, and it was those families, through the Council of Churches in each community, that lobbied hardest for Father Fred's dream. The goal was $300,000 to build an ecumenical home for the 3000 residents at the hospital and the surrounding community. The church building had been designed by a Traverse City architect to include two chapels, Catholic and Protestant—along with another space for Jewish services—so that people of all faiths could be served. As the money started pouring in, groundbreaking was scheduled for spring, with completion expected in early 1965.

A visit from the Weaver brothers came one afternoon as Lucy was folding letters into envelopes to be picked up with the four o'clock mail. Georgie and Harold knocked politely, and then entered the tiny office she shared with Father Pete.

"Lucy Greene!" announced Harold, "We've come bearing gifts, like they say in the Bible."

Lucy laughed, "It was actually the poet Virgil who had a character say that," she said, "but it does sound like the New Testament."

"Close enough for a J-J-Jew like me," Georgie remarked.

Harold glanced sideways at his friend. "I didn't know you were Jewish, George. You never told me that."

Georgie poked him in the ribs and laughed, "My great aunt T-T-Tabitha, on my mother's side. Th-that makes me 1/16th J-Jewish."

"Geez, Georgie. What a kidder!" Then, to Lucy, "Okay, so Lucy Greene, we hear you are *Sister* Lucy, so you can't be Jewish too."

"Yes to the former, no to the latter," Lucy responded. But here, I'm just Lucy Greene, *Sister* Lucy only if you insist. But yes, I am a nun from the Society of St. Joseph. So is Anna in Ward 3, Sister Anna Jorgenson."

"Well, I'll be d-d-darned. My pa was C-Catholic, but then after the first war, he c-c-c-came back an atheist. Said God would never allow the th-th-things he saw to happen. He n-n-never went to ch-church again."

Harold broke in. "C'mon, Georgie. Not now, okay?" Then, to Lucy, "Lucy Greene, we brought over a table runner we made. It's for the new chapel. Here." He handed Lucy the paper sack and out of it she pulled a ten-foot white runner with a brilliant red cross in the middle, smaller crosses populating both ends.

"Another beautiful work of art," Lucy said, holding the

runner up to the light. "Father Pete and Father Fred will love it. Thank you so much. You bring so much joy into the world. Thank you."

"Th-that's what weavers do," said Georgie.

"Yep," said his friend. "That's what we do."

When not working, Lucy spent much time with Anna, whose recovery was much slower than anticipated (slight improvement in one eye, just enough for her to make out shadows). In whatever "free time" she was able to carve out of her busy days, she sought opportunities to learn more about side effects of medications. She still suspected a connection between Progrol and Anna's blindness. Neither Dr. Turner, Dr. Gordon, nor the ophthalmologist ever said definitively what caused Anna's microaneurysm. *No certain known cause*, she figured, meant anything *reasonable* could be causation. But Progrol had not even been mentioned as a possible cause. Curious.

On the morning of November 23, Lucy went to Ward 3 as the usual first stop of her day. In any given week, she tried to visit each woman in the ward, if only for a few moments to say hello or bring a candy treat or a magazine she had found discarded somewhere. Since most of the women in the ward suffered from varying degrees of aging-related disorders, few could remember why they had been institutionalized or even what family they had somewhere. Most had not been visited by relatives or friends in years. For most, Lucy was their only contact with the outside world. Lucy tried to get to the ward by eight o'clock, between breakfast and the dispensing of medications, when the women were inclined to be more alert and receptive.

Such was the case on this blustery November day, when Lucy stopped to visit Alice, *before* medications. It was her intention to follow up on the advice given her by Smit— "get the lowdown on side effects straight from the horse's mouth," he had said.

Alice was standing at the window, her back to Lucy when she knocked on the door. She wore a faded red cotton shift, a white T-shirt under it, and black leather slip-on shoes. She turned to greet her friend, her Baby Sally wrapped in the familiar white blanket and lying on her shoulder as Alice bounced slightly up and down as if to soothe the doll's imaginary distress. A broad smile crossed Alice's face when she saw Lucy.

Lucy motioned her to sit next to her on the edge of the bed. Then she pulled out a baby rattle from her purse and handed it to Alice.

"This is for Baby Sally, Alice. Here, you can hold it for her. Shake it and see if that doesn't calm her down."

Alice shook the little plastic rattle in the doll's face as she leaned into it and kissed a cheek.

"Alice," Lucy continued, "I wonder if you could put your baby down to rest for a little while? I have something I want to ask you about."

The woman placed her doll on the bed pillow and carefully wrapped it in its blanket. Then she turned her full attention on Lucy.

"What is it, Sister? We can talk now. She's asleep."

Lucy explained that she wanted to know what Alice thought about the medicine she was given every morning after breakfast. She was curious: Could Alice help her understand, what was her experience with the medicine?

Alice looked at the door to the hallway. It was closed. A troubled look passed over her face, and Lucy guessed what it was.

"Don't worry, honey. The doctors won't know whatever you tell me. This is just between you and me. I'm just ... just wondering if you're different from how you are now. Because I see you *after* you take your medicine, just as I see others here. And, well, you seem different. But I'm not inside you to know how you feel. Inside. That's where it matters most, see?"

A spigot opened, and truth cascaded out. No one had ever asked Alice *this* question. In fact, no one had ever asked any of the women on this ward or any of the other wards, as far as Lucy knew. She herself had observed the effects and the side effects on patients, but nowhere had she ever heard patients themselves talk about either. Their voices were excluded from the data that doctors and nurses routinely gathered. Lucy suspected that because patients had no legal rights, and because they were considered mentally unstable, their lived-through experience, their voice in their own affairs, was irrelevant. Worse, because so many had been abandoned to live in institutions, few people on the outside cared what the patients themselves had to say about the ways medications affected them. After the lab rats and spider monkeys, they were, in fact, the first humans on whom the pharmaceutical industry experimented. From her "seminars" with Nancy Brownell, Lucy recalled Nancy saying, "Patients are a captive audience, with no legal rights, and no people to advocate for their best interests."

"Oh, Sister Lucy," Alice began, "It's like night and day for me. I know I'm not all right here." She pointed to her head. "That's why Ray—he's my husband—wanted me to come here. He said I couldn't take care of our children anymore. I kept losing track of who was who, there was so many of 'em, kids I mean. Then I started leaving them behind at places. Left little Jeremy or maybe it was Johnny, in the grocery store one day and didn't know it until I got home, and Ray noticed.

"But then it got worse. I don't remember it, but they say I dropped Baby Janie from the attic window and she fell all the way down, down, and there she was on the driveway. She never cried, though. Ray, he said I had to go away and get help, he couldn't trust me anymore. So, my mum and da took some of the younger ones. And the older ones, I guess they just had to shift for themselves 'cause Ray had to keep his job and all. I never did learn how they all fared once I was gone. Ray said I did other things too, but I don't ever remember any of those. Doctor told me I was just getting old before my time. But heck, I'm only ... I don't know how old I am."

She looked over at the doll wrapped in that white blanket. "At least they let me bring Baby Sally here. At least I have *some* family. I don't know where the rest of them went to. Some days I think I'm back home and they're off to school or work, but then I realize no, I'm here and they're there. I get so confused. I'm sorry, Sister. I'm just so sorry. I've been good, but maybe I did something bad."

Lucy put her arm around Alice, who leaned into her just as Anna always did when she felt safe. "No, sweetheart. You just have a sickness in your head. It's not your fault. You are good, you are ... loved."

They sat in silence a few moments. Then Lucy asked, "How are you after you take your medication in the morning, Alice? How do you feel?"[16]

"My whole body goes crazy. I can't hardly walk or sit or stand without almost falling over. I feel like my face is falling off, you know, like the skin is peeling away, so I scratch at it and pull at it. The ladies out there (she pointed toward the hall) they think I'm making faces at them, but I'm not; I just can't stop my skin from, just, getting all shivery. I can't hardly talk. I know what I want to say, but I can't get my tongue and my lips to say the words. Sometimes, my legs start to quiver, and my hands shake so much I can't even hold a spoon. All I can do is go to bed and sleep. Or I just sit here and look out the window at the birds and the trees. I just don't care about anything—eating, going to the bathroom, talking, anything. Then it's dinner time and I go, but no one talks there, and I don't, for sure. Then we come back here and then it's time for bed, even if the sun's still shining. Then I sleep and then it's morning and I don't want morning-before-medicine to end. It's the only time I

---

16. "The drugs I had taken for so many months affected every part of my body. My eyes kept going out of focus, especially when I tried to read. My mouth was dry, my tongue swollen, my words slurred. Sometimes I forgot what I was trying to say. My body was puffy. I hadn't menstruated in months and I was able to move my bowels only with enormous amounts of laxatives. I had no energy at all. If walking around in a constant haze is supposed to be tranquility, I was successfully tranquilized" (Judy Chamberlin, *On Our Own* [New York: McGraw-Hill, 1978] 52).

"Some patients experienced the drug-induced change in brain function as a positive, reporting that the drugs made them calmer, less fearful, and even clearer in mind" (Robert Whitaker, *Mad in America: Bad Science, Bad Medicine, and the Enduring Mistreatment of the Mentally Ill* [New York: Basic Books, 2002] 176-77).

feel like a person. Even if I am crazy, at least I feel like a person."

A knock at the door; they both turned. Nurse Hemley stood in the doorway, one arm cocked before her, her face staring at the watch on her wrist, the forefinger of the other hand pointing at the watch.

"Medicine time, Alice. Your turn, sweetheart." The nurse, older and grayer compared to so many of the others, had a face that seemed to alternate between sternness and compassion, her job one of guiding Alice to the nurse's station for meds, while awkwardly commiserating with her reluctance. Lucy thought she could detect tension in this nurse's tone and choice of that word, *sweetheart*. Did most nurses feel this way? Did most feel an unsettled mix of duty and compassion as they herded patients along to their appointed time, like it or not, resist it or not? Lucy wondered what Nurse Hemley would do if Alice flat-out refused to go with her. But no, Alice would not be one to resist. She would follow the rules. Alice was a "good patient."

Alice turned her face toward the window and stretched her neck to see a flock of barn swallows swoop by and land on a sycamore tree in the arbor below. As she stared, the delight in her eyes and the crease of a smile faded; it was as if she longed to have a barn swallow's freedom to glide effortlessly in the wind and alight where she wished. It was also as if she did not hear Nurse Hemley's words. She put her hand down on Lucy's, squeezed it.

"Alice," said the nurse, slightly louder this time, "Come on, dear. Let's not keep Nurse Angela waiting." She cocked her arm again and pointed to the watch just as Alice glanced over at her. "It's time."

Alice removed her hand from Lucy's and stood. She straightened out some wrinkles on the front of her red shift, so that the vertical buttons down the front aligned, and she stepped a foot or so away from Lucy. She was determined to delay politely as long as possible. Lucy stood too, and the two women looked deep into one another's eyes.

"I'll bring you a present tomorrow," Lucy whispered. "Would you like something for Baby Sally? A teething ring? A ribbon for her hair? A ribbon for your hair?"

Alice smiled again. "I like ribbons for both our hairs," she said. "Red. My favorite color in the world."

"Red it will be, then, Alice. And if I can get a Polaroid camera, I'll take both of your pictures, so you can send them to Ray. Would you like that, sweetie?"

"Alice? Time!"

Alice followed Nurse Henley out the door, turning for just a second to look back at Lucy, then past her at the windows. She said nothing, her eyes focused on the swallows settling on the trees outside, her expression blank.

Anna was sedated, but Lucy spent a couple of hours bathing her with wet cloths and rubbing her with lotion in those places where the dryness had set in again. Then she read aloud from a Bible Anna had in her dresser. Psalm 23: "The Lord is my shepherd; I shall not want." It had been Anna's favorite reading in the convent, and it seemed to comfort her now. She lay still, her eyes closing slowly, her mind drifting to faraway places.

She kissed Anna on the forehead, promised to return later in the day.

Chapter 17

LUCY SAT IN THE CANTEEN SIPPING A MORNING COFFEE. SHE HAD TAKEN A rear booth, where she recorded notes from her meeting with Alice. She tried to capture the human interactions between nurse and patient—the tug-and-pull of authority tempered by tenderness. How to capture in words the nuances in their interactions, she would leave for another writing time; for now, she wrote down the exact words Alice used to describe her experience of side effects, and she tried to describe the way Alice's face longingly tracked the movement of the swallows outside her window.

Out of the corner of her eye, she spied Muriel Putney, the patient pursuing an FBI investigation into the state hospital. Muriel stood in the doorway surveying the canteen patrons. Her eyes alighted on Lucy. She glanced around at other tables as she made her way to Lucy's booth.

"Friend," Muriel said in a low voice as she sat opposite Lucy. "Friend. Twenty-two letters and I got nothin' back from the FBI, so now I'm gonna tell the president directly what's going on here." She unbuttoned the top two buttons on her blouse and pulled a sealed envelope out of her bra.

"They outdid themselves this week, friend. First to Mrs. Glaussen, even though she deserves everyone's insults for the way she steals food and cigs from us. When she was in the shower, which they forced her to stay in for two days, they put peanut butter in her underwear so it looked like you-know-what, and they put bristles in her best gabardine slacks so when she put them on, they stuck to her skin and gave her a case of red welts like you never seen before. That was just to her. They stole my car too, the one my dead brother-in-law gave me when they took him away to jail back then. Now I got no way to get outta here when Escape Day comes. But I told it all to the president here."

She slid the letter across to Lucy, who still hadn't said a word.

"I know I can trust you, friend, and you'll mail that for me, won't you, friend?

Lucy glanced down at the mailing address: *President, Big House, Washington DC, America.*

Lucy smiled kindly. "You can trust me, Muriel. I'll mail your letter today."

Muriel stood and looked around. "Spies," she said. "They're everywhere. And you can't tell who they are 'cause they dress just like non-spies. But I know they're here. I *know*."

Muriel made her way back to the door, turned to look at Lucy once more, put a finger across her lips as if to swear her comrade to secrecy, and then disappeared into the hall.

Lucy tucked Muriel's letter into her purse, finished her coffee, and then set out to find Mr. Frederick. Now that she had taken some time to understand how Alice experienced her medications, she needed to have more data from Mr. Frederick, and then other patients too, if she could find the time. She knew Mr. Frederick had taken up residence in Cottage 24. She heard that he had made two more unsuccessful attempts to escape the asylum—once by running (fully clothed this time) into the hills that bordered the west side of the grounds; the second time by making it past Division Street on the east side, where Traverse City police captured him hiding in some tall shrubs in a back-yard on Twelfth Street. He told police he was a Canadian seeking political asylum, but they brought him back to the state hospital anyway, where he was promptly placed under close supervision in Cottage 24, where the staff-to-patient ratio assured he would remain under constant surveillance.

Mr. Frederick sat in a rocking chair in the cottage parlor, a wool blanket on his lap and a Chicago Cubs cap on his head. He eyed Lucy with curiosity when she came in. His eyes remained on her as she spoke with the attendant on duty and then came over to sit next to him. He recognized Lucy from Sundays at church service, and so he trusted her, knowing she was not hospital staff. She was surprised to discover him alert and articulate, not sedated. She pulled up a wooden stool and sat next to him.

She asked him why he ran away so often. Why was he so afraid of taking medications?

He spoke in whispers. He said he had tongued his morn-ing meds and then spit them out in the toilet. He was pre-tending to be calm, and he would pretend to sleep when staff came around. So they wouldn't know. He hated the medication because they made his muscles twitch and they clogged his mind; his jaw locked up and he chewed the inside of his mouth until he bled; and he felt like doing absolutely nothing. Then he would sleep, and his mind wouldn't clear until the next morning. He said he ran to avoid all of that.

"But," he said, "there's something else. A good thing. When I take the medication, the voices go away."

"Voices?"

"In my head. I hear a loud man named Arthur telling me to do bad things or to stop doing things I should be doing;

some voices sound like a woman screaming my name; some just tell me to yell at people or call them names. See, I don't want to do things like that, but the voices, I can't stop them. The doctors say I have schizophrenia and the voices are part of it. I believe that. I hate taking the pills, but they get rid of the voices and let me have some peace. The problem is that I can't have it both ways, see. I can't stand the voices and that's why I'm in here. But then I get all those other problems when I get drugged up. I can't win for losing. No way out. No way."

He pulled the blanket up to his face and began to cry. He wiped his nose and eyes on a corner of the blanket. Lucy stood up next to him and put a loving arm around his shoulder. He leaned into her, sniffling.

"Doctor Wilson says if I can just be patient with the drugs, the side effects might be less, but so far, not so much. I want to get better, I do, and he says maybe I can go home someday."

Lucy stroked his thinning hair with her free hand. "Would you like that, Mr. Frederick? Would you like to go home?"[17]

"Yes. Well, no. I don't know. I had a grocery store. Fred's Market, in Gladstone. I had a family too. Wife and two teenagers. We were all so happy then. Until the voices

---

17. "We know why nine of ten of those who relapse, relapse.

"They blow up because there's no medical supervision to see they keep on with their medications at home, or to regulate the doses. They relapse because there is mismanagement of many patients put out to family care homes. The state doesn't pay the family care people enough per day to make it worth their while to be attentive or considerate to their newly sane guests.

"And there's often a failure, or a lapse of tender loving care on the part of the relatives to whom the newly sane folks have returned" (Paul De Kruif, *A Man Against Insanity* [New York: Grove Press, 1957] 219).

began, and then all the trouble started. But it's all gone now. Anyway, if I went back, who would take care of me? My wife, Frances—I called her Francie—she went off with some truck driver. The kids are all gone who knows where. So, who's going to make me take my medicine? The dog? No one. What good is a cure if you don't have anywhere to be cured at? This here is the only home I got any more. I run away to escape the willies, but I'd always come back, see? I got nowhere to run *to*."

He wiped his nose on the blanket and then pointed to another man sitting at a table in the dining area, his head resting on the table over which he slumped. "See Davis over there? He's schizophrenic too, or at least that's what they say because he hears voices sometimes, but he can't think clear on a good day and he has these delusions that get him into trouble when trying to make sense with people he's talking to."

Lucy stood up and looked toward Davis. "Does he talk with you about his meds?" she asked.

"Not much, but one day he told me that the docs think he could go home to his family if he stayed on his meds. So, he takes them religiously and he swears they work for him. No voices, no delusions. Nothing. Just sort of drowsy all the time, like how he is now, see? I suppose he could go home and, maybe that's a good thing as long as there's someone there to take care of him and keep him on his pills. But here he stays. I didn't ask him, but I figured he's been gone so long no one wants him back, crazy *or* sleepy. None of my business, Sister. But since you asked, there you have someone whose medicine works. His side effects aren't like mine, so maybe he *could* survive out there. Who's to say?"

Lucy took this in as more data and thanked Mr. Frederick

for sharing his knowledge. She would keep what he said to herself.

"I don't really care what you do with it," he said. "It's neither here nor there with me. For every Davis and me, there's a hundred more. All of 'em have their own stories to tell. We're just a bunch of different fish in a great big hot kettle. And we're all slowly boiling to death."

Lucy promised to come by to see him more often, and she would look for him at Sunday Mass. She left convinced that, for this patient, his chemical regimen was working, but only in part. Given the side effects, the drug was not perfect, to be sure, but they rid him of the voices that had ruined him otherwise, and, in that sense, the drug *was* effective. The same could be said for Davis: *Effective*, however narrowly defined. This was not the data she expected, but it was data she needed.

Where she had been expecting something black and white, what she was realizing was a complicated gray.

Her next step was to reestablish contact with Tom Oakes. How long had it been since he'd asked her to review the draft of the article he'd written on the narrative? What a whirlwind of weeks had consumed her since they last talked! Now she had to get him back on board; he would be instrumental in getting this other story out—*if* she could count on him.

He sat at his desk, cutting up copy for the hospital newsletter, positioning and pasting headlines and text as he readied the next issue—a cover article on the new garden being developed west of the old livery (the herd of work horses had been sold in 1956, not long after the final vestiges of the farm program had closed down); a lesser article on the grand Thanksgiving dinners that would be served a week hence; and, on page two, a profile of five new nurses arriving for duty in December, along with the announcement of an upcoming visit by some low-level dignitary from the governor's office in Lansing. All in all, Tom figured, it was a fine newsletter—rote, but fine. While putting together newsletters ensured his weekly paycheck, they also reminded him just how underused were his true writing skills.

His smile was broad as his large hand extended to meet her tiny hand when she sat down across from him. A few moments of pleasant catch-up followed—where she'd been for nearly two months, if not more; how consumed she'd been with Anna and with her work for the chaplains. Her apologies for not getting with him to review the article he had drafted on Anna and her were met with both of his hands up in the air before him and a kindly, "If nothing else, I am a man of great patience."

She would take the draft with her and mark it up for accuracy and add any suggestions she thought appropriate. With her part securely on the ledger, she reminded him that they had agreed that in exchange for her permission to submit this article, he had agreed to support her "research project." She judiciously placed the stacked pages of the draft on his desk so that they lay between the two of them. She knew what she was doing; he didn't seem to notice, though the effect must have registered subconsciously. Colluding with her, although she considered it might jeopardize his job, might also become his ticket out of his dead-end job and out of northern Michigan for good.

"So, Mr. Oakes ... "

"Tom."

"Sorry. Tom. Has it been that long? My goodness. We talked, you and I, about my having doubts about the medication that Sister Anna was taking. I didn't feel comfortable with what I thought were negative side effects."

"Ah, yes," he said. "That was Progrol, as I recall."

"It was. For a while she was off the medication, but then it was restored. I have reason to believe that her taking that drug affected her vision. She was in Munson Hospital for a bit, you may have heard, and they think she suffered from temporary blindness. Though she's back here, the situation with her vision hasn't improved much."

He said he was sorry to learn all this, but he'd not heard of anything like this vision problem with other patients. To what did the doctors attribute her condition? Was it Progrol?

"Apparently, that was not considered, at all," she said. "But, interestingly, no certain cause was determined—neither by the Munson doctors nor by the doctors here."

He asked if Dr. Turner had weighed in, but she deflected the question by saying that the questionable circumstances surrounding Anna's condition caused her, Lucy, to renew her investigation into side effects of medication generally, at the hospital. And that she thought she was on to something—"a line of inquiry, if you will"—that had her piecing together a larger picture.

"Larger? How so?"

She didn't want to be premature, she explained, but she had some thoughts about certain ways in which relatively untested medications were being administered to patients who had no formal rights to accept or refuse taking them.

She didn't want to go into much detail—yet—until she had more time to investigate. Lucy was deliberate in using the word *investigate*, as would shortly be apparent. She looked past him at the five-shelf bookcase behind him. All but one shelf was littered with stacks of manila files, bound and plastic-covered reports of various thicknesses, worn two-inch reference books, and an assortment of knickknacks and postcards that seemed to find themselves wedged in here and there. But the third shelf stood out for its order and pronounced prominence: this was where Tom Oakes kept his most prized books—and they were all on the art of writing. She could make out four titles: *The Elements of Style*, *Understanding Fiction*, *How to Write Novels that Sell*, and *The Secret to Magazine Publishing*.

"How can I help you, then, Sister? I know we talked about something like this before but help me remember."

"Thank you. I would like to engage your skills as a professional writer in what I would call investigative writing. In college, I read works by Ida Tarbell, who was a social activist who exposed monopolies in the oil industry; I also read other American social protest writers, like Upton Sinclair, who wrote about the Chicago meatpacking industry. Surely, you've read *The Jungle*?"

Tom interrupted: "Of course! A great novel! But let's start with Henry Thoreau and *Civil Disobedience*. *Uncle Tom's Cabin*, one of my all-time favorites. We could even go back to colonial America and ... "

She cut him off mid-sentence. She had struck a vein of passion.

"So, you see, Mr. Oakes—Tom—I, too, come from social activist stock. That is my religious mission; in a way, that is what brought Anna and me here. I'm not sure what sort of written product will come of this investigation of mine, but I do know that writing—and making the results of one's inquiry public—can bring about change. I have the investigative skills, but not the professional writing expertise you have."

Tom's eyes sparkled at this tiny bit of praise and recognition. She had successfully played on his vanity.

"Well," he said, "whatever I can do to help."

She continued, now playing the ethics card. "You seem to be someone who not only knows this field of writing for publication, but also a man who shares with me a keen sense of right and wrong."

Lucy knew she was right on the former, less so on the latter, but her felt sense for Tom Oakes's professional aspirations and the direction of his moral compass steeled her.

"You are a woman after my own heart," he blurted out, then revised himself. "Oh, but you know what I mean, Sister. It's a figure of speech." He blushed.

"Yes, Tom. We are very much alike, so let us help one another in our little quests for stardom. We have nothing to lose, and much to gain."

Between his vanity and her incertitude, she had won him over. Her "team" had cemented itself. She picked up the manuscript that had been positioned between them on the desk, and started to leave.

At the door, his manuscript under one arm, she turned back to see him sitting there, a grin of satisfaction spread over his face. He held up a thumb-up fist and winked at her.

She started on her way back to Ward 3, where she would

check in on Anna again. But on the first floor in Building 50, her attention was broken by a loud cry from down the hall. A nurse's voice sounded: "Oh my God," then, "God, no!" She hurried toward the voice. As she approached an open door, she could see the backs of nurses and attendants gathered in the doorway.

She heard, "No! This can't happen!" She reached the back of the group and, on tiptoe, tried to peer into the room. She heard a voice on a television, a deep voice that she recognized as the CBS newscaster, Walter Cronkite.

She could only make out some of the words being broadcast—"President and Mrs. Kennedy ... Dealy Plaza ... 12:30 Central ... grassy knoll ... rushed to Parkland Hospital ... massive ... "

Another audible gasp went up from someone in the front of the pack. A male this time. She could hear a woman sobbing. The broad back of a male attendant standing in front of her turned aside to let her in closer. Between heads and shoulders, she caught glimpses of the screen. Scores of people were running down streets or standing still, holding on to one another. Women clutched their babies, women clutched women, men clutched women and men alike. All were either crying or looking about themselves, as if caught in a slow-motion movie. Walter Cronkite's voice said, "Police are actively searching buildings surrounding Dealy Square, hoping to find a suspect or suspects. We have reporters on the ground there but no word of any progress in that search. Here at Parkland, Mrs. Kennedy is with her husband in the Emergency Unit. Governor Connally, we are told, is heading into surgery. An attending physician told CBS News that he believes the governor is in stable condition. The wounds do not appear to be life-threatening. We are trying to get that report verified at this time."

Lucy stood, frozen, her ears and eyes glued to the television report. Gasps and words of denial floated in the group. They huddled, shoulder to shoulder, as if sheltered from a storm. A nurse next to Lucy leaned into her. Lucy put her arm around the woman. Behind her, she heard Williams' deep voice, "Son of a bitch. This can't be happening." Someone in front mumbled, "This is insane." The incongruity of that comment, made in this institution, was lost on Lucy.

FBI was engaged in an active search throughout Dealy Plaza. Witnesses said they saw pigeons alighting from the roof of the Texas Book Depository just when they heard shots ring out. The building was sealed off as officers began a floor-by-floor search. Shortly after 1:00 p.m., a Texas police officer was shot and killed within miles of the Plaza; it was not known if that shooting was related to the shooting of the president. News reports were pouring in as pandemonium broke out in the center of Dallas, and immeasurable grief broke out across America.

And then, Walter Cronkite's voice—gravelly, punctuated by his distinctively calm cadence, pronounced what every American watching most feared: President Kennedy was pronounced dead at 1:00 p.m., the exact time Governor Connally was undergoing surgery for a gunshot wound to the chest. Two thirds of Kennedy's cabinet, including Secretary of Defense Dean Rusk, were in a plane over the Pacific en route to Japan.

"Assassination," said Williams. "God help that plane. This has to be a conspiracy."

Chapter 18

As Walter Cronkite's voice trailed off and a street reporter picked up the broadcast from the hospital, Lucy wormed her way out through the stunned crowd in the doorway. A day that began with blue skies and sun had turned into a rainy, cold evening as a "lake effect" storm from Lake Michigan made its way across the northern lower peninsula. She had walked the ten blocks to the hospital that morning, and hadn't dressed for this unpleasant turn in the weather. Walking back to her home, she ignored the rain that soaked her wool overcoat and saturated the leather half boots she had purchased just the week before. Her hair hung in wet strings and her ungloved hands stung from the cold.

Still, she did not hurry. She *could* not hurry. The wet cold had slowed her, but the death of President Kennedy had numbed her. Had she fallen on ice and ended up on a slushy sidewalk, she wouldn't have cared, not about her shoes, not about her soaking wet coat, not about her health. Since the news about the president, she didn't care about anything. The world had gone mad; evil had shown its ugly head once again in her life, and she was devastated. She walked in silence, the way she used to walk the corridor in the convent, praying as she meditated, the way Buddhists do. In many ways, she was a Buddhist—the awareness of suffering, the solitude, the intense fidelity to peaceful ways of being. She walked mindfully. She prayed for Mrs. Kennedy. She prayed for her darling children. She prayed for the cabinet members on the plane to Japan. For the brave officers and agents who had risked their lives in Dallas. For the frantic doctors and nurses in the Dallas hospital. For Vice-President Johnson, who would be sworn in before the sun set in Texas. And she prayed for the country, that it would have the courage to face whatever truth was to emerge from this time of tragedy and grief.

She turned the corner onto her street, now completely exhausted. Physically. Emotionally. Spiritually. Her heart had been drained with constant worry about Anna; renewed doubts about the integrity of those very doctors who oversaw Anna's health; troubling discoveries about possible overmedication of patients (and flagrant violation of the civil rights they *ought* to have but did *not*); suspicion of the drug industry's power to influence medical professionals and overstate its nascent claims. She longed for those halcyon days at the convent school when the world was so much smaller and friendlier, the future so much broader and rosier, her faith in her mission and agency in pursuit of justice so much more robust. She was a novice then, in every sense of the word. But life had done what it does to all novitiates—it teaches the inevitable hard lessons that come with living.

The beating in Alabama, the rape of Anna, the daily worry about Anna's recovery, the isolation and loneliness of the life that had been handed her—they alone were enough to wear down the strongest, most resilient person, enough to threaten one's belief that good would prevail, that the work would all be worth it. But now, on top of all that, this senseless murder had shattered her belief that good ultimately *would* prevail. Even her recollection of Dr. King's inspirational words—"Darkness cannot drive out darkness;

only light can do that. Hate cannot drive out hate; only love can do that."—couldn't relieve her heavy heart on this dark, wet evening. Her exhaustion exceeded words.

Lucy dropped her purse and coat on a chair by the front door. She pulled off her boots and left them in a puddle by the steaming radiator, where they would be cracked and curled by morning. She lowered the venetian blinds throughout her apartment, closed the curtains in her bedroom, then ran bath water until the bathroom filled with steam, and she soaked for a long time. She put on her best nightgown and long sweat socks to keep her feet warm. She pulled back the covers on her bed, curled up, and went to sleep.

She dreamed terrible dreams. She is with Sister Anna again on that bus, and their attackers swing their wooden staffs and baseball bats, blood spattering the windows and speckling her white blouse. They wear animal masks— ferocious tigers and fanged boars. They have long talons dripping with blood, Anna's blood. She crouches behind the seat as the Negro woman seated next to her is struck in the back by a hatchet. Her body heaves atop Lucy's, protecting her as repeated blows come one after the other. Screams, blood, vile shouts from vicious mouths.

And then silence, except for the moans and the crying and the sounds of beatings from outside the bus.

Then she herself is outside the bus, stepping around bloodied and crying people stretched out on the pavement and in the weeds. She is running, screaming, searching.

She woke in a sweat, breathing in heaves. Icy rain pelted her bedroom window. In minutes, she slipped back into sleep. The dreams again: toothless men with long rifles and bayonets—uniformed, filthy, saliva dripping from their mouths, eyes wild red and glowing, their weapons sticking in the faces of patients she almost recognizes, men and women she had soothed—Alice, Jane, Thomas, Mrs. Einstill. Their heads burst open, flesh and bone and brain, with the bullets raining from every direction. President Kennedy, his head spurting blood, slumped to his left, and Mrs. Kennedy climbing over the trunk of the car as burly men pull her to safety. And then the laughter, barbaric and primitive—Anna being violated again and again until she falls silent—the raw male peals erupting like demonic shrieks in the dark, celebrating power and hate and brutality.

Awake later in the night, she knelt beside her bed and prayed the rosary. In the morning, she made toast and dipped it in her coffee. She called the ward to check on Anna, as she did every morning before nine. She asked for Nurse Bennett, the gentle one who called Anna "kiddo" and who brought her popsicles every Monday. Nurse Bennett, unofficial private nurse to Anna, everyone's doting younger sister. The one who said Anna was *her* favorite (every nurse had her favorite), who made sure Anna always got a daily touch of rouge and her nails trimmed weekly. But Nurse Bennett had drawn a line: she would *never* take Anna to the station for medication. The other nurses understood; they had drawn their own lines for their own favorites, and so they covered for one another as needed, regardless the task. It was what nurses did; it was their unspoken code of respect and camaraderie.

"Dressed for the day," reported Nurse Bennett. "But something does seem odd this morning. Anna is dragging her right leg a bit, and she's also slow with her right arm. She may have slept wrong on one side. Happens to a lot of patients, even me. I wheeled her to the cafeteria. She poked at her scrambled eggs with her fingers and left the bacon. That's unusual because she loves bacon. No change in her vision as far as I can tell, but that's hard to decipher anyway. I brought her back and then I made the call."

Concerned, she had called Dr. Gordon, but he was tied up in the men's infirmary with two acute cases. She called Dr. Turner, but he was somewhere on the campus escorting some bigwigs on a tour; his secretary didn't say who they were except that they had pulled up in a limo and were upset about the mud. She finally got through to Dr. Parker at his home, and his wife said he'd just left in his car. He would be expected on Ward 3 in thirty minutes or so.

The nurse decided to get a waiver for Anna's daily meds, until one or another doctor appeared.

"No sense mixing apples and oranges in case there's something new," she said. "Not an emergency, Sister, but you should come by when you can."

Lucy would be right over. She cleared the table and left everything in the sink. She said a prayer that Anna had indeed slept on the wrong side: prayer aided the return of hopefulness.

As she dressed, she listened to the morning news on the radio. The vice-president had been sworn in on the plane taking President Kennedy's body back to Washington, where he would be laid out in the Capitol Rotunda in the coming days and then taken to Arlington Cemetery for final arrangements. Governor Connally would recover. A man named Lee Harvey Oswald had been arrested and was being held by the police. He had been charged with murdering the president and a police officer named Tippit. There was uncertainty if other killers were involved. The plane carrying cabinet members had escaped any threat and was headed back to Washington.

Lucy stood, yellow rain slicker on and purse over shoulder, at her kitchen table. She had lingering images from the dreams, but, through silence and meditative prayer, she was trying to mend her spirit. Even in the midst of an unprecedented national tragedy, the ordinary and extraordinary demands on the lives of people like herself continue; challenges pile on top of one another like cement blocks. They sit on shoulders, weighing people down. Those who are not immobilized, they carry on—because there is no other choice *but* to carry on.[18] Sister Lucy's heart was large: it had capacity. Her strength had been tested, but it was not depleted. On her refrigerator, a favorite handwritten quote from Dr. King gave her daily strength. She paused to read it before she left:

> *The ultimate measure of a man is not where he stands in moments of convenience and comfort, but where he stands in moments of challenge and controversy.*

It was shortly after ten o'clock when she opened the large door to Ward 3. She expected to see a familiar daily

---

18. We shall overcome
    We shall overcome
    We shall overcome, someday
    Oh, deep in my heart
    I do believe
    We shall overcome, some day
(*We Shall Overcome*, Traditional gospel song that became a protest song in the 1960s. These lyrics were performed by Joan Baez during the Civil Rights March on Washington, August 29, 1963).

tableau: patients sitting in straight-backed chairs lining the walls, heads bowed and occasionally twitching upward or sideways; patients lounging in upholstered couches watching daytime soap operas or game shows; attendants sweeping or mopping floors, cleaning rooms, or smoking and chatting with one another; nurses filling in daily logs in the nurses' station or assisting patients with daily hygiene in rooms or the hallway.

Today was different. Today the attendants worked on the floors as usual, but with lethargic motions, as if their mops had weights on them, as if they had to struggle to lift and dip them in buckets of cleaning solution, as if the brooms were strangely adhered to the tile floors. Where there had always been a low chatter, a friendly back and forth among the attendants, there was now only silence, eyes downward, the work the focus.

And the nurses. Some sat in their station as always, but their eyes were glued to the television screen in there. None wrote in the daily logs; none put lipstick on the patients who insisted on being spruced up daily "in case their date showed up early."

The strangest sight was what appeared to Lucy to be small vignettes where patients and staff had reversed roles. She passed the first room on her left, peeked in to see an elderly patient she knew as Minnie hugging a nurse, patting her back, murmuring, "There, there, sweet one. There, there." Lucy stepped closer, heard Minnie say, "He's in heaven now. Gone, not forgotten. With the angels and the saints. Where we'll all be one day. We'll all be there."

Glancing into other rooms and down the corridor as she advanced, Lucy took in similar patient-nurse interactions—the hugs, the patting of the backs, the gentle words to console. A patient still in her worn gray robe brought a hand-crafted origami bird to the nurses' station, handed it to Nurse Bellamy. Another walked over to the television where a game show was just beginning. "No games today," she announced as she turned off the television. "Today we are sad."

There is beauty here, Lucy thought, *Love lives here. Hope.*

The aftermath of the Kennedy shooting had spread its shroud over all of Ward 3. The grief was almost palpable, the pain apparent in every face that was capable of understanding the tragedy that struck every being personally, in her or his own way. *I will always remember what I was doing the day the president was shot*, Lucy thought. *And I will always remember the comfort given to the comforters in the asylum. Some here may have lost their minds, but none have lost their hearts.*

Anna's door was closed. Nurse Bennett leaned against the wall next to Anna's door. Her eyes were red, and her mascara had run below her eyelids. At her wrists, tissues extruded from the sleeves of her cardigan sweater. She looked exhausted too. She opened her arms when Lucy approached and stepped forward to hug.

"We're all in quite a mess here today, Lucy. Just going through the motions. The news, you know, about the president. He was the first president I could vote for. I felt so proud. He was such a good man; he was one of my heroes. And now ... just like that ... "

Lucy patted her back as they embraced. "I know," she whispered, "I know." They separated, Nurse Bennett grasped the knob to Anna's door, and opened it slightly.

"Sleeping," said Nurse Bennett, her finger vertical across her lips to signal quiet. "I helped her to breakfast but after a few pokes at her eggs, she stopped eating. Like I told you. I brought her back here, she seemed so exhausted. God knows, who's *not* exhausted around here today, what with all that's happened? Do you think she knew about the president? I can't say. But it could be. It's always a mystery to me what she knows and doesn't know. Sometimes I think she hears me, but then other times she doesn't respond to anything. Anyway, her eyes were closed before we even got to her room. I prettied her up the way I always do, even though she was sleeping. I left her flat on her back sound asleep, about 9:30 it must've been. I put in for a waiver on her meds until she seems better, so no meds yet."

Lucy pushed the door halfway open. She would just peek in on Anna, nothing more if she were still sleeping. Somewhere behind her, the television went on again, this time tuned to a news station where a reporter was talking about Dallas.

"Nope," said Nurse Bennett. "Can't allow that to be on here. Some patients really can't handle this news. We have to have some controls over that." She quickly stepped away, waved at the patient who had turned up the volume, and nearly sprinted to the television. Lucy only heard the name *Oswald* before the volume went down and the screen went blank.

Lucy entered quietly. She took off her slicker and put it on a chair. The blue curtains were pulled, the room was dark. With the windows closed to the wintry air, the radiator had raised the humidity to what seemed to be stuffy with the door closed all morning. Anna lay stretched out on her bed, fingers interlaced on her chest as if she were praying. Lucy turned on a small desk lamp on a table by the door. It provided enough light for her to make out that Nurse Bennett had applied rouge to her friend's face, faithfully combed her brown hair back and tied it into her characteristic bun in the rear of her head. As she advanced further into the room, Lucy became puzzled by what she thought was a smile on Anna's face. She peered closer, but then noticed the absence of much movement of Anna's abdomen. *Dark as Hades in here*, she thought. *No wonder Anna is asleep.*

Lucy went to the window and pulled aside the blue curtains to let in more light. Outside the window, on the stone sill, a nuthatch landed; its head jerked and twisted, as if it were trying to peek inside.

Lucy turned back to get a better look. Anna's abdomen was still, not even a slight motion. She moved closer. Eyes closed. Skin color slightly gray. She put a finger on Anna's wrist. No pulse. She leaned her head down over Anna's face, ear to mouth to listen. No breath.

She dashed into the hall and waved at a male attendant approaching with an armful of fresh towels. "Anna," she said, "She isn't breathing. Call a doctor, anyone." The attendant dropped the towels and ran to the nurses' station.

Lucy went back into the room. But she knew. Anna's gray color told her she'd been gone for some time. Lucy stood there, suspended in time. She would savor the precious final moments she would have with Anna, before others appeared. It was time she would carry in her memory for life. Anna's and her time.

She stared at the peaceful face before her. Lucy placed both of her hands behind Anna's head and pulled her up toward her own. Cheek to cheek, in the moment of supreme intimacy we must all share when death calls, she whispered her goodbye to the most important person she had ever known—and loved.

"Go in peace, my lovely, lovely Anna. I will be with you one day."

She held Anna's head with one hand, caressed her brown hair with the other. Then she gently returned Anna to the pillow. She straightened a collar on her blouse, pulled down a cuff so it lay even with the one on the other arm, secured an errant clasp on a bead bracelet. She adjusted Anna's silver chain, placed her silver crucifix perfectly on her friend's breastbone.

She laid both her hands on Anna's still arm, stood and bowed her head in prayer. The door sprung open as Nurse Bennett rushed into the room. Lucy heard the nurse catch her breath as she stopped abruptly a few feet away, stood still as a statue. She gasped, "Oh no! Oh my god, no! Please, no!"

Lucy glanced at the nurse and then back at Anna.

In the doorway, Nurse Bennett, in her youth and her inexperience and her immense affection for Anna, was hysterical.

"I called them all, one after the other," she said through mucus and tears. "But none of them could come. Dr. Parker was on his way. I just thought she ... she needed more rest. Oh my god. Oh my god. It's all my fault! I let her die!"

Nurse Brownell hurried over from rounds in the cottages and desperately tried to calm the nurse. Nancy pulled the nurse's head to her shoulder. "No, Sarah. You did the right thing. It's not your fault. Sometimes, we just cannot get here in time. It just happens. It ... just ... happens."

"And, and then … Sister Lucy was here, and she went in, and I … I should have done something, before it was too late."

Nancy held her close. Patients had now gathered around the two of them.

"Now, now, nurse, please don't cry," said Mrs. Walters from her wheelchair.

"We all gonna die some time," echoed Gloria, standing behind the wheelchair, blind from birth and the mind of a ten-year-old.

Lucy sat on a stiff chair, elbows on knees, her head in her hands, silently crying.

Nurse Bennett broke free of Nancy's arms, went to kneel before Lucy. She leaned close to Lucy and whispered, "Dear Sister. Please forgive me for what I'm going to say at this tragic time, but I worried about that damned medication they were giving her. I never said anything. I couldn't say anything. But I had my doubts. Please forgive me for not doing something."

Lucy pulled Nurse Bennett up, and, eyes staring wide into the nurse's eyes, she angled her head slowly to the right and then to the left; she smiled, ever so slightly, a look of keen understanding.

"You cannot be forgiven for what you have not done," she said, her voice loud enough for only Nurse Bennett to hear. "You have been Anna's savior every day, her crutch, her special angel. I have only thanks for you, only gratitude. Be kind to yourself. Where Anna is now, she loves you still."

And then, Lucy stood, pulled the nurse up to stand next to her and, in an even lower voice, whispered to her, "If her passing was due to her history, or her medication, or if it was just her time to leave this good Earth, it matters not, right now. For now, all we can say is that it *was* her time. The rest may be learned, some day."

Dr. Gordon signed the death certificate as approximately 9:45 a.m. on November 23. Cause of death: Stroke. Hours later, Dr. Turner cosigned the death certificate.

Chapter 19

LUCY'S FIRST INCLINATION WAS TO DEMAND AN AUTOPSY TO DETERMINE cause of death. Was Anna's death truly the result of a stroke? Or was it brain damage? Or could it have been related to *Progrol*? But the immediate period following Anna's death was one of such overwhelming grief, she could not think clearly enough to ask for an autopsy in an institution where autopsies were performed in only the rarest of cases. Further, she was sure Dr. Turner would object to anyone doubting what he and Dr. Gordon had determined to be the cause of death, much less would he tolerate Lucy raising the specter of Progrol again.

In her bereavement, it was too much for her to take on. She would bring Anna home for a proper Catholic burial. It was all she could do to manage just that.

Lucy proceeded to make initial arrangements from her home phone. Anna would be transported to Kalamazoo in an ambulance Wednesday morning. Lucy would follow in her car. The sisters at the Kalamazoo convent would comfort Anna's parents personally and contact other friends and relatives. They would console the parents, a priest would visit, others would bring soups, fresh-baked breads and desserts, as the custom has always been in Catholic families.

On Thursday, there would be a viewing in a funeral home arranged by the sisters. The funeral Mass would be held on Friday in the Nazareth College chapel. They would do it all—the flowers, the liturgy, the songs (Sister Katherine would play her guitar; she and Sister Helena would sing "Abide with Me" and "Be Not Afraid"). Sister Geniece, her dear friend and first mentor, would give a eulogy that would leave no dry eyes in the entire church.

Sister Anna would be laid to rest in Mt. Olivet Catholic Cemetery.

Having the support of the convent made a world of difference to Lucy. She could not have gotten through this time without their support. Father Pete and Father Fred drove down from Traverse City for the funeral Mass; Nurse Bennett and Nurse Brownell came with them. Even Williams and Smit came to pay their respects, both giving Lucy warm hugs, their own hearts broken, tears in their eyes throughout. Father Pete brought condolence cards from nurses and doctors, attendants and even a few gardeners whose vases of flowers and greens always graced the tables and windowsills of Ward 3 rooms. Father Fred produced a large envelope full of hand-written letters from patients, many decorated with drawings of Anna and Lucy or the artists themselves with large, sad eyes and upside-down smiles.

As Lucy was leaving the grave-side service, her parents on either side of her and walking arm in arm, she nodded to Smit and Williams standing off to one side. They both wore ill-fitting suits with narrow ties. With a bow of his head, Smit returned a solemn greeting. Then he put up one hand to signal could he have a word with her? She motioned her parents to go before her, wait at the car.

Williams held back, waiting beneath a bare-limbed old maple tree, a few red leaves clinging in the chill of that late November day.

Smit leaned in toward her, his hand grasping her own. "I just wanted to say, again," he struggled for words. "That I am so sorry, that, you know, she ..."

"She had a good life," Lucy interrupted, removing her hand from his, "until that senseless day on the bus. I will miss her more than anyone can imagine. Thank you, both of you, for your kindness and your special care—for us, for me. But the Lord had other plans for her. And now she is gone. And I am here. It will take time; *I* will take time. But we sisters are a hardy bunch. We are prepared for tragedy as well as comedy."

Lucy waved at her father, whose head had peeked out from the rolled-down car window.

Smit took a step backward. "Sorry, Lucy. I just wanted to. ... you know ..."

"I do," she said, "and I appreciate it very much. Very much. You're a dear fellow and a dear friend. We'll be in touch. You take care now."

Lucy held up well, all things considered. In a crisis, she always held up well. After all, she was the one to take the lead, the one to *get things done*, however distasteful or unpleasant. She knew she would make it to the end and beyond. She needed to live through her profound sadness. She would never lose that sadness, but she had to see the most intense part to its end. She would spend some time with her own family in Kalamazoo; she would take long walks along the icy banks of the Kalamazoo River and around the perimeter of Gull Lake out toward Nazareth College. She would return to Anna's aged parents' home and share photo collections of her and Anna at the hospital, the Cherry Festival Parade, the West Bay beachfront, and the dunes at Lake Michigan. Her father's eyesight was beginning to fail with cataracts; and her mother had lost some capacity for retrieving words; more often than not, she would sit and listen without joining in the conversation.

At home with her own family, she spent time alone, for the most part, grieving silently—and thinking. Lucy's parents welcomed her, knowing that she needed the solitude to restore her spirit. Except for evening meals together and occasional checks just to see how she was doing, they kept a respectful distance.

Lucy used this time to look deep within herself, to take the long view of her life up to now and the longer view of her life not yet lived. "Be grateful every day," Sister Geniece used to tell her, "even if it's for the simplest things, like enjoying a steaming cup of tea or seeing deer on the frosty lawn in the morning."

And she *was* grateful for so much. For her curious mind and her empathy for those less fortunate. For years of schooling that led her to the convent. For the convent itself and all the love and devotion paid her by her fellow sisters. She was especially grateful for her long friendship with Anna, who always brought Lucy out of the doldrums with the way she would contort her face in a screwball way until Lucy burst into laughter. For Anna's silly jokes too: "If you can guess how many jellybeans I'm holding behind my back, I'll give you both of them."

But she was not grateful for her decision to move to the South and the risks she and Anna took during a time when threats and violence lurked everywhere. She regretted that decision, not because it was the wrong thing to do, but because of the harm it ultimately brought to them. But even in the terrible aftermath of that time, she was grateful for the months she had with Anna in the state hospital, as challenging and as difficult as they were.

The Christmas holidays were a bittersweet time for Lucy, one to get through rather than enjoy. She went through the motions with her family and with her friends at the convent, but her depression lingered in spite of her mom's famous eggnog and her dad's imitation of Jimmy Durante at the annual New Year's Eve party in their home. When January 2 finally arrived, she was glad.

Now it was 1964, and she was at a crossroads. It was time to decide. She knew she did not have to return to work in Traverse City; with Anna gone, what purpose would returning there serve? Anna's belongings could be sent to her parents; in a few hours she could gather her belongings from her apartment and return to Kalamazoo. Surely Father Pete and Father Fred could find a local person to take over her work responsibilities. They would understand.

There would be other opportunities for her now, to use the many talents she had honed as an organizer, an activist, a teacher, a secretary, and a caretaker. She could rejoin the sisters at the convent. She would be needed.

But would she be happy? Would she ever be happy? Anywhere?

She got a surprise phone call one dark evening in that dreary first week of January. It was Smit calling to see how she was doing.

"Just checking up on you, Lucy. Up here in the hinterland,

people miss you. The patients ask, where did that red-haired one go, the one who always brought us mints and rye whiskey?"

For the first time in weeks, Lucy laughed. "Oh Smit, I never brought them whiskey."

"Oh, sorry, they must have you confused with someone else. Or maybe it was Rice Crispies? My hearing is not always that great, you know." On her end, she imagined him smiling broadly.

She laughed again. "It's good to hear your voice." A few more niceties followed as they caught up on what Smit called the Adventures at the Asylum.

Then, he put it directly.

"How are you doing? I don't mean that as a greeting, but as a serious question from a friend. I've been, well, worried, no one hearing anything from you in weeks. It's like you just dropped off the planet. Not that you don't have the right to do that, but, you know, I'm just wondering. Do I sound like I'm hemming and hawing? I suppose I am, filling up the space between us, trying not to pry, but ... um ... caring. There, I said it."

"My dear friend. No, you are not prying. I'm sorry I didn't contact anyone, but I've been in a dark place since Anna's death, and I have had to go inside myself. I had to do that. And now, I'm just trying to figure out what to do with myself. But I'm okay, really. Just ... going slowly, very slowly."

There was a long pause on the other end. Then Smit said, "Okay, well, that's some relief then, Lucy. But listen to this. This may cheer you up—or, at least, it may give you something to think about. I'm going to tell you this just in case you intend to continue what you call your ministry here—and what you call your research project."

"I'm listening."

He continued. "I made a connection, through some friends in Ann Arbor, with the ACLU office in Detroit. And, well, I called them up, and, you won't believe this, but I was put through to a woman who listened to me tell a vague story about your—our, actually—questions about patient rights, and the whole mystery about medications. I hope you don't mind, and I didn't mention any names, but when I told her that one patient had passed away recently and there may be reason to think her medication had something to do with her death, she became even more interested. Well, it turns out that this woman has a cousin who was a patient in the Traverse City asylum, so she has a connection with the hospital. She actually visited here ten or so years ago, when there was a farm, and everything was more natural. It was before the wonder drugs era anyway.

"So, I just wanted to tell you, in case you're thinking of not coming back here, that there are people out there beyond our little circle in Traverse City, who may be able to help your research. Oh, and, listen to this. She knows an attorney in the Chicago ACLU office who's actually doing research on the civil rights of mental patients. That's as far as we got on the phone, but I have her name and direct number and she invited me to call back. Which you could do yourself, if you wanted."

Lucy thanked him for making that contact and for sharing it with her. Yes, she would think about it more, and yes, she did feel better knowing there are others beyond her tiny circle who are asking similar questions. But she remained undecided about what direction her life should take now.

"I have someone here," she told him, "a trusted friend who has always been a confidante. I need to talk with her. I know I need to make some decisions. Whatever I decide, I'll not keep it from you and the others who care about me there. I have your number, I'll call you, I promise."

The next morning, she drove to the convent to see Sister Geniece. She had doubts and she needed advice. She found her favorite mentor in the kitchen just pulling a batch of cookies from the oven.

Over tea and warm peanut butter cookies, Sister Geniece listened.

"It was hard being there," Lucy said. "I tried to cheer Anna up but, you know, she just couldn't respond other than with a little smile once in a while. I know she knew I loved her and would always be there for her, but there were times when I just ... doubted—myself, and my strength to carry on. In my most frail moments, I was ashamed of myself for being weak."Tears welled up in Lucy's eyes. Geniece pushed the plate of cookies her way.

"But you *did* carry on," said her friend. "Right up to the end. You must look back on all that with pride, not shame. I'm so sorry you have felt shame. For all you know, Lucy, you may have been the very reason Anna hung on as long as she did. Maybe you gave her reason to live."

Lucy stared off into space, lost in memories of the hospital. "I suppose so," she said. "I wouldn't know what else to do other than what I did. But there were other things there that kept me going, questions I had about how patients are medicated, about side effects, about patients' rights, as citizens. There was—is—gross unfairness in it all. In a way, being there, I discovered a calling, as much as it had seemed a calling when I entered the S.S.J., or when Anna and I went into the South. We were eager to try something new."

Sister Geniece sat back, a broad smile coming over her. "Lucy, as long as I've known you, embracing newness has been part of your very being, though you know, sometimes you've had to be nudged a little in that direction. Anna was your main nudger. But *now*—now you have to nudge your-*self*. For you the question always was, could you make a meaningful difference? As a sister ministering to the needy, as an activist for those most deserving of justice, or as a patient advocate. But, please, tell me more about what the Traverse City State Hospital still means to you. With Sister Anna gone, that is."

It was the very question Lucy needed to have asked of her, for it went to the very heart of her indecision. She described her "research project" and how she had enlisted the help of Tom Oakes and set in motion their collaborative writing ventures. She told about Smit and Williams, and about Nancy Brownell. She named patients who depended on her and other attendants and nurses who knew and loved her. She told of Smit's connection with the ACLU in Detroit and the attorney in the Chicago office.

"What do you think will come of that?"

"I honestly don't know. He just told me about that on the phone last night. I'm sure Smit will have more to say about it—if I see him again."

Sister Geniece reached across the table and put Lucy's hands in her own. "God has mysterious ways of pointing us in certain directions," she said. "What I hear you saying is that you are *not* alone up in Traverse City. You have a community and you have purpose. Anna may be gone, but your work beckons. That's what I hear your heart saying, Sister."

She was right. Lucy wasn't alone at all, she realized. She hadn't felt part of something bigger than herself in a long while. The last year had sapped so much of her activist energy. But now, she felt the beginnings of a renewal, and that old feeling returned.[19]

Sister Geniece let go of Lucy's hands and sat back in her chair. Her voice tender, her eyes brimming with kindness, she said, "Remember the Gospel of John. He asked us to walk as Jesus did when he said, 'Whoever claims to live in him must walk as Jesus did.'

"My dear Sister Lucy, you seem to be to be eminently ready to walk as Jesus did."

The next day, a determined Lucy Greene returned to Traverse City.

---

19. It's been a time that I thought
   Lord this couldn't last for very long, oh now
   But somehow I thought I was still able to try to carry on
   It's been a long, long time coming But I know a change is gonna come
   Oh, yes it is
(Sam Cooke, "A Change is Gonna Come"[Recording, RCA Victor, 1964]).

Chapter 20

A FRESH BLANKET OF POWDERY MID-JANUARY SNOW COVERED EVERY-thing; the temperature dipped below 20 for the third straight day. The boilers in the big brick powerhouse across the street pumped hot water through the tunnels and into the pipes in Building 50 so efficiently that some orderlies were working in T-shirts.

In the asylum canteen, Smit sat opposite Lucy in a rear booth—two cokes and the remains of a bag of potato chips between them. It was late in the afternoon, a few minutes after Smit's shift had ended. The place was nearly deserted.

Her head had just jerked back as if she didn't hear correctly what he said. Her eyebrows closed toward one another. It was the *I-can't-believe-you're-asking-that* look. She laughed as her eyes lowered to meet his.

"No, Smit. We were not like that. We grew up together, went to school together, best of friends since first grade. We went into the convent together, same college, and then on to our life's adventures. We took a vow of celibacy. Oh, I suppose that wouldn't have ruled out a more sexual relationship, but that wasn't us. We loved one another, like siblings. And no, I'm not attracted to women sexually. Even nuns can be attracted to men, in spite of their vows. Now, does that satisfy your curiosity?"

He had a sheepish look. He had to ask, he said. He always wondered about nuns, and what they liked and

217

didn't, never having had any contact with them other than seeing a few on the Michigan campus.

"But they wore all those robes and whatnot," he said, "and those halos." His *let-me-entertain-you-with-my-deliber-ate-malapropisms* grin returned.

She stifled another laugh. "Habits," she said. "They're called habits. My order stopped wearing them a while ago, though some sisters never ... "

"I know," he interrupted with the expected bad joke, "they never lost the habit."

She smiled at the pun. "Okay. I deserved that one."

"Well then," Smit said, stirring his cola with a straw. "In spite of your vow of cerebralcy" (a hint of a smile).

"Celibacy."

"That too."

She put the back of her hand to her mouth, stuffed another laugh. She liked Smit more every time they were together. He was funny and witty, and he was able to control the side of him that brought forth anger, like talk about the troop buildup in Vietnam.

"In spite of that," he said, "if I invited you to go somewhere, would you go?"

She rolled her eyes, blinked a few times in succession, and shook her head side to side ever so slightly, as if she had misheard for the second time.

"Oh my," she said. "Are you ... asking me out on a date? Is that what you're getting at, Smit? Or was that just hypothetical, like you're constructing your theory of nun behavior."

He was dead serious, and he was beginning to resent that she was making it into some sort of game. But the truth was that he *was* asking her out. And the further truth was that his asking made her uncomfortable. No man had asked her for a date since she had entered the convent at age 18. So, this was as awkward for her as it was for him, especially since she had to admit she liked him, a lot. Even his looks she found attractive. She treated his invitation lightly because it made her nervous.

"Absolutely not, on both counts," he said. "I'm just curious."

"You're lying! I can tell when you're lying. Your nose twitches. Just a little."

"Okay, I'm lying then. See, I like you, and I have *friends* kinds of feelings for you. But if we were to go out, we'd just be going out as friends. Like when I was at Michigan. I went out with dozens, well a few, girls—women—just because we like to do things together. Oh, there were a couple that I was more serious about, but those didn't last long. So, I'd like it if we could just go have some fun. It wouldn't be more than that, what with the cerebralcy thing and all. I'd like, kiss your gloved hand when I drop you off as a sign of my chivalry."

She gave him the *incredulity* stare, "What have you been reading lately?"

"Arthurian Legends. What makes you ask that?"

"Well, other than the fact that you seem to be hallucinating from some place in the fifth or sixth century, not much. But I think we were talking about you asking me out."

"Well, now that I know you would be interested in dating *me* rather than Nurse Jaworski in Cottage 33, the answer is yes. So, what do you think?"

She shook her head, her amusement continuing to make him squirm uncomfortably on his side of the booth.

"Oh my," she laughed. "You are so sweet, and I am so flattered. But I can't go out on a date with you. You must understand. I just wouldn't do that sort of thing."

He looked across the canteen and waved at someone he recognized. His gaze fell back on her when he spoke next.

"All right, then. I get it. You're the linguist, so the semantics are important here. Look at it this way: it's not a, quote, *date*, unquote. It's what they call an *outing*, like when staff take patients out for a day at the beach or on a picnic. Would you like to go on an outing? No hand holding like on a date. No flowers or chocolates. No 'I'll have your daughter back by 9:30, Mr. Greene, you can count on it, sir.'"

She nearly burst a mouthful of cola all over him. She wiped her mouth with the back of her hand and then with a paper napkin.

"All right, then. I'll go with you on an outing. But I insist on wearing my habit. Will that be okay with you?"

"Your habit? You actually still have a habit? Oh my! This I have to see. Yes, please wear your habit. Like the Swinging Nun.

"The Singing Nun, Smit. But what about Williams?"

"What about Williams?"

"Don't you two do everything together?"

"Ah hah. I see what you're getting at. Tit for tat. No, we don't do everything together. Especially lately. Not since Janice came into his life. New girlfriend from Detroit. Gorgeous. Smart. Talented—she plays viola in a symphony. They dated in Ann Arbor and then graduated and went their separate ways. But now they write back and forth, and he spends a fortune on long-distance calls to her in

Detroit. She has a great job there, in advertising—the first Negro female in the company and she's doing really well. And Williams, well, to put it lightly, he's in love. They talk long into the night sometimes until he or she or both of them fall asleep on the phone. Now he's talking about taking a second job just to pay for the phone bills we're getting. Way deep in love, that man is."

Lucy was happy for Williams. He often seemed lonely being one of the few Negro people in Traverse City. She imagined that he must feel singled out wherever he went around town, like that night at the U & I Lounge. Most people in this part of the state couldn't identify with that kind of difference—Traverse City was strikingly Caucasian. But she could identify with his need to connect with his racial community. She didn't have to be Negro herself to know that; it was the first lesson she and Anna learned when they landed in Mississippi—because they were white, they would never find a natural place in the Negro community; they were there to support people in their fight for equality. They were outsiders who needed to make meaningful connections with their fellow activists at levels below skin color. Still, she knew she could never know the struggle for civil rights the way a dark-skinned person could. And that was all right. That was as it should be.

Smit left *not-a-date-but-an-outing* behind as he reached into his worn leather brief case from his college days. He pulled out a letter and slipped on his black horn-rimmed reading glasses as he opened the envelope.

"I have something for you," he said, unfolding the paper. The envelope bore the logo of the University of Michigan. "It's from one of my profs there, not Higgins, but one of his colleagues in Poly Sci. At Anna's funeral, I told you about the call I made to the ACLU and how they gave me a contact in Chicago."

Lucy had been thinking on and off about what that contact could possibly mean for her; she was eager to hear more. She beckoned to the waitress, raised two fingers and pointed at their empty coke glasses. "Go on," she said. "I thought a lot about what you said that day. It's part of the reason I came back. I'm intrigued."

They were the only patrons in the canteen now, their privacy secure. The cokes showed up in less than two minutes.

"Good," he said. Smit read the letter aloud, line by line. This was a Professor Andrews, who had been asked by Smit's Professor Higgins to share with Smit and "other interested parties at the TC State Hospital" his research into the recent history of the rise of the pharmaceutical industry in the U.S.

"This is preliminary work," Smit read, "as this corporate enterprise has only been a major player in the world of medicine for a relatively short time, fewer than ten years." But with the phenomenal success, in the 1950s, of Thorazine to treat schizophrenia, drug manufacturers were quick to develop other drugs—Haldol, Serpasil, Prolixin, Ritalin. Together, these drugs constituted the first generation of pharmaceuticals that have had *some* clinical trials, "... although those trials," in his opinion, "were not held to the highest standards or for the longest trial period that they should have been in normal circumstances."

Smit put the letter down and pulled off his glasses. "Andrews goes on to speculate," he said, paraphrasing: "Have some drugs been rushed to market because so many people in so many places desperately wanted to *believe* these were wonder drugs? Would science finally win in the battle against mental illness?"

He continued reading then. "Was this the same wishful thought process that, in the recent past, promoted the 'scientific' faith in medical therapies widely used in institutions? First, there was hydrotherapy, popular since the beginning of the century, which ranged from soothing warm baths to near drowning, all with little effect in spite of the claims. Then came insulin-induced comas. In this therapy, patients were injected with insulin that produced comas over a period of days, and they came out of the coma feeble and needy, sometimes with lasting neurological damage. This was followed by Metrazol-induced seizures, in which patients experienced explosive seizures, the result of which was that patients would be so dazed and disoriented they would no longer have problematic behavior—they, too, often suffered brain damage. Electroshock therapy used electrical currents to induce seizures that left patients stunned and dazed and consequently submissive and easy to manage. And, of course, there was the prefrontal lobotomy, in which portions of the front part of the brain were severed, thus robbing a person of what makes him human and rendering his behavior to that of a household pet."

The back of her hand to her mouth, Lucy uttered, "My goodness!"

"I know," said Smit, continuing to read aloud, "I'm almost done.

"All approaches were well-intentioned as cures. All were done under the auspices of science, in the interests of helping patients who had no rights for refusing treatment. All were marketed toward the medical establishment. All made money for someone, somewhere. And all failed to produce any lasting results or viable cures.

"Further, the letter says, there is sufficient evidence that today, the pharmaceutical industry is marketing drugs directly toward the doctors, in the very same institutions, who continue to have total control over which patients get which medicines. There is doubt that many of these medications are being held to the strictest standards of testing; in some cases, only six-week trials, not long-term trials, are the norm. Hardly a scientific standard.

"But the important point is that control over who gets what places an enormous amount of power in the hands of relatively few physicians and psychiatrists. We know, from history, that power placed in the exclusive hands of the few can be dangerous. Which is not to say that there is anything amiss at present, only that, if history ever does repeat itself, there may be cause for concern—until more is known about not only the efficacy of new medications but also the ethical imperatives of the distribution system."

Lucy frowned. "Hmm," she said, "That's a lot to take in. I'm really shocked to learn that some drugs get so little testing before they are approved. I heard that about Progrol, the medication Anna was given. I don't understand why the government—is that the FDA?—became lax about their own standards? I thought they were dedicated to safety standards. They have to meet scientific criteria and those criteria must be rigorous in order to qualify as a *bona fide* clinical trial. What's going on?"

Smit shook his head, "Good question. But he talks about that here."

He continued reading and paraphrasing. "Professor

Andrews says that some drugs are rushed to market because they produce *some* positive results, enough to convince the government gatekeepers that it would be *inhumane* to withhold promising—'sometimes they say *proven*,' he writes—'treatment protocols for those who suffer the most.'" His letter asks if anyone at the Traverse City State Hospital has any insights to share that might illuminate his findings so far.

The second round of cokes arrived. Lucy and Smit sat silently as they peeled the paper covers from their straws. The waitress out of earshot, Smit remarked, "Professor Andrews, he's careful to couch suggestions of right or wrong in vague language, so I can't really tell from this letter how he intends to frame his research. He has to be careful to avoid liability, I'm sure. So, he speculates rather than comes to any premature conclusions. Besides, he's doing preliminary research on something that does not have an abundance of resources available; I'm sure there aren't a bunch of corporate reports and marketing plans just lying around for the taking."

"I see the picture here," Lucy said. "It would take Congress, I suppose, to investigate something this big. Don't you think?"

"Well, sure," he said, "but then there are scores of corporate lobbyists running around Washington wining and dining our lawmakers even as we speak. I'd put my bet on academics to do valid research. Independent of the drug companies. But you can imagine what a large team it would take to challenge the research findings of a major industry like this. Chemists, doctors, clinicians, attorneys, just for starters. Of course, they, too, could be bought off by the industry—to validate the research that the pharmacy industry is doing on its own product. Even academic researchers can be bought off, you know, through grants and fancy labs."

"That's called *sponsor bias*," she said. "I've done my homework."

"I figured you, of all people, would have a word for it," he returned. "Anyway, corporate has a huge stake in getting positive outcomes, and they have little tolerance for uncertainty. Heaven forbid that the research should prove that X doesn't do Y, or that X has Z side effects that would prevent it from coming on the market."

"Of course," Lucy smiled, "the research itself—good, bad or otherwise—is tainted by the fact that its sponsors want it to prove that a medication works."[20]

"Not *is*, according to Professor Andrews, that's too strong a word at this point. But *may be* tainted puts the emphasis on, and the need for, truly objective research—the third-party variety, from sources independent of the corporation. The FDA is supposed to be regulating this kind of product research, but you know how murky and tangled Washington can be, especially when so many people want the drugs to work! Who knows what pressure is put on

20 "Starting in 1959, (Tennessee Senator Estes) Kefauver directed a two-year investigation by the Senate Subcommittee on Antitrust and Monopoly into drug-industry practices, and his committee documented how the marketing machinery of pharmaceutical firms completely altered what physicians, and the general public, read about new medications. Advertisements in medical journals, the committee found, regularly exaggerated the benefits of new drugs and obscured their risks. The 'scientific' articles provided a biased impression as well. Prominent researchers told Kefauver that many medical journals 'refused to publish articles criticizing drugs and methods, lest advertising suffer'" (Robert Whitaker, *Mad in America* [New York: Basic Books, 2002] 149).

the FDA? I think this tale would make for a good mystery novel: it has intrigue and grit and motives!"

"I'm sure it would, Smit, but let's stay on track."

"Right. Back to the resources. My guess is Professor Andrews doesn't go into his resources, and that is because they're pretty lean and hard to find. But that doesn't mean they don't exist or that they can't be found. Like he says, he's just in the early stages of his research. He's fishing around ... maybe because he smells something fishy."

"So why would he write this then? To strangers in northern Michigan?" Lucy could barely contain her curiosity.

Smit shook his head. "Like I said, I'm not sure. My guess? He heard from Higgins that some people up here at this hospital are asking questions about medical treatments for patients and he senses some relevant data, even of the anecdotal kind. I'm pretty certain my old professor would have mentioned it to him because Higgins and I have talked about it, the asking questions part. This is how the academic world works, Lucy. One person drops a comment in conversation; the other sees something in it and begins to ask questions. Soon he talks with others or brings it up as an aside at a conference. Pretty soon others engage with the question and then they're feeding off one another's curiosities. In political science, ears really perk up when money and politics and power get involved. As a matter of fact, you have that same sort of curiosity. Maybe you should get a Ph.D. and ... "

He stopped when Lucy glanced up as two doctors in white coats passed through the canteen. She didn't recognize them. "Greed," was all she said, almost to herself, but loud enough for Smit to hear.

"Maybe," he continued, "but let's remember that the pharmaceutical industry is out to make money. Period. They may talk of humanitarian missions, etcetera, but the bottom line is the bottom line. You don't see them out in the jungle harvesting natural remedies from plants and trees. Even if natural remedies *worked*, that's too labor-intensive and costly, and it doesn't smack of the *scientific* and the *modern*. They want *new*. They want *tested*. They want high-powered marketing that uses words like *safe* and *latest* and *miracle* and *wonder*."

Lucy had not thought deeply about how drugs are *marketed*. But now! Now she considered that the drug industry must have a distribution system that penetrates that soft area where doctors and psychiatrists are the gatekeepers between corporate sellers and lay users. She eased her spine against the soft cushions that lined the booth.

"I have a lot to think about," she said. "I can't thank you enough, Smit, for sharing this letter with me."

He folded up the letter and passed it across the table to her.

"Sure. I would have shared this with you sooner, but I figured you were in no shape to hear all this right after Sister Anna died. So, on my own, I called him up right away and he said I should call the ACLU office in Detroit, just in case they may be looking into the same things. But that was just wishful thinking on his part, I figure, because their hands are all tied up in *racial* civil rights, not *patient* civil rights. That's why they put me on to that woman in Chicago, the one I called you about. Funny how one person knows this, and one person knows that, and before long, if you're persistent enough, you get to the right person. That's what happened, I guess. Who knows what this person in

Chicago has going on? Could be something or could be a dead end."

"I'll contact this person in Chicago," Lucy said, "but there's more I have to do here first."

He sat back against his own booth cushion. "That's the spirit, Lucy." Then, after a pause, "So there's that part, about the letter. There's more. But it's gonna cost you something."

She put her hands up to her face, fingers on her cheeks, eyes tightening. "Is this about the *outing*, Smit? Are you trying to put the squeeze on me? Some sort of *quid pro quo*?"

"Sister Lucy, you know Latin. I can barely master English, knowing I came from Hamtramck, not Gross Pointe Farms. I wouldn't know a *quid pro quo* from a *quid pro* wrestler.

Besides, we already agreed on the outing, didn't we? It just needs a day and time for the first one."

"Uh huh," she said, a quirky grin spreading across her face. "The *first* one?"

He ignored her. "What I meant is that it'll cost you another bag of chips. Fritos if you don't mind."

"Okay, but this better be good." She waved at the waitress and pointed to a rack of Fritos above a display case. She held up one finger. The girl brought it over to them.

Smit then launched into a lengthy account of the reconnoitering he and Williams had been doing for the past few weeks—since Lucy had asked them to linger a bit around the open doors of offices. They listened when doctors saw patients. And, especially, being in the immediate vicinity when Dr. Turner was on rounds—they listened to how he spoke with patients and nurses, noting his turns of phrase and his ways of finding out what ailed patients, even his timing of utterances. Anything that might qualify as *linguistic data*, she had suggested. Keep notes if possible, she urged them, or jot them down as soon as possible after they notice something. Date and time too.

They did just that, both of them, together and separately. Williams was fortunate enough to have, as part of his regular cleaning assignments, the hall where Dr. Turner's office was located. And Smit's supervisor had given him a small crew of three men who would clean wherever Smit saw the need, whether it be in the Building 50 wards or in the cottages. As a result, he could pick and choose where he and/or his crew would work.

Between Smit and Williams, they had many opportunities to listen and watch what went on. They jotted down notes in little spiral notebooks they carried in their pants pockets. At night, they would write up more elaborate notes from the scraps of information they jotted down in their notebooks.

From his briefcase, again, Smit produced a manila envelope that contained two short stacks of papers, all handwritten in two distinct styles—his and Williams's. He slid each one, in its turn, across to Lucy.

In the first group of notes, titled *WAYS OF TALKING WITH PATIENTS*, Lucy read about Smit's and Williams' observations of how Dr. Turner interacts with patients on rounds. How when he enters a room, he tells other doctors on rounds that the patient suffers from this or that psychiatric disorder, so that anyone new on the rounds team has a preliminary mindset before even meeting the patient.

Lucy scrunched up her nose. "So what?" she said. "What's odd about that?"

"Probably nothing," Smit said, "but then he adds some

remark that describes the patient in unflattering ways, like, 'We'll next meet Mr. Webster. He's a hypochondriac, so if he says he is sick or has a medical problem, take that with a grain of salt.' In the notes, there's another episode I wrote up. When he went with the team to visit a young female patient in Cottage 23, a gal who'd lost her whole family in a car accident, he warned the docs that they couldn't really believe anything she might tell them because she was psychotic and she wouldn't likely tell the truth."

"Ah," Lucy said. *"Prejudicial qualifiers.* They're used to bias observers before they have an opportunity to view raw data. So, if a doctor doesn't like a patient or if he has had previous negative experiences with a patient, he can interfere with what should be an objective interview with a patient."

Her thought went to Anna, and how Dr. Turner so often referred to her having been attacked in Mississippi. Could it be, she thought, that, deep down, he harbored negative feelings *because* she had been raped? Or could he himself harbor negative political views against the Freedom Riders, and could those prejudices prevent him from being objective in his care for her? She hated to think this possible, but she didn't really know him well.

Smit passed another paperclip-bound group of papers across the table. It was labeled *TIME ISSUES.* "Here's something else I noticed. He instructs the docs he supervises to waste little time with an individual patient. He's always saying things like 'Let's not dwell on this patient's complaint. We have so many more to see today.' Or he might say, 'She'll go on and on like this for hours if you let her. Let's get moving.' I can understand that they have a lot of people to see, and so time is of the essence, but sometimes, I think a doctor just needs to slow down and listen, even if the patient is unbalanced or unreliable for whatever reason. These are people who need a doctor to take time with them. In fact, they need *more* time than people who are *not* institutionalized.

"But Turner, he just seems to want to cover the territory without soaking up the landscape. So, the other docs end up doing what he does. He's their boss, after all. A couple of times I actually counted out the seconds before he interrupted a patient. Eight seconds the first time I counted. Six seconds the second time. The older docs, like Doc Gordon, they're slower, they listen more, probably because they have some history with their patients; they know them better; they care more, it appears. That's my opinion, for what it's worth.

"But the new docs, they learn to do the same thing Turner does—don't really listen, just interrupt and talk over the patient. It's like *they* know best; *they* know more; *they* have it *all* figured out beforehand. And the patients, bless their souls, they just pipe down like it's God speaking to them. Sorry. Bad choice, again."

Lucy thought about how people are socialized to talk in certain ways depending on who's got the most authority. And the power of authority determines patterns of speaking. Unless others challenge that power.

Smit rolled right along: "Another thing, and this really bothers me, is that if other doctors express any uncertainty about a patient or a patient's complaint about his health, he jumps to conclusions right away. He says things like, 'She had this condition a year ago and now it's back. Case closed.' I actually heard him say that there's no time for uncertainty in the wards. He said, 'You have to make decisions and then go with them.' It's as if being uncertain about a diagnosis just doesn't fit into his worldview. Which may be okay some of the time, but what if that fear of uncertainty causes a doctor to make a rash diagnosis? People have died from such things, haven't they?"

Lucy was lost in thought. Anna again. She remembered the day Anna lost her vision, how puzzled Dr. Turner was at first, but then how quickly he concluded that the condition was temporary, how swift he was to diagnose her with episodic blindness. And then when she asked if Progrol might have something to do with Anna's blindness, how quickly he denied that possibility. His certainty was dogmatic. And then there was that ophthalmologist at Munson Hospital, how swiftly he determined the cause of Anna's condition from what he already knew from the record Dr. Turner had sent over: that Anna had suffered brain damage and that *must* have been the causal agent. Could that decision, Lucy wondered, have closed down any alternative diagnoses to consider? Could it be that Anna actually did have some sort of early stroke? Could her "episodic blindness," brought on by "brain damage," actually have been a harbinger of what would later be a major stroke? And could that stroke have been prevented? Did both doctors stop searching for *the* cause because a more convenient and available cause presented itself?

A shudder went through her. Where was all this leading?

Another clipped-together group of papers slid toward her.

"These are from Williams," Smit began, "and I can just summarize it all for you. You can read his notes at your leisure. Over the course of weeks, if not months, what he noticed is that our Dr. Turner gets many visitors wearing fancy suits and driving fancy cars. They come to his office and they talk there, sometimes for hours. Williams, he's sharp, you know. So, one day he stops one of the suits as he's leaving the building and he asks him if he's from the CIA. No reason given, just working off a hunch. And the suit laughs and says, 'CIA? Hell no. I work for a pharmaceutical company you've probably never heard of.' Williams ignored the implication that a Negro attendant would be ignorant of the names of big drug companies. Pretty funny, huh?"

"Pretty sad."

"My thought, exactly. Anyway, these suits are coming and going all the time. He often sees them bringing large paper sacks full of something. Williams noticed that on the days these men visit him, after they've all left, Dr. Turner often leaves for home carrying shopping bags full of something. Williams thinks they're gifts of some sort, but he doesn't know for sure, just guessing because one day a suit brought Sheila, she's the secretary, a huge bouquet of flowers. Another time a suit brought her a leather purse."

Smit flipped through the pages. "Then Williams wrote, right here, how when Dr. Turner is gone for a few days, Williams comes by his office to mop or sweep and strikes up a conversation with Sheila, and she tells him that the doc is in Las Vegas with his wife, or that he flew to Miami, with Mrs. T. again, for a few days of fishing in the Keys.

"Williams puts two and three together and comes up with five. The paper sacks full of gifts and the trips to pretty exotic locations. With his wife too. Nice new cars for both of them. The other docs drive Fords and Plymouths. He drives a Lincoln and the Missus drives a Cadillac. Do I see a pattern here?"

"I think we know there is a pattern, don't we, Smit? This is the most influential doctor at this institution. He supervises all the other doctors, and he's the one person who can persuade them to use whatever drugs *he* deems appropriate, from whatever companies *he* recommends. When it comes to purchasing decisions, his opinion matters more than anyone's. By the looks of things, he is not in a position to be entirely objective. I think what we're seeing is the dangerous intersection of science and money and medicine and power. And it may well be the future for all of mental health care, happening right here, in tiny Traverse City. And it's probably going on in who knows how many other hospitals in the country."

Smit said, "Not probably, *certainly*, if Professor Andrews' research has any merit."

Chapter 21

IN THE JANUARY NEWSLETTER, "THE HOSPITAL ORGAN," TOM OAKES PUT in festive photos and heart-warming stories of patients enjoying the Christmas holidays and the New Year's Eve "formal" dance. He was deliberate: He did not mention the increased threats of suicide and patient assaults on one another that always seemed to increase during the winter holidays as the Christmas blues sounded their intense alarms. His newsletter was not intended to reveal ugly truths about patients' lives, but rather to present the illusion that all was well, now that patients' mental health had been so dramatically improved through the newest medical interventions. As Dr. Turner never hesitated to remind him, "The newsletter is PR, plain and simple." Still, in Tom's mind, he was quite capable of writing the truth, though that would have to be in another time and another place.

Lucy, meanwhile, had renewed her determination to continue her research. In the second half of January, she was busier than usual. Father Pete had taken some time off to tend to his own aging parents in Ohio. That left Lucy as the main support to Father Fred at the very time the architectural and interior design plans for All Faiths Chapel were being finalized, more letters soliciting donations were written and mailed out, and the groundbreaking ceremony planned for what everyone hoped would be the mildest

March on record—an ambitious prospect indeed, given the unkindness of March in a good year.

Thus, it was with only the hint of a joke that Father Fred often mentioned a sixth century saint at Mass: St. Medard or Medardus, a venerated French bishop who, legend has it, was invoked for bringing good weather (or rain, depending on what one meant by "good" in one's prayers) and for relief of toothaches. Though St. Medard's normal feast day would have been celebrated on June 8, Father Fred joked that a candle lit for the good bishop every few days in the two months preceding March might not be a bad idea.

Following the busy daytimes supporting the chaplain ministry, Lucy spent evenings compiling pages of notes on her research project. She typed them on a Smith Corona she purchased second hand. She carefully organized everything she'd learned from Nurse Brownell in the "seminars" she'd had with the head nurse, though she didn't put Nancy Brownell's name on anything because notes from that source became melded with her own observations of patients and her own reflections on Anna's time at the hospital. With Smit's and Williams' notes, however, she found she had more questions for them as she typed. And so she kept their names prominent at the tops of each page so that she would know whom to contact for more information.

She read a recent note penned by Williams. It said Dr. Turner had just returned from a professional excursion to San Diego, where he gave a talk at a national pharmaceutical conference entitled "Deinstitutionalization through Medical Miracles." He had been gone for ten days. While he was gone, Williams was able to charm out of Sheila,

Dr. Turner's secretary, the interesting fact that not only had Mrs. Turner accompanied her husband on the trip, but the happy couple were also afforded a lovely hotel room on the ocean at La Jolla.

The rest Williams wrote as dialogue meant to entertain:

"Wow," I gushed. "I should-a-been-a doctor."

"Not only that," Sheila blabbed, "they were given an extra week, all expenses paid by the people who invited him to give a speech. All that on top of his honorarium! He's very important, you know."

"Oh, I know," my guileless voice said, "I know."

None of this came as any surprise to Lucy, who made note of the trip and Sheila's remark in her own typed notes, under the heading *PERKS (from Williams, 1/1964)*. Frequently working late at home, she sat at her desk, reviewing and revising her notes as if they were to become the groundwork for a more comprehensive document—an article for a magazine, or a report to some official, as-yet-unidentified organization. She wouldn't really know what she had until she completed this stage: it was an organic process. As she shifted through notes and wrote little comments on them, she searched for what she called "centers of gravity," patterns of information that would cluster around major points. For example, she knew that Dr. Turner was the opinion leader at the hospital when it came to drug selections for patients, and she knew that he was often rewarded in monetary and material ways by the companies that made and sold the medicines. She knew that very few medicines were being prescribed for a broad range of conditions. Too broad a range, given the nascent state of pharmaceutical invention. And she knew that side effects were much greater and more unpredictable than anyone would admit, patients and most nurses excepted. What more centers of gravity might there be? She would leave that to the next person who would lay eyes on the research notes: Tom Oakes.

More the gatherer than the scribe, Lucy would rely on Mr. Oakes, the writer, to sift through the many pages for what it all might mean to an interested reader, like the ACLU, or a member of the Michigan delegation to Congress. If Tom Oakes were true to his promise, he would put it all into some coherent whole. If he were true to his long-held aspiration to become a freelance writer, he would turn that whole into an article for publication, and that would be his ticket to fame and longed-for path out of a job he loathed.

She appeared at Tom Oakes' office shortly after nine the next morning. He looked disheveled again—tussled hair where a comb had not found its purpose, a two-day stubble on his cheeks and chin, mismatched shirt and tie, and eyes that shone red and blinked a lot. Heavy drinking the night before, she figured. Sober now and more likely to be available for a serious conversation.

Which he was. She accepted his offer of coffee. He went to a portable coffee maker on a cluttered side table and, his back to her, poured a cup for Lucy. She noticed that his back was turned to her longer than pouring a fresh cup ought to take, which meant, she guessed, that he had poured some whiskey into his own before returning to his desk. She figured the flask had disappeared into the clutter.

She apologized that she still did not have ready her notes on the story he had drafted on Anna and her history. She would have it to him shortly. Apologies accepted.

Then she laid a thick brown expanding file on the desk between the two of them and reminded him what she was delivering. Did he remember their agreement? Yes, of course he did: it was to compile a mass of notes into some organized fashion that would constitute a readable something or other that would be used for something or other and sorry, Sister, but I'm a little off today and what was it again that we're to do with whatever I finally come up with?

She tempered her impatience. She'd had only one hangover in her life, and she remembered well how debilitating it could be; she could not imagine having one virtually every day. She could have simply picked up her file and said thank you, I'll do this myself, but she had made a promise to a man who needed to raise himself out of a dead-end job and gain some professional respectability. She would not go back on her promise to help him help himself while helping her help *her*self.

Not yet, anyway.

"All you need to do is search through the notes, look for patterns and compare those to what I labeled as the centers of gravity notes in the last section in the file. Start by reading the raw notes themselves, Mr. Oakes. Look for themes and connected ideas. I think I see them myself, but I may be too close to it all and I need someone to look it over who is more dispassionate, less involved in what I would call suspicions and doubts arising from my own personal bias. It needs an *objective other* perspective with a good command of the language.

"Is that still you, Mr. Oakes?"

Of course it is, he assured her. And he'd get right on the project just as soon as he could.

"But, you see," he said, "I have this other task," pulling out from a manila file a small stack of typed pages, "that I'm under time pressure to finish. Another of Dr. Turner's articles. I'm the ghostwriter for this one too. The ghostwriter does all the work, but he gets all the credit. Oh, and I'm not bitter, you see. That's just how the game is played. Fortunate or unfortunate, that's my job."

He lied. He was, in fact, bitter. But he was also resigned to what his life had become. She was sorry for Mr. Oakes, and she sincerely hoped that her research project might offer him a way to spare himself from his own self-destructive ways. *Who knows*, she thought, *a first-rate article with his name in the byline might just make a difference.*

"Imagine your name on two bylines, Mr. Oakes. One on the Lucy and Anna story, another on this writing project, however it turns out. Wouldn't that be grand?"

In Tom Oakes' mind, there was no doubt that the project had promise for his lifelong dream of becoming Tom Oakes, Writer. He opened the file and began leafing through the clipped-together sheaves of papers. He spread them out over the other papers he had strewn on his desk.

She said, "I just clumped and grouped them according to who told me what or by what topic went with what."

She pointed out the names of Smit and Williams on some of the sheets. "Do you know these names?" He did not.

"They are attendants—two of my sources—and I kept their names prominent so I could double back to them to ask questions or clarify something in their notes."

"All right," he said. "I'll mark those passages where I have questions, so you can go back to them if necessary. All of this seems rather well organized as is."

"Well, you may see some other way to organize. I leave that to you, Mr. Oakes. Once you have a sense of what goes with what, and what you see as potential emphases in the written product, please call me and we'll talk about all that—and what product or products you may be writing. An article? A report? Maybe both. We'll see."

"Got it, Sister. Can do, will do. I'll tinker with this material in between other things I'm working on. I'll let you know when; a few days at most. I'm planning on writing an article, at the very least."

She noticed that ink from the pen stuck in his shirt pocket had leaked onto the cloth. She said nothing about it. Instead, she stared at him, the look that said *I'm putting my trust in you. Don't let me down.*

"A few days, Sister. I promise."

"And I'll have your manuscript back to you in a matter of days, too. I promise."

Minutes later, Lucy sat in her little office, thinking. She would meet with Dr. Turner that day, if possible, and she had one goal—to create discomfort in the doctor's otherwise comfortable life. It was time to act on her principles, and on the data that had convinced her something was terribly wrong at the hospital. She would make him aware that his professional ethics were suspect, his attitudes toward patients problematic, and the way he handled Anna's decline and death disturbing. And what might come of all this agitation? At the very least, he would be made aware that she harbored suspicions that something in his professional behavior wasn't right, that he needed to be held to the professional ideals espoused in the Hippocratic Oath: *First, do no harm*. To patients who deserve respect and dignity in spite of their station in life. To colleagues who depend on him for thoughtful, principled leadership. And to himself, for willingly becoming the pawn of greedy pharmaceutical companies eager to line his pockets with easy rewards.

It all came down to personal ethics. It always does.

She thought of Rosa Parks refusing to give up her seat on that bus in Montgomery: how a singular act of determined resistance could launch irreversible consequences. *There may be winds of change bearing down on America's asylums*, she thought, *and they may be inevitable. But there is no inherent place in that change for injustice, malfeasance, or mistreatment.* She thought of Dr. King writing that letter of resistance from a Birmingham jail cell.[21] How he perfectly captured the inescapable interconnectivity of all forms of injustice.

And the need to speak out against them.

Lucy called Dr. Turner's office. Would Sheila put her on the doctor's calendar for that afternoon? Yes, he had time later in the day and what was it she wanted to see him about?

"Oh," Lucy said, "just tell him I have a few questions ...

---

21. "Injustice anywhere is a threat to justice everywhere. We are caught in an inescapable network of mutuality, tied in a single garment of destiny. Whatever affects one directly, affects all indirectly" (Martin Luther King Jr., *Letter from Birmingham Jail*, April 16, 1963).

about patient care; and I need his guidance, his expertise, to make some decisions about ... my work."

She felt that was sufficiently vague—and pandering. She would not be oppositional, even though what she had to say would likely be interpreted as oppositional. She hoped it wouldn't come to that. She would keep what she had to say quasi-friendly: she told Sheila she just had some things that she was trying to figure out and could he help her with them?

"All right, then," said the secretary. "I've got you penciled in for 4 p.m. I'm sure Dr. Turner will be able to help you with your problems, whatever they may be. Why, he helps so many people! He's the smartest man I've ever known, okay? And the kindest. You know, he brings back gifts for me when he goes to those conferences. Why, just last week, he brought me a huge seashell from California that he found on the beach. It's called a conch and it's very rare. I love how shiny it is. If I put my ear on the open part, I can hear Lake Michigan!"

In the name of truth, Lucy's first instinct was to set gullible Sheila straight by telling her that conch are found only in the Caribbean, that what she was putting her ear to had almost certainly been found in a San Diego airport gift shop.

But it would be pointless, she thought, *and cruel*, to dispossess Sheila of her own truth.

Speechless, Lucy simply said goodbye and hung up. She had to prepare for her meeting with Dr. Turner. She had her notecards in her purse, each labeled with a crucial question, each filled with scribblings that would serve to elaborate on the question if needed. She had her paper sack lunch with her today, and so she sat alone in her office space munching her baloney sandwich and reviewing her notecards until she had each committed to memory. In a barely audible voice, she practiced her delivery—to find the right tone (respectful but insistent on getting to the truth), the right balance of knowledge and curiosity (*based on X, I wonder Y*), and the judicious use of key words (*ethical, personally beneficial, appropriate disclosure, conflict of interest, corporate gifts*).

Chapter 22

SHORTLY BEFORE FOUR O'CLOCK, LUCY SAT ACROSS FROM SHEILA ON A gray, cushioned parlor chair graced with elaborately carved leaves and blossoms on the rosewood back. Sheila appeared hard at work adding up columns of numbers in an accounting book. She snapped and cracked her chewing gum. Every once in a while, a weak "Oh, darn" came out of her, followed by a furious application of eraser to numbers. She looked up every now and then and smiled at Lucy. She glanced at the wall clock, then shrugged her shoulders and said, "He's in there but, golly molly, I can't just knock on the door and disturb him, you know. I can see here on the phone console that he's on a line."

He's very important, Lucy recalled from Williams's notes. She would be patient.

"I'm content to wait," Lucy said, "I'm sure it's very important."

"Yes," Sheila said between a snap and a pop, "I'm certain it is."

At four-fifteen his door opened. Appropriate apologies for having to take a call from New York that was unavoidable but please come in and would you like tea (a look to Sheila, the tea)?

"No tea, thank you. I'm fine."

He boasted a suntan. She asked how his trip to the west coast went.

246

"Great trip," he beamed. "Great place, San Diego. Have you been?"

"No, unfortunately I have not been west."

"Well, so good to be in a sunny clime at this time of year." He glanced over her shoulder to see the snow flying outdoors.

She pressed. "I'm happy for you that you can get away like that. Do you go on trips like that often?"

"Oh," he said. "I wouldn't say often, but frequently, yes. I'm a bit of a consultant for a company that supplies our hospital, and they seem to like the little talks I give. So, they pay the expenses and all. This time they tacked on a few extra days for R & R. Hard to say no to that, let me tell you!"

"Yes, that *would* be hard. This talk you gave. What was it about, if you don't mind my asking? I've heard you give mini-lectures to the new docs on rounds, and I'm always eager to hear more."

His face lit up with enthusiasm.

"Well, it was about which medications are most effective with our population. How we are using them. What therapeutic effects they're having. What we see as the future for mental health care. That sort of thing. It was a good audience; they had many questions."

"I'm sure they must really value your expertise on medications. After all, you would be the one person at this hospital who would know the most about that topic, wouldn't you say?"

"Indeed. But then again, that's my job. Or, I should say, that's a significant part of my job. The other medical staff, they have their hands full with such a large patient load.

Few if any have time to keep up on the research literature. That's one reason why I'm here late into the night more often than not—reading the latest reports and such."

"I understand late night research. I do it myself … "

He interrupted, "So, you *know*. In my case, they depend on me to inform them about best decisions for patient care. And, with so many medicines on the market, and with new ones coming every year, someone has to be the most informed. *Some*one has to lead."

"And liaison with the medicine makers?" she said.

"Oh," he said. "That too. Yes, of course. It goes with the territory, so to speak. But here now, enough about me and trips west. What's on your mind, Sister Lucy? I haven't spoken with you since Sister Anna … passed away. Such a fine person. Such a huge loss, for all of us, but especially you. How have you been holding up?"

Lucy said she's doing better, with time, thank you. It's been hard, but she's getting her old spirit back, slowly.

His condolences again, how much he liked Anna, how much she'll be missed. Then, after a glance at his watch, what was it she wanted to discuss with him?

"Since Anna's death," she began, "I've thought a lot about how she suffered—the headaches, the uncontrollable fits of anger or confusion, her episodic blindness, as you called it, and then the circumstances of her death, and her … "

"Yes," he interrupted, "such a terrible sequence of events, so many challenges in such a short time. Tragic, just tragic. I wish we could have done more for her, more to, ah, ease her pain, give her more relief. She suffered so much."

"Yes," she tried to continue but he cut her off again.

"I've seen cases like hers before where a traumatic brain

injury leads to all sorts of complications. Like the blindness, for example. Otherwise inexplicable behaviors and complaints ... "

Lucy now cut *him* short. "I'm sorry, but those were not complaints, Dr. Turner. Calling them *complaints* makes it sound light, as if she had had a pulled muscle or ingrown toenail. I'm surprised to hear you call her behaviors *inexplicable*, because I don't recall that you ever used that or similar words. In fact, as I recall, *nothing* appeared inexplicable. If you ever did feel the least bit perplexed or inclined to offer a tentative opinion, I never saw that side of you. This is one of the things I wanted to ask about."

His eyebrows rose a bit above his now-narrowed eyes as he sat wondering, *What is this woman, who has no medical credence at all, getting at? Where is this going?*

"Ask away. I'm a captive audience!"

Lucy caught his forced upbeat tone.

"I'm curious about language and how it's used in social settings," she continued. "I'm not sure you know this about me, but I studied linguistics in college. At that time, a new field called sociolinguistics was just getting off the ground in the academic world. The big universities were starting up entire programs in sociolinguistics. My college was very small, so we had to bring in visiting professors from other universities to give some of the lectures to supplement our more traditional linguistics program. They were fascinating lectures; I was hooked after the first one. Have you heard of sociolinguistics?"

Not one to be bested by a more knowledgeable woman on *any* topic, he quickly deconstructed the term and replied, as if he *were* familiar with the field, "Of course, language and social ... things." *Things* gave it away. He had no idea.

A neutral smile enveloped Lucy's face. Her eyes stayed on his. She wanted to capture his complete attention as she unraveled a train of thought that would likely increase his uneasiness.

The die would be cast, and the result would be irreversible.

"Sociolinguists try to understand how people use language in social situations, like a corporate organization, a classroom, a political body, or a family. And it tries to understand how social factors like race, class, authority, and gender impact human communication. In a hospital or institution like this one, a sociolinguist might analyze doctor-doctor talk, doctor-nurse talk, doctor-patient talk, nurse-nurse talk, and even the ways laymen talk with doctors."

"Ah, yes," he said. "Interesting, but … "

"And since my time here, I've taken to noticing how language is used in many situations, and it fascinates me."

He listened with great intent. *This woman*, he thought, *who claims to have some expertise in this area, is driving at something. But what is it?*

"You have my attention, Sister. I can see that this would be a rich arena for studying how people talk to one another. Please, continue."

He exuded polite curiosity. Beneath the cordial veneer, he was beginning to feel discomfort. Tiny beads of sweat broke out on his brow. He wiped his forehead with a handkerchief, which he then folded neatly and placed in a desk drawer.

She leaned slightly toward him for emphasis. "When you were with Anna on rounds, I noticed a number of things that puzzled me. And, actually, I've seen these same things when you are with other patients, so it wasn't just with Anna. It seemed more general."

He sat back, elbows on the desk, hands folded before his mouth, listening.

Lucy had manipulated the "conversation" exactly to the point she had hoped for: The superficial niceties were wearing thin; he knew that what she had to say was serious; and she had imported a certain edge into her tone.

She called up the large visual field on note card #1: *Observations of Doctor-Patient Discourse*. She could have gone through her list of his discourse styles—abrupt interruptions; self-assured diagnoses; avoidance of the appearance of uncertainty; closed-ended questions that elicit yes and no rather than probing questions that elicit from patients helpful insights into their conditions; reluctance to respond to patients' emotions, and more. That, however, would have been overkill.

"What exactly did you notice?" he asked. "Regarding Anna." With this question, he had narrowed the field *for* her.

She affected the ignorance of a neophyte. "I don't have a name for what I noticed, but it's like calling up a stereotypical frame of reference when profiling a patient instead of looking directly at the patient him or herself for who he or she really is—or what he or she is really trying to say."

"I don't understand. What are you saying?"

"Well, with Anna, you told the doctor at Munson that she had suffered a brain injury way before he was able to come to his own conclusions. As if that explained her blindness and that was that."

"Look, Sister. That *was* that. She had classic symptomology. That doctor had to know her history in order to treat her appropriately."

"Dr. Turner. With all due respect, I beg to differ. What you told him gave him a frame of reference *before* he could form his own causal frame of reference. What if what you said to him took away his objectivity? What if she was experiencing the first signs of a stroke? What if Progrol had induced an adverse side effect that *caused* her blindness? If there had been a more open discussion of *possible* causes early on, she might have received different medical treatment. The bottom line is, she might not have died."

He stood abruptly. His face was livid when the questions spewed from his lips: "What are you accusing me of? Malpractice?" It was his own offensive linguistic strategy to jump to the worst conclusion; that might serve to ward off any further incriminations. *Pushing the envelope,* she recognized, is a classic way of exercising one's power—and shaping the subsequent conversation. She had to head that off.

"No, Dr. Turner. I am not. What I *am* doing is attempting to satisfy some curiosities. And, if you will allow me just another minute or two, I would like to ask just a couple more questions. Please. Remember that it was *my* best friend who died, *my* source of strength and meaning, *my* ward for whom the courts have made *me* the party most responsible for her health and care. It is entirely possible that *I* am the one who will be guilty of malpractice—because I did not ask these questions then, because I shirked my moral responsibility when it was most needed. So, no, doctor, this is not a threat to you, but rather a search to redeem myself.

I hope you can sit back down and see our conversation from this broader perspective. Please."

He sat down, rearranged some pens and unopened envelopes on his desk—buying time for his nerves to calm down. Finally, he spoke, a reasoned, deliberate tone void of any emotion. He was back in character.

"You have my attention, again."

"Thank you. I know this is hard ..."

"No, actually, it's *not* hard. I'm nothing if not professional. I'm trained, let us remember, to deal with all manner of talk, including adversity." Then, as if to pour some salt in an open wound, he added, "Whether the adversity is real or concocted."

She took a deep breath. *Don't fall into that trap*, she told herself.

"You had other questions?" he said.

"Curiosities, actually," she said, picturing note card #2: *Corporate Gifts*.

"I'm also curious about how the pharmaceutical industry had made such significant inroads into patient care in state institutions. I notice that the industry touts medicines as wonder drugs and the public has eagerly accepted that line of thinking. For good reason too: They want cures as much as any of us do; they want to believe in what some people call the 'medical model of patient care.' (*Nancy Brownell's exact words*, she recalled.)

"I notice that this same industry has a huge financial stake in promoting their products. They must have giant marketing departments and those marketers must be very active in influencing doctors to endorse their products. I can imagine a company showering doctors and psychiatrists with a wealth of perks, from expensive dinners, trips, and gifts, to lucrative financial awards for such services as speeches and endorsements. These benefits might flow more often to those who are in positions of leadership, it seems to me. I mean, it makes sense for a company to put its energy where it will get the most traction. Sorry, mixed metaphor."

She paused just long enough to picture note card #3: *Civil Rights.*

He sat back in his chair. He eyed her with venomous suspicion, yet he remained silent. A fox waiting to pounce on its prey.

"As I said, all this is mere speculation," she said. "I must repeat, I'm a curious person. As you know, Anna and I were activists for civil rights. That activism did not end when we left Alabama. What I have discovered here is related, I think."

"Ah," he said, a skeptical voice. In his mind, he thought, *Activists looking to make trouble everywhere they go is really behind all this bugaboo.* "And how would that be?"

"Patients have limited rights once they have been committed. Whether it is right or wrong is another matter. Which is exactly what has been the issue since Jim Crow. I wonder if patients' rights are being well served when medications are so liberally given to them, when side effects are so little known, and when so few medications are expected to treat so many disorders. I've come to believe that, for all the good intentions behind using drugs to treat mental disorders, it is just too early to assert that only a *few* can correctly and effectively treat such a great number of conditions. It's like saying that one size of shoe will fit everyone in an entire family. Ten, twenty, thirty years from now, with multiple clinical trials that meet the strictest scientific standards, and with greater diversity of applications, maybe *then* we can safely say they are wonder drugs. But to make that claim now is simply overstating the facts. It is premature."

He smiled, sardonic, almost mocking. "Hmm. Was there a question in all that?"

"Oh, yes," she said.

Card #4 flashed: *Patients' Civil Rights.*

"Do you think patients' rights as citizens are being violated?" she asked.

"I do not," he said, "since they have no rights in the first place, having been committed and legally under our professional care.[22] No, one cannot have one's rights violated if one has no rights to begin with. That would be, to use your language, a logical fallacy, wouldn't it?"

"I suppose it would," she agreed. Then, "That's why I see the connection with the civil rights movement. Which leads me to my last question. And thank you for being such a patient audience, Dr. Turner. I do so appreciate it." Fawning, obsequious.

---

22. "Until patients mounted their legal protests in the 1970s, American society had always pretty much taken for granted that it had the right to forcibly treat the mentally ill. There had been a number of legal battles in the 1800s and early 1900s over society's right to commit patients, but once patients were so committed, forced treatment seemed to follow as a matter of course. Mental patients lacked competency to consent, and—or so the argument went—the state had the right, in the absence of such competence, to act as a substitute parent and determine what was best for them. While there was an understandable rationale to that argument—how can a psychotic person evaluate a proposed treatment?—the history of mad medicine also showed that it invited abuse" (Whitaker, Robert. *Mad in America.* [New York: Basic Books, 2002] 212).

"And that last question is?"

#5: *Ethics.* "Well, I don't quite know how to say this, but I'll try if you'll bear with me."

He had that sardonic look again, the one that signaled certainty and superiority, now that Lucy had intimated her own uncertainty. That was, of course, by design, and it was intended to inflate his ego while setting the stage for getting to some very unsettling raw truth.

"You seem to be doing just fine, Sister. Please, fire away."

"All right, then. My question is this. Given that the development of new drugs to treat mental illness is fairly recent, say 10 years or so; and given that the producers of those drugs stand to make a fortune if their products are successful; and given that those drugs are heavily marketed toward individuals who are the most influential people in getting those drugs into treatment programs on a grand scale; and … "

"Yes, yes, yes," he said, voice raised to indicate his impatience with her logical string of premises.

"I was saying, given that all this makes fertile ground for potential abuse, do you think the medical profession has an ethical responsibility to assure the public that its members are not personally benefiting from the marketing of medicines? I mean, the potential for conflict of interest seems large, don't you think? Can you imagine a future where the pharmaceutical industry conducts its *own* research on its *own* products with its *own* scientists? I don't know, maybe that's happening right now. Or a future where the very medical professionals who prescribe treatment protocols for powerless patients have a vested interest in the products that make up that treatment? I shudder to imagine that world, don't you, Doctor Turner?"

The game was up: The friendly nun come for a friendly visit. A few questions to satisfy her alleged curiosity. Things she has noticed about how things are done. A slow, methodical building toward ethical accusations.

Somehow, she knew things. She was much, much smarter than he had ever suspected. But what *was* her intent?

"Sister Lucy," he said, glancing down at his watch again. "I have no idea what it is you're getting at, but I don't like the insinuation you seem to be making. I think it would be best if we ended this conversation. I have a meeting, and I cannot be late. I wish you well in your efforts to satisfy your ... curiosities."

That was it. He stood, she stood. No hand was extended from either. No final words spoken. She turned and walked toward the door. Before opening it, she turned and looked out his window toward the snowy-white expanse of the Great Lawn.

"You have a great view from here," she said. "It must be nice to be so high up that you can see almost everything that goes on below."

She closed the door gently behind her. Sheila looked up from a magazine she was leafing through, quickly closed it and put it aside.

Lucy smiled as she walked past and said in a low voice, "I love Cosmopolitan Magazine," she said. "I just wish it would rattle a few cages, don't you think, Sheila?"

"I don't actually read it, Sister. I just thumb through it now and then. You know, now and then."

There was no meeting the doctor had to get to. He sat at his desk, thinking.

She's on to something that I don't like, he thought. *And I can't tell where she's going with it. She harbors strong opinions that border on accusations. She is a dangerous person—to the future of medicine, to this institution, and to me personally. She has already suggested she'd go over my head to get someone to listen to her, and even though that didn't happen, she's capable of doing that, and she may even go outside of this hospital, given what she's learned in the civil rights movement. Is she acting alone? If not, then who is she collaborating with? What are they up to?*

Lucy had created doubt. He considered the big picture. His credibility might be threatened. Some people might see him as a pawn to the pharmaceutical industry. Some might look more closely at the articles he had published, the claims he had made there, and they might call him to task on those claims. People in Congress could do that, he knew. They had done that, in fact. He could not be perceived as being part of a drug industry scandal, if that were to be an outcome of this woman's ploy.

This much was clear: He had to protect himself. He would get to the bottom of this Sister Lucy problem one way or another. And he would, somehow. But one thing was more pressing—he needed to get over to Tom Oakes' office and get him to tone down the rhetoric of that article he was ghost writing for him. He needed to back down overreaching claims that had dubious evidence to back them up. He needed to qualify any claims he had made that could be interpreted as overstated, if not downright false;

and he had to prevent any appearance of fawning to the drug industry. Doing so might well disappoint his benefactors in the industry, but once this Sister Lucy crisis passed, he could easily reclaim his authority in another article, another speech, another convention address.

But for now, first things first.

Chapter 23

Dr. Turner went over to Tom Oakes' office to discuss the article on which they were working. He expected that Tom would have put the final flourishes on the article by now and would soon return the copy to the doctor for final approval. But it was seven o'clock by the time he got there, and the door was locked. Tom was gone for the day.

Likely drowning his sorrows at Sleder's Tavern, Dr. Turner muttered as he sought out an attendant with master keys to open it for him. It was long past the gloaming hour, that time just before dark when one must turn on the lights to see indoors. Most people had gone home for the day, save a few attendants who roamed the halls with brooms or cleaning rags, and a solitary nurse guiding a patient in a wheelchair. Most patients would either be finishing dinner or preparing for bed or staring at the final television show for the day before it is turned off at eight o'clock.

The office was dark and empty. He flicked on a wall switch and moved toward Tom's cluttered desk. He hoped to find the article himself, take it back to his own office to tone down some of the claims he had made about the effects of certain medications on patients—a few qualifications here, a few word changes there; it shouldn't take much. He would be careful to downplay recidivism rates: He would only mention those patients suffering from schizophrenia who, he knew for sure, had been released back to their

260

families and who were being closely monitored to ensure they continue on their meds.

He would ignore those patients who had been returned to their homes but who had no supports there to guarantee continuity of care. The ones who had to be readmitted once their debilitating symptoms returned. Recidivism, he decided, would have to wait for another article, one that he hoped might land him another week in La Jolla as soon as next year, when he could address the same corporate audience.

He pulled his reading glasses from a coat pocket and put them on. He moved some books and assorted hand-written pages to find a manila envelope with his name on it and the title of the article— "Medications and the Promise of Deinstitutionalization."

Then his eye caught the heading of one of the hand-written pages strewn about the top of the desk. The header was printed in all caps, bold black pen: *WAYS OF TALKING WITH PATIENTS*. Under that, the notation *from Smit* appeared. He glanced through two pages, skimming, but reading close enough to determine that some of what he saw were the very words he himself used when visiting patients. He picked up another sheet, this headed *SUPERVISION OF OTHER DOCTORS ON STAFF*, also *from Smit*. Skimming again, he read about such things as TIME DEMANDS, with direct quotes under that subhead that sounded just like himself, again, on rounds. He went on to read bullet lists with quotes that were strikingly similar to his own words.

On another sheet, he read at the top, *VISITORS TO THE DOCTOR, from Williams*. His eyes opened wide, he gasped as he read dates and descriptions of visitors he had

had in the past few months—"corporate types, well-suited, driving big fancy cars ... some bearing shopping bags full of who knows what, but I would hazard to say gifts, as I saw sticking out the top of one bag what appeared to be the handle of a woman's purse." The notes went on to say that many of the cars had out-of-state license plates, and all the visitors were males past forty, "usually traveling in pairs or threes, only occasionally alone."

The doctor dropped into Tom Oakes' swivel chair. He stared at the mass of pages before him. One off to his right caught his eye because it had SISTER LUCY & ANNA neatly printed across the top of the first page of a few pages clipped together. This he read through word by word. It chronicled key events, rendered in detail, that related to Anna's decline and eventual death. He read direct quotes attributed to him as well as to other nurses and doctors; descriptions of Anna's symptoms at various times; and a stinging list of "Curiosities" that were unmistakably identical to those Lucy had presented to him just that afternoon.

He returned that stack to its home on his right and leaned back, the chair moving with him until he was looking up at the ceiling, his mind calculating slowly, methodically.

"What do we *have* here?" He said aloud. Then, glancing over all the notes before him, he muttered, "What *do* we have?"

While he could not determine satisfactorily what he had before him, he did know some things with certainty. For one, he knew he had two employees of the hospital who had been observing him very closely. For another, he knew he had one patient advocate who had taken meticulous notes while he provided medical treatment for her dear companion.

Make that one of my patients, he thought to himself, *under my care*. Anna was *his* patient, first and foremost. And *he* was the doctor, not her friend. In saying that to himself, he realized he was becoming defensive—and for no apparent reason—for what these notes amounted to was not at all clear. But they *did* amount to something, that was certain.

For yet another, he knew his trusted community relations director was deeply involved in whatever this was. He could no longer trust Tom Oakes any more than he could trust Lucy Greene. Smit and Williams? He didn't know who they were, but it would only take a call to Employee Relations to find out. Were they attendants? Nurses? He would know by morning.

He sat back again, reflecting on the mild threat Lucy had suggested when he tossed out the word *malpractice*. Though she denied any such intent, he now suspected that she had cleverly defused that possibility as she drew him out on other fronts. *She was fishing for something*, he thought, *and it smacked of something legal, if my instincts are right. Something to do with Anna's death; it must be that.*

He grabbed a clean sheet of paper from beside the typewriter perched on a small rolling table off to the side. He pulled an ink pen from the breast pocket of his sport coat. He stared at the inscription on the pen: Progrol. In his careful script, he wrote a note that Tom Oakes would discover the minute he sat down at his desk the next morning:

Dear Mr. Oakes,

I came by to pick up the deinstitutionalization article to make a few last-minute changes. Sorry I missed you, but it was pretty late. I couldn't help but notice these other papers on your desk. I read through them with great

*interest as they seemed to have an awful lot to do with
me. I am eager to talk with you about these pages, as
I'm sure you would like to help me, as your supervisor,
understand what you and your—shall I say, Colleagues?
Chums?—are planning. Or would
Conspirators be the favored term, you being, after all, a
wordsmith yourself, and I, a mere doctor?*

*At any rate, since these documents seem to bear heavily
on me and my practices with patients, I've taken them
with me for a closer look. I'm happy to return them to you
once I understand what value they have, what purpose
they are intended to serve.*

I do hope to hear from you tomorrow morning.

Sincerely,

Dr. A. Turner,

Assistant Medical Superintendent

They are all in this together, he muttered as he switched
off the light. *And they will all hang together*, he snarled, closing the door, gently.

By nine the next morning, Doctor Turner had the names
of Percy Williams and Vivian Smit, attendants, same home
address, same home phone number, from Employee Relations. Hired less than two years ago, right out of college
where they were roommates.

"According to this application," said the voice on the
other end, "the two of them are preforming alternative service to the draft. Spotless records here as far as I can see."

Dr. Turner sat back in his leather chair. He twirled a pencil in one hand, thinking. Vivian seemed an odd name for a male attendant. He poked his head out the door to ask Sheila if she's ever heard of a man being named Vivian.

"Well, sir," she said, "As a matter of fact, I had a cousin in Indiana who was named Vivien, with an *e* in it. My Aunt Doris loved French names, and she wanted to name him Vivienne, but My Uncle Walter said it had too many i's and e's in it, and why don't you name him something simple like Bob or Bill, but Aunt Doris, she had to have her way, okay? So, she shortened it to Vivien, but it turned out that Vivien with an e is actually a girl's name. But by then it was all official and too late to go through all the trouble of changing it, so they left it Vivien with an e. He hated that name all the way through school; everyone called him a girl and picked on him, you know how kids are. So, when he was old enough, he changed it to Vinny. He had a long crooked nose and greasy hair, so it sorta fit when he was a teenager 'cause he looked sort of Italian (she pronounced the word "Eye-talian"). Then he died. But they put Vinny on his stone, 'cause, you know, that was the right thing to do, poor soul dead and all. Fell off the tractor and cracked his head wide open on the plow."

With a gruff "I see," he closed the office door. "Percy's not much better," he muttered as he got back on the phone to Employee Relations. He asked, would that office prepare letters of termination if, as assistant medical superintendent, he believed an employee should be fired. Yes, but the person in question must be given a 30-day notice, and the reason must be stated in the letter. This protocol is required by the State Civil Service Commission.

He asked, for what reasons an attendant could be fired?

Poor work evaluations. Gross misconduct. Drinking on the job. Deviancy of most kinds. Damaging property. Theft. "Homosexuality?"

The response was quick: "We would never allow homos to work here."

After hanging up the phone, he went over to a tall bookcase and pulled out a brown leather volume, The Diagnosis and Statistical Manual of Mental Disorders (DSM-1). This first edition had been published in 1952 and not updated since. The DSM-1 classified all known (at the time) mental disorders and was used by doctors, psychiatrists, clinicians, and researchers to determine a patient's mental disorder after an evaluation. He thumbed through until he came to the "Sexual Deviation" classification. There it was: homosexuality, along with transvestism, pedophilia, fetishism, and sexual sadism.

There we have it, he thought, a broad smile crossing his face. *Homos. These two, they work and live together, starting in college and now at the state hospital. Secret lies, secret lives. I could threaten them with an evaluation to make the diagnosis stick, but why would these two allow that, knowing that a positive finding by yours truly would result in their never finding work again in any state institution. No, they would quit rather than be subject to that sort of thing. This should be easy.*

Tom Oakes would also be easy. Everyone knew he had a drinking problem, had been a drunk for years. It would not be hard to make that case, what with his many demonstrations of inability to be fully functional. Everyone knew but turned the other cheek. It was always known that Al Turner wanted him in that position, and for whatever reason, protected him. And indeed, he also did just that.

Because he relied on Tom Oakes to make him look good. But now, now that he had enough reputation, he no longer needed Tom Oakes. He had reached that point where his corporate backers themselves would weave some magic into his articles. In fact, that would be even better. Tom Oakes would not even merit appearing in a never-read-anyway footnote again. He was expendable. But first, he needed to be shamed.

Lucy Greene? She might be more difficult. If her intent truly was to file a lawsuit, that would have to be on her own hoof, and she didn't strike him as having that kind of money. Then there was the liability protection he enjoyed by working for the largest employer in Traverse City. They had their own lawyers and they would quash any attempt to sully the name of the hospital. Besides, she had no proof of any deliberate wrongdoing or intent to do something wrong. He supposed a case could be made for negligence, but her silly theories about how doctor talk can derail patient care was pure girlish whimsy.

He could not fire her, but he could limit her access at the hospital. He could deny her permission to visit the patients. His rationale? That he saw no significant purpose in her continuing to advocate for patients. There was no evidence that her presence on the campus made any difference in the overall quality of patient care. Patient care, he would remind the chaplains, was the exclusive province of the assistant medical superintendent. If Lucy wanted to stay on to assist the chaplaincy, Dr. Turner would have nothing to say about that, but she would be denied access to the wards and cottages until further notice.

This will spur her to move on, he figured. *By her own*

admission, she needs to follow a higher purpose. Typing endless letters for the priests and arranging altar flowers will drive her nuts in a week. She would be a fool to stay.

It was a simple plan, one that could be done quietly and without involvement from higher up. Even if Lucy did go above his head, the chief medical superintendent would not relish any negative attention should any of the information contained in those notes be made available to the public. As the person ultimately responsible for all operations at the institution, he would be put in an uncomfortable position. Dr. Turner knew one thing for certain: His boss could not afford to have the hospital besmirched by feckless accusations of negligence or impropriety. Dr. Turner would not worry about that possibility.

He would reduce Lucy's presence on the grounds to a mere whisper of what it had been. He would destroy those notes; whatever she had up her sleeve would not see the light of day. Lucy Greene would drift away to some other corner of the globe where her eccentric language theories and her religious fervor for civil rights would find another garden in which she could flourish. Or wither.

Then, is a satirical *sotto voce*, "Sorry, Sister, mixed metaphor."

Tom Oakes arrived shortly after ten o'clock. He was shown in by Sheila, who lingered in the doorway as Tom made his way to the visitor's chair opposite his boss.

"Coffee, Mr. Oakes?" she said.

"Please, black, no sugar."

He had begun drinking at the office as soon as he read Al

Turner's letter. One shirt tail unceremoniously hung over his belt, and his front pocket on his white shirt had ink marks showing through the bottom stitching. He was nervous. He blinked a lot.

"You wanted to see me?" he said.

From a side drawer Al Turner produced a stack of papers and plopped them down in front of Tom Oakes, whose blinking increased wildly. Dr. Turner's eyes squinted with displeasure. Then, head dropped enough to be able to look over his reading glasses at Tom Oakes, Dr. Turner turned over the notes, page by page, feigning reading. No words passed between them for long moments. Dr. Turner was masterfully putting on the squeeze.

"Let me see here," he finally mumbled to himself, delaying the inevitable as long as possible. Sweat broke out on Tom Oakes' hairline.

Tom looked down at his shoes, then at his fingernails, then at his shoes again, then over toward the wall where he desperately wished there had been a window, so he could have pointed toward a herd of deer or a lone fox crossing in the snow. Anything to break the eerie silence. He felt like a seventh grader called to the principal's office, sitting there knowing he was about to be suspended for looking up a girl's skirt in math class. Sheepish could not begin to describe his features.

"Ah yes, here we are," began Dr. Turner, as he replaced single pages back on the stack and pulled the pile closer to himself. He placed his hand squarely on the stack. "I am interested to know how you came by all this ... all these ... papers, with such different handwriting throughout, as if they had been penned by different hands. Who are the authors, Mr. Oakes?" He said nothing about the contents of the papers. He would let Mr. Oakes broadly incriminate himself.

Tom squirmed, cleared his throat, mumbled something unintelligible.

"I'm sorry, Mr. Oakes. I can't make out what you just said. Can you say that again?"

"I said," he muttered, barely audible, "that, uh, if what you have before you is what you removed from the top of the desk in my private office last evening,"—he paused to let the idea that invasion of privacy and an act of thievery may even have taken place—"if that is what I think it is, then I'm not really at liberty to say who wrote them. It's ... confidential."

"Ah-hah, confidential, is it? And why is it confidential, Mr. Oakes, if you don't mind me asking?"

"Well, sir, it just is, confidential, is all. If I were to say who, or why, then it wouldn't be so confidential anymore."

Tom Oakes was sweating though his shirt now. And his head was aching even more than it had an hour earlier. He would have given anything for two aspirin and a shot of whiskey. He cleared his throat, and noticed that his shirt tail was hanging out. He leaned back and tucked it into his pants.

Dr. Turner smiled, sat back in his cushioned chair, head cocked slightly to the right, arms behind his neck, as he looked past Tom Oakes and toward the door. His eyes returned to Tom just as his words did to his subject.

"I see. Well then, would you agree that if I were to have seen names of people on these papers, names that I recognize as being related to the operations of this institution, that there's a possibility that these very names match the hands that penned these notes? Or would I be way off?"

Tom glanced around. His attention alighted on a painting of a white horse charging through a green forest, reins dragging alongside him. He wished he were on that horse at this very minute, riding off into the distance, never to return. His gaze fell back on the stack of papers.

"Mr. Oakes? Would I be way off?"

"Sir, I could use that coffee now."

Dr. Turner pushed an intercom button. Sheila answered. "The coffee? Coming right up," she said. "I had to run down to the canteen to get a supply. Just bringing it in now. Sorry for the wait."

In she came. Sheila handed Tom a cup and saucer. He sipped, then sipped again, wishing he could just sit there sipping for the rest of the day. Sheila's look to Dr. Turner asked if there would be anything else. He shook his head no, and she left, but not before casting a furtive glance at Tom Oakes, who struck her as oddly miserable.

Abruptly, Dr. Turner changed the tenor and tone as he leaned forward, his chest inclined toward Mr. Oakes, his inquisitor eyes glued on the blinking eyes of his captive. His smile morphed into a chilling pursing of the lips through which his words had the slightest hiss as he spoke slowly and deliberately. He relinquished all politeness by dropping both *Tom* and *Mr.*

"All right, Oakes. Enough pussyfooting around. What the hell is this all about? All these notes about how we do things around here, how I talk with patients, how I supervise others, the whole nine yards. Come clean. You're a loathsome fool and you know it. Don't waste my time."

It was a moral crisis for Tom Oakes.[23] He had been buf-
feted about by this self-righteous man for years now.
Always told what to do. Never asked did he *want* to do
this or that. Never asked his opinion, always given an opinion. Belittled when he made a mistake. Praised so seldom
he could not remember ever feeling good about himself.
And the humiliating process of ghostwriting articles full of
self-aggrandizing masquerades!

He'd had enough. He'd given far more than he'd received.
He'd nearly abandoned his life-long dream of becoming a
real writer. Until Sister Lucy came along. Then he thought
he had a chance to write something he could be proud
of. Something worthwhile. And those two attendants,
they trusted him with information they had clandestinely
obtained. He didn't even know them, but he knew he was
connected to them on a plane where truth and moral justice
mattered more than pandering to one's superior.

What kind of man would he be if he got Lucy and Smit
and Williams in trouble? What kind of man would betray
their confidence and lose their trust, the only people who
had given him a modicum of self-respect? The only people
who had helped him restore purpose to his otherwise meaningless life, a life made all the more meaningless by the very
man sitting across from him. No, he would not be the kind
of man who would betray his comrades, come what may.

Tom placed his saucer and cup before him on the desk.
He took a deep breath as he grasped the arms of his chair.

"Dr. Turner, you will have to arrive at your own conclusions

---

23. "The courage of life is often a less dramatic spectacle than the courage
of a final moment; but it is no less a magnificent mixture of triumph and
tragedy" (John F. Kennedy, *Profiles in Courage* [New York, Harper and
Row, 1956] 246).

about what these papers mean. I can only say that, as you have never acknowledged, I am a much better writer than what you think of me. I have a voice and I have ideas. I have technique and I have style. I have come to know the story of Sister Lucy's and Sister Anna's journey, and I have discovered that theirs is a much bigger story than simply how they came to be at this hospital. That story is just now writing itself. That is all I have to say to you, sir."

The ambiguity in Tom's comment about the story writing itself was not lost on Dr. Turner, who saw in it an implied threat. The acid in his voice filled the room as he stood abruptly and swooped the papers off his desk. They fluttered onto the floor. He stepped on top of them and stood before his ghostwriter.

"Then, as of this minute, you are on notice, Mr. Oakes, that your employment here will be terminated. The letter informing you of such is already in preparation. You will have 30 days to clear out, and you will have no more tasks to complete on behalf of this hospital. We will immediately begin to seek your replacement. Which, I might add, we will likely find among the dropouts from the community college on the other side of town. You began here as a schmuck and you will leave unchanged."

Dr. Turner stormed over to the door and placed his hand on the knob. He opened the door just wide enough for anyone in the anteroom to hear what he was about to say.

"And now, sir, you may leave. And you may leave your notes here on the floor, since the paper on which they are written is hospital property, and since you are an ex-employee, you have no right to them anymore. Now get the hell out of my sight."

Tom Oakes showed himself out. The last thing he heard was Sheila's "Hope you have a swell day there, Mr. Oakes."

He would walk to his car parked in a lot on Green Drive. He would brush a fresh covering of snow from the windshield. He would slowly drive the few blocks over to the Little Bohemia Grille, where he would sit at the bar for hours, working up the nerve to call Sister Lucy and tell her what had happened.

The hardest part, he would eventually say, was that he was unable to retrieve the notes. The materials had been stolen from his office, yes, but that theft would not be considered criminal, given the authority of Dr. Turner and his niche in the hierarchy at the hospital. Still, he felt some pride for how he had conducted himself. It kindled in his heart a feeling of worth that he hadn't felt in decades.

Though Dr. Turner would easily enough discover who Smit and Williams were, he himself had not revealed their identities on principle. Plus, he did not disclose what article Sister Lucy and he would write. That too was honorable. He had lost his job, but he had regained his personal integrity. Being fired actually brought with it a sense of relief. No more would he be forced to grovel or waste his words propping up someone else's ego.

After five whiskeys, the hard truth struck him. Though he had acted with integrity, it cost him dearly. He had no job. He had no savings. He was not a famous writer.

It was all a mistake, he thought, *getting involved with writing an exposé that only held a vague promise that it would launch an illustrious new career. Maybe Dr. Turner is right, maybe I am just a schmuck. A self-deceived, loathsome schmuck.*

Chapter 24

ONE BY ONE, LETTERS ARRIVED FROM THE OFFICE OF EMPLOYEE RELA-
tions. Tom Oakes received his letter three days after the
deplorable meeting with Dr. Turner. He carried the
unopened letter around with him for an entire evening as
he went from one bar to another, sitting alone in a corner,
fingering the envelope. He knew what it said. He read the
letter the next morning after three cups of black coffee at
Dill's Café. Then he folded it up again and walked in the
snow over to a liquor store on West Front Street to buy a
bottle to take home.

Smit and Williams had a brief meeting with Dr. Turner.
They knew what was coming. Lucy had given them
advance notice after talking with Tom Oakes. They had a
choice to make, Dr. Turner explained, looking serious and
amused simultaneously, if that were possible. But he knew
there really would be no choice.

He had heard rumors, he said, that they were homosexuals. Did they know that the medical profession and the
military consider homosexuality to be a mental disorder?[24]

---

24. In 1949, the Department of Defense distributed a memo unifying
the military services' regulations relating to homosexuality. Unlike the
wartime policy, there was to be no "rehabilitation" of gay and lesbian
personnel. The memo stated:
> [H]omosexual personnel, irrespective of sex, should not be per-
> mitted to serve in any branch of the Armed Services in any capaci-
> ty, and prompt separation of known homosexuals from the Armed
> Forces is mandatory. (Cited in Berube, 1990, p. 261).

And did they know that that "little gem of information," if made public, would prohibit them from being employed at any state hospital? An evaluation would be required, of course, to determine if they suffered from this disorder. Dr. Turner himself would conduct it. He could not predict what he would find, but in his experience, "rumors generally turn out to have an element of truth."

He let that last thought settle in before offering them the alternative.

Which was, they could terminate their employment themselves for any reason they wished to give, although the civil service did not require *any* specific reason. Should they make this choice, they would have up to thirty days before departing, but they could leave any time they wished. If they were to apply for a job at another state hospital, and if that prospective employer asked for a reference from the Traverse City State Hospital, Dr. Turner would be obliged, ethically, to disclose the rumors, whether or not he could substantiate them. He would also have to disclose the fact that neither of them volunteered to be evaluated.

"I would just have to say that you chose to leave rather than submit to an evaluation."

Smit and Williams stared at one another, shook their

The memo urged more careful investigations of suspected homosexuals and the establishment of better communication between the military branches to facilitate the exchange of information concerning homosexuals. The Department of Defense also recommended that each branch of the military give lectures about homosexuality modeled on existing venereal disease lectures (Berube, 1990) (Rhonda Evans, "U.S. Military Policies Concerning Homosexuals: Development, Implementation and Outcomes." Report prepared for The Center for the Study of Sexual Minorities in the Military, University of California at Santa Barbara, Assessed February 22, 2020, https://www.palmcenter.org/wp-content/uploads/2017/12/evans1.pdf).

heads in disgust, and then looked back at Dr. Turner, who studied a fingernail. He was unable to contain a smirk.

Handwriting on the wall, they said they'd choose the second option. Williams volunteered that, speaking for himself, he "couldn't take another winter up here anyway." What Smit had on his mind was that if their draft boards got wind (from some malevolent, unnamed source) that they had been labeled homosexuals, it would go on their selective service record that they exhibited "signs of mental instability." Then they would never get a respectable job that amounted to anything meaningful. As long as there was a draft.

Dr. Turner's smug look was evidence enough that he would willingly write to Smit's and Williams' draft boards were they to resist what was obvious blackmail.

Their letters arrived at home four days later. They would take whatever portion of their allotted thirty days they needed to plan the next steps.

Lucy was never contacted by Dr. Turner to have her day of reckoning. Instead, he called Father Pete to let him know that Lucy would no longer be granted visitation privileges at the hospital. He explained that there was no evidence that her presence on the campus made any difference in the overall quality of patient care. That in fact, her visits to patients always came unannounced and nearly always interfered with doctors or nurses tending to patient needs.

Father Pete, of course, had no way of proving or disproving this assertion.

"The last thing patients need is distractions," Dr. Turner said, "and things have, unfortunately reached that point." Then, in a sentence filled with convolution and equivocation, he intimated that he would hate to see "a little thing like this" affect Father Pete's own ministry at the hospital. Father Pete took it all in, not sure what Lucy had actually done to deserve it, but he could hardly argue against what seemed to be a *fait accompli*. Dr. Turner made it clear that he would not tolerate an appeal to change his mind.

When Father Pete asked Lucy what had happened, she asked *him* to respect her privacy in not discussing the matter with others. "Suffice it to say that we had a significant disagreement on principle and practice after I questioned his medical decisions related to Anna," she explained. "Some things are better left unspoken," she continued, "What's done is done." She assumed a deferential stance, saying that she regretted if she had interfered with patient care in any way and that she was not comfortable with entering into any dispute with hospital administrators. To do so might have a negative effect on others' work at the hospital, and she would not allow that to happen.

Father Pete was beside himself with curiosity and regret, but he would honor her wishes, however much he disagreed with her decision to keep things to herself.

"I've known you too long," he said, "and I know how good you are with the patients. There's something else going on here, and frankly, it stinks."

"There *has* been a falling out," she said, "but that is now history. However, there *is* also something else, something more essential," she said. "With Anna gone, I don't see any purpose in my remaining in Traverse City. Even with the patients lately, I'm not myself. I'm distant, abstracted. That itself may be sufficient cause for Dr. Turner. Perhaps he's seen what you and others have not. At any rate, it really doesn't matter anymore."

Lucy spoke on the phone with Smit and Williams about

them being fired and what course their lives would take from here on out. Neither of them knew exactly what they would do, "But I do know this," Smit said, with a sudden burst of enthusiasm, "We need a party!"

"A party?"

"A grand, going away party," he said. "You, me, Williams, Oakes, and that head nurse that you spoke so highly of."

"Nancy Brownell."

"Yeah, I'd like to see her one more time too. I'll bring the wine. Williams will bring the cheese puffs, pork rinds, and moon pies. He's become very health conscious, you know, since that woman entered his life."

"Smit," Lucy said, "I'm so sorry, I ... "

He cut her off. "Nope, can't go there, Mother Superior. No regrets for being morally grounded and for taking on the hard work of the world. Let's end this vacation on a high note. Things change, we change, the world changes. But in the end, it'll be good that survives. It always does, it always will."

"Oh Smit," she said, a little shaky in her voice, "You're ... just ... so ... "

He cut her off again: "Napkins and glasses, plates and a corkscrew. That's all you need to bring. The others can bring something that goes with pork rinds and pop tarts. What'd you say, Sister Lucy?"

Lucy planned the party for her apartment the next weekend.

Tom Oakes was invited via a note Lucy taped to the front door to his home in town. *Just a few of us,* the note said, *I'm sure you'll know them all. A time to say goodbye before we all go our separate ways. We may not leave much behind,* it said, *but we will never lose our friendship, so I hope you will join us. Snacks and drinks provided.*

Repeated phone calls to his home and his office went unanswered. According to a clerk in accounting in the office next door to his own, he had not been seen in the office at all, even to begin packing up.

Tom Oakes hadn't been seen anywhere in nearly ten days.

Lucy was worried.

No longer permitted to visit patients, Lucy poured herself into her work for the chaplains. The new chapel project was moving ahead full steam now that it had the blessing of the diocese and now that contributions to the $300,000 needed for construction had begun coming in. An A-frame design was approved, and groundbreaking was scheduled for April, at the corner of Elmwood and Eleventh Streets. The chapel would have three sections—one for Protestant services, one for Catholic services, and one for Jewish services.

In the days before her final weekend in Traverse City, Lucy surreptitiously made her own "round" in the hospital—always keeping an eye out for Dr. Turner—to say her goodbyes to staff and patients.

Nurse Bennett took the news hard. Her ever-tender heart seemed broken when Lucy told her she was leaving. With Anna gone, it was time for her to move on to other opportunities. Nurse Bennett wiped tears on the back of her hand as she embraced Lucy and held her tight.

"I will never forget you, Sister. I was so inexperienced when I started here, but Sister Anna was the first patient that I took special interest in. Not only because of who she was, sweet loving soul, but also because of you and how much I learned from you about how to make women comfortable, even happy, in spite of their troubles. I feel so much more mature now, *because of you*. *Seasoned*, that's the word that fits better.

"Every day you came, you were like the sun on a gloomy day, your kindness and gentle ways just lit up the ward. I learned how to smile no matter how I felt, and I learned to listen, really listen, the way you do with every patient you visit. The little gifts you always bring? Now I bring them too! Little things like Find-A-Word puzzles and lemon drops, things that bring back the smiles that seem to get lost so easily here, especially around holidays and birthdays. Especially for the ones whose families have forgotten them. And for the really tough women, gosh, I even bring cigarettes, can you believe it? Even after the surgeon general's announcement just this month about smoking and cancer. But what do they care, those women, if a cigarette brings them some joy?"

They agreed to write letters. They would be friends for life.

Heavy snow fell for the fourth day in a row. The shovelers had been out since dawn, carving walking paths throughout the grounds that more or less followed the sidewalks. These paths were lined by four-foot snowbanks which grew by the foot with each day of continued snow. Lucy walked on a narrow shoveled path past the laundry building to the Weaver's Shop adjacent to the water tower. She leaned into the window and squinted through the frosted glass. Georgie and Harold worked next to one another at two large wooden looms. Harold was carefully setting up the yarn on one loom, while Georgie worked the shuttle and heddle on another. Harold glanced up when Lucy wiped snow from the window and peered in at the two men. He raised a hand to signal she should come inside.

Lucy shook snow off her shoulders. Georgie and Harold stopped their work. It was a short but sweet ten minutes of leave-taking. Lucy explained that the time had come for her to move on, that she had nearly completed the work of her calling at the hospital. She would likely return to Kalamazoo and then on to yet another of life's adventures, as she put it. The two men hung their heads, nearly unable to look her in the eye, they were so saddened by her news.

"G-g-g-onna miss you, Lucy Greene. G-g-gonna miss you a lot."

"You said it, Georgie. We'll *really* miss you, Lucy Greene. Everybody will!"

"I'll miss both of you too," she said. "But I'll be coming back to visit. Tell you what, how about if I bring back some special yarns, wool from Scotland or Australia, and you can make another one of your beautiful scarves for me. What do you think?"

A big "whoo-hoo" came out of them simultaneously as both men threw their arms around Lucy and the three of them stood there hugging for a good five seconds, swaying side to side. Lucy could think if no sweeter way to say goodbye, and as she left Georgie and Harold, eyes glistening, they were waving at her through the iced-up window as she made her way back through the tunnel of snow toward Cottage 24, where she would check on Mr. Frederick.

Before she got halfway to his cottage, a white security patrol car pulled over next to her on Red Drive. Two uniformed officers leaned forward to peer at Lucy through the passenger side window. The officer on the passenger side rolled down his window and held up a paper, his eyes moving back and forth from Lucy to the paper. He put the paper down and opened the door as the other officer emerged from his side.

"Ma'am, afraid I'll have to ask you to hold up a minute."

Lucy slowed to a halt, the wind engulfing the three of them in a whirlwind of snow as the officers approached. Lucy wondered if Mr. Frederick was on the loose again and these officers were warning her to be on the watch for him. But that was not to be the case.

"Ma'am. I'm officer Barrett from Security," said the man with the paper now tucked into his coat pocket, "and my partner here is Sargent O'Dell." Both men tipped their caps in a gesture of respect. "Would you be Lucy Greene?" he continued.

Lucy pulled her coat closer to her cold neck as the snow swirled past them and across the street.

"Yes, that's me. What can I help you with?"

Sargent O'Dell took over. "Well, Miss Greene, we have an order from the administration that you are not allowed in the buildings on this campus, except for the chaplain's area in Building 50. And if we were to see you on the campus, we were to escort you to that location or off the hospital grounds."

Lucy was taken aback. Was she now considered a trespasser?

"Straight from the assistant medical superintendent, Dr. Turner, ma'am. I'm mighty sorry. You don't look like a troublemaker, but I ... we ... don't know the circumstances. We just carry out orders."

Lucy could now see it all falling together. Dr. Turner did not trust her to stay away from the patients—although, indeed, she had no intention of staying away, until she left for good anyway. But this! This was not only humiliating, but also far, far, over the top. All she could figure is that he was very worried about what threat she posed to him.

He had revoked her visiting privileges. He had *not* banned her from the buildings. *Though apparently,* she thought, *they are one and the same.* Either way, her access to everyone is now virtually gone. What was especially hard about that is she would not be able to say goodbye to her favorite patients, like Mr. Frederick and Alice. Fortunately, she *had* been able to say her goodbyes to Nurse Bennett and Georgie and Harold, and she *would* be able to see her friends Nancy Brownell, Tom Oakes, and Smith and Williams at least once more.

She pulled her hand-woven scarf down from her face. "So, what would you like me to do, then, officer? Now that I've been identified as an undesirable."

"Well, ma'am, I'm sorry for whatever has caused this, but understand we're just following orders and ..."

"Gentlemen," she interrupted, "It is not your fault. I do not hold you responsible for doing your job. But tell me this: would it hurt anything if you were to allow me to stop in Cottage 24 for just ten minutes, to check on a favorite patient, just a few minutes. You can even come in with me. I just ..."

And here she pulled out her religious card with the photo of the Mother of Perpetual Help. "I just want to share this prayer with him. It will make him feel very good. Is that asking too much, Officer? Is it?" She would pray for forgiveness for lying.

She initiated the *long slow stare of innocence* mixed with polite solicitation.

The officers glanced at one another.

"Jerry?" said Barrett, "Seems all right with me. What can ten minutes matter?"

"Well," his partner returned. "I suppose it'll be all right. But look here, Miss Greene. You can go on ahead and we'll wait for you outside 24 and then we'll escort you to wherever it is you need to go."

Lucy thanked them as they climbed back into their cruiser and turned the corner at Blue Drive, pulled over next to Cottage 24, and sat there, motor running, as Lucy followed them on foot. She went up the front porch and entered. Mr. Frederick was seated in a cushioned rocker, a wool blanket stretched over his legs. He was asleep. He stirred as Lucy shook the snow off her coat and approached.

"Why, if it ain't my favorite spring blossom," he said with a wide yawn. "To what do I owe the honor of your little visit today?"

She pulled an empty straight-backed chair up next to him and sat down.

"My dear Mr. Frederick. I just have a few minutes to … to see how you are doing."

"Why Sister Lucy, how kind of you to ask. Besides being cold as can be on this winter day, I'm actually doing pretty well. They put me on a new medicine, and guess what, I'm feeling almost normal lately."

"No voices?

"No voices."

"What about side effects?"

"Nothing like they used to be. Nothing like the all-day sleeping and the way my mind got all confused. Biggest thing is I don't feel like a zombie anymore. And that's worth it in spite of the other stuff."

"Other stuff?"

"Oh, the shakes, and the cotton mouth. And the tiredness. And the days when I'm just feeling bad, so bad I can't even play checkers or cards. But what's a schizophrenic to do? I can't have it both ways, can I? I can't get rid of the voices and the violence without something else getting in the way. My life, it's better. Not great, but better. Maybe one day it'll be great. I keep hoping. But I'm not going anywhere anyway, so I got plenty of time for them to find a better medicine for me. I don't know, maybe God forgot about me. Maybe there's no such thing as God. I don't know anymore.

"Anyway," he said, "like what Popeye says, 'I yam what I yam.'"

He chuckled at his own joke, a sure sign that he was feeling his real self that day.

Lucy had tears in her eyes. *No man should have to suffer so,* she thought. *No good man who never hurt anyone.* She would have to pray hard for strength and renewed belief in the goodness of her Savior in a world filled with suffering.

Lucy glanced at the wall clock and then out the window. The white cruiser was still there. Her time was running out.

"Well, Mr. Frederick, I know how that doubt feels. Personally, I struggle with it too. But I just want you to know that in my time here, I've come to admire your tenacity and your forbearance. You have taught me a lot about resilience. And I thank you for that." She put one hand on his shoulder as she stood.

"Oh, dear me," he said, putting his own hand over hers.

"You talk like you're going away. Are you going away, Sister Lucy?"

The horn sounded from the street.

"I am, my dear friend. I just wanted to see you once again to say goodbye in person. It is time for me to go on another of life's journeys. It is time to leave."

She kissed him on the forehead before he could utter a word. She placed one finger across her lips to signal no more words. She put her coat on, tossed her scarf around her neck and across her face.

"I'll miss you, Sister Lucy."

"I'll miss *you*, Mr. Frederick."

At the door, she waved, turned, and left. At the street, she got into the cruiser and asked to be taken to the chaplains' office in Building 50.

Chapter 25

At 4 o'clock sharp on Saturday, Smit showed up at Lucy's apartment. Williams arrived a bit later, having spent time on the phone to Ann Arbor securing a six-month lease on an apartment for the two of them.

Moving boxes lined the walls, some taped shut, others half-filled and open. Two suitcases stood just inside the bedroom door. Books were stacked tall here and there. In the kitchen, potted plants on newspaper filled her kitchen countertops and table. Her guests leaned this way and that to navigate carefully around the clutter.

Smit lay half stretched out on a couch while Williams poured wine. Lucy came in from the bedroom carrying armfuls of clothing and plopped it all down on top of a large moving box in the corner.

She sat down as Smit put up a glass, "Here's to us and here's to the future." She wiped at the corner of an eye.

He said, "Don't cry because it's over. Smile because it happened."

Two "Hear, Hear's" followed as they each took a drink.

Next, Williams: "We started with a simple hello and we will end with a complicated goodbye."

"Hear, Hear!" from Smit was followed with another sip of wine.

Lucy: "I'm glad you were a part of my life. I will miss you both."

"Hear, Hear!" said Williams, "but let's not get all gushy

and sad. Remember? It's a P-A-R-T-Y, not a E-U-L-O-
G-Y. Let's remember some good stuff."

The mood alternated as they relaxed and reminisced
about patients they had come to love or find immensely
entertaining. At times the mood was as festive as Smit
insisted it should be; at other times, they sat quietly reflective as a fog of sadness filled the room.

"Alice Banks," Lucy said. "She was in Ward 3 with
Anna. I just loved the way she cared for her doll that she
thought was her own little girl. She held her so closely and
talked endlessly to her. And how Nurse Bennett treated
Alice with such respect. As if Alice weren't senile at all.
I learned so much from those two about accepting without judging, and about connecting to patients on emotional
levels, dwelling there, seeing life through their eyes."

They nodded, staring down at their wine. They each
had learned so much.

"They were our teachers, you know," Williams said.
"They taught us something every day. How to love one
another. How to care for one another, the way *they* cared
for one another. Oh, sure, there were catfights and dog-
fights, and sometimes I wanted to strangle one of them or
one of them wanted to strangle me, but for the most part,
there was more peace than discord. For many of them, their
minds may have been gone, but they still know, in their
hearts, how to care for someone else. That's what I take
from this place."

"And the docs," Smit said. "They do some great work
here with some very tough cases, like the fellow in Cottage 41, I forget his name, the one who called everybody
the filthiest, most vile names and wouldn't cooperate at all
some days. Then Dr. Gordon would show up, not say a

word, set a checkerboard on a little table in front of the guy and sit opposite him. Still not talking, the doc would pull out a Milky Way, cut it in two, and push half across the table. The patient would call him every name in the book, but Dr. Gordon, once he'd set up the checkers, would say, in a real low voice, "You're down two games to my three, buddy. And I'm putting two bucks down on this one." He would pull out two dollar bills and lay them on the table. Next to them he'd put a little bowl with some pills in it and a bottle of Pepsi next to the pills. The foul-mouthed guy would look at the money, look at the doc, look at the pills, look at the money again, and then wash the pills down with the pop and rub his hands together as if he were about to win the lottery. Dr. Gordon, he knows his way around the most difficult patients. They ought to rename this hospital for him. He taught me a lot about saying little and doing a lot."

There was another long pause as Smit's anecdote sunk in. Smit and Lucy nodded in agreement.

"On the lighter side," Williams said, "there was Mr. Frederick, in the early days. When he'd strip down to his skivvies and run for the hills. Attendants were hardly fast enough to catch him, including me. He'd scream and laugh all the while; it was all I could do to just trot after him, I was laughing so hard. I hated to catch him too. He's put his big arms around me and say, 'Willy—he always called me Willy—now you just let me go and I'll set you up with Nurse Wolfson or anyone you want from the ward.' But I couldn't let him go 'cause the others were always right there too, but I think they didn't want to capture him either. I always wondered where Mr. Frederick would end up if we just discharged him."

Lucy added, "I think he'd come back. I had a good talk with Mr. Frederick one day. I was surprised to learn that he actually thought his medications help him. They give him side effects, but they eliminate the voices he hears. His conundrum is that he thinks he has to choose between hearing voices that command him to do things he doesn't want to do—or having side effects that make him sick."

"Sounds familiar," Smit remarked. "Someday they'll have a pill for schizophrenics that doesn't make them so sick. I hope so, at least."

"*Some*day," echoed Williams.

"At any rate," continued Lucy, "it was so sad talking with him because he no longer has a home to return to, or even some relatives who could take care of him. He's lost so much." She wiped tears from her eyes with a napkin.

Smit saw the mood turning again, and so he piped up with, "I'll miss Phillip B. Jamison. He insisted we call him by his full name all the time. 'Good morning, Phillip B. Jamison,' and "Would you like some soup, Phillip B. Jamison?' That got to be old, so one day in the dining hall I tried his initials. I said, 'How's your dessert there, PBJ?' and he threw his key lime pie at me, said I was never to make fun of his name—it was all he had left, he said. Imagine that, a guy who thinks he has nothing worthwhile in the world other than his name. PBJ: He made me laugh and cry at the same time."

They went on like that, one patient after another, one nurse after another, the entertaining ones mixed with ones whose natural end of life came at the asylum, the ones who attempted and the ones who committed suicide. They'd all seen and heard enough of those cases.

Shortly after five, Nancy Brownell arrived, bringing

with her a big chocolate cake with Bon Voyage spelled out in sprinkles. She poured herself a glass of wine and joined the group. She looked distressed, her red eyes suggesting some crying before she had arrived.

Tissue in hand, she patted her nose. "All I want to say is how sorry I am for all of you," she said. "Had I known things would have turned out like this, I would have, I don't know, I would have done *something*."

Williams reached over with his hand and patted her hand. "No, no," he said. "None of us have any regrets. We all did the right things. The long view of history will be on our side. We're stubborn, determined, and proud. Am I right, or am I right?"

Two "Rights" followed in quick succession.

"Well, then," Nancy said, raising a glass, "here's to stubborn, determined, and proud."

"And right," added Smit.

"And right."

Then Nancy said, "I don't know what will happen to you. In our own ways, and following our own paths, we have come to shared values that do not match with the values of the powers that be. I long for the old days when patients could contribute to the community we built here, through farm work, maintenance, kitchens, clothing shop, and all the rest, but I realize those days may never return. We nurses—and some doctors—have tried so hard to keep the human spirit alive here, each of us doing what we can in our own little way. Personally, I have been fighting that fight for many years now. But when you arrived, Lucy, and when you two pitched in to try to right some wrongs, I had hope."

"We haven't given up,' Lucy said. "We've just stalled a bit."

"That's right," said Williams, "We'll come out of this stall, you'll see."

Nancy took another sip of her wine. "I admire your spirit, again," she said, "but the truth is that each of you is going on your way to other places where you will pursue other goals. I myself will remain. To continue my work."

She sighed, stared down at her wine. She continued, "The world of this asylum is changing too fast, and there remains an unresolved debate about the quality of patients' lives. What does it mean to care for an *individual* person as opposed to a *type* of person? What do we do when someone violates *our* professional code of ethics? *Should* patients give up all rights once they have been committed? For me personally, I ask, in the face of an uncertain future in patient care, what *is* my responsibility to my nurses? Will our mission—which is to comfort thousands of poor souls who have nowhere else to go, or whose family will not or cannot welcome them back—remain the same? What will be asked of us that threatens our own integrity?"

Smit sat back, placed his wine glass down. "Those are big questions, nurse. Philosophical. Your nurses are so lucky to have your leadership."

"Yes," she responded, "They are philosophical questions, and they are the backdrop to the practical decisions nurses make every minute of every day. I try to coach them to think in these ways. As you say, Smit, in big question ways. So when they lose their equilibrium, they have some way of making sense of things, some way of connecting the small events of life with the bigger ones.

"And so, that aside, when all is said and done, you three will leave, and I will remain, as I always will, to support my nurses no matter what new challenge comes our way. I can no more desert my nurses than can one of them desert a patient."

The tears returned to the corners of her eyes as she stood, unsure of what to do with herself. Lucy went over and put both arms around her friend. They swayed for a few moments, rubbing one another's backs softly, gently. Smit and Williams sat in silence, lost in thought.

"Now then," Nancy said. "Enough of that. Pour me a fresh glass, please, while I go out there and cut us each a big piece of the best chocolate cake in Traverse City."

Lucy went to the front window and pulled a curtain. She hoped Tom Oakes would show up. But the street was dark now and a fresh coat of snow had begun falling. She retrieved a second bottle of wine from the kitchen, brought in the plates of cake along with a platter of fruit and crackers and cheese, and put everything down on the coffee table.

Nancy returned and sat back down. The four of them stared at their slice of cake in silence. Nancy broke the lull.

"I know we said no regrets, but I must ask anyway: *Do* you have any regrets?"

"I have only one," said Smit. "I never did have that outing with Lucy here."

"Outing?" said Nancy. "I don't understand."

Lucy laughed. "Oh, it's just a silly private joke."

Smit said, "Private, yes. Silly joke or missed opportunity? Either way, I regret that it never happened."

Williams' eyes shot at Smit, then Lucy, then back to Smit. He understood.

Lucy broke through the mild tension with a change of focus. "Well, for me, I regret ever getting Mr. Oakes involved. I should have known that he might make a huge mistake. Leaving our papers out in the open was unfortunate. I'm sorry I misjudged."

"Who could have known Turner would come sneaking around?" Smit said. "I just hope Mr. Oakes is not too hard on himself."

"I worry about how he's taking all this too. I hope he doesn't feel responsible," said Lucy.

Williams came next. "Lucy, something would have happened one way or another. I think we should just say it was a matter of time, though when the time did come, it was premature. As for me, I have no regrets. I kind of enjoyed playing detective, and I really enjoyed our one night out on the town with the roller skating and the Motown party. Except for all the white folks there at the U & I Lounge, I almost felt like I was with my own people."

They all laughed as the mood changed once again. Nancy said, "I regret that I cannot be as open as the rest of you. My position here, you know, demands that I keep a low profile when it comes to rocking the boat. I ... I cannot jeopardize my nurses' education, and that includes their moral education. I hope you understand."

Williams responded with, "A toast to Nurse Brownell! For her integrity and honesty!"

Cheers all around as they downed another sip of wine.

"Now then," Nancy said, "I must know what each of you has planned. I want to stay in touch, you know."

One by one they told of their plans.

Williams and Smit would move back to Ann Arbor, to a

little apartment they could afford for at least a couple of months on what they'd saved. They would need another income stream to stretch the two months out longer.

"For me," Williams said, "It was just a matter of time before I got back there. There's this girl, you see, she's in Detroit, and she and I, well we're pretty close."

"Janice?" said Lucy.

"Yeah, Janice. I could rent an apartment for less than I'm paying in long-distance calls to her. I had to borrow money from Smit to pay for the last bill and that can't continue, what with the interest he charges on one of *his* loans!"

"One hundred forty-seven dollars and counting," Smit reminded his friend.

Williams continued. "So, we'll live there, I'll get a job somewhere until I figure out some things, and I'll drive over to Detroit on weekends or she'll come to visit me. We'll see how all that goes. It's a temporary plan. But my friend Smit here, he has other ideas for himself. Tell 'em, soul brother."

Smit was more pensive than his friend. He didn't have a girlfriend to buoy him. He would miss Lucy so much. Leaving her would dash any hope he had for, who knows, getting serious—in spite of her religious vows. He just could not let the thought of her go. But he also could not bring that topic up again tonight; it was too personal.

Instead, Smit talked about the danger he and Williams faced from their draft board.

"We'll lose our exempt status," he said. "That'll take a few months, so we'll have some time to figure out what to do next." He told them about an organization that had been on the U of M campus since 1960. It was quickly gaining national attention as a radical group opposed to the Vietnam situation and the draft.

"It's called the Students for a Democratic Society, the SDS, for short. They wrote a political manifesto called the *Port Huron Statement*," he explained. "It's critical of U.S. foreign policy, the arms race, even racial discrimination, and it advocates for non-violent civil disobedience as a way to bring about genuine democracy. That sound familiar, Lucy? There's this guy I knew in my senior year named Tom Hayden. He's now the president of the SDS and I'm going to look him up when we get there and see how I— Williams and I, I hope—can get involved."

Lucy chimed in, "I guess that makes activists of all three of us."

"Looks like it," said Williams, "Each in their own way."

"So that's the plan, for now anyway," said Smit. "But to make things even more complicated, I just learned that Johnson is sending another 8000 troops to Vietnam this spring, and we can expect that number to just keep growing. Folks in the SDS tell me that the number could get as high as 100,000 by next year. Unless Johnson ends it all, the draft will only get bigger and bigger. The way I see it? For Williams and me, our days are numbered. Unless Williams gets married. That would earn him a deferment."

"Not gonna happen," added Williams. "Janice likes me, but marry me? Way too soon for that kind of talk. I'd need a real job before her old man ever lets her marry me. And I'll never get a real job before Uncle Sam suits me up and sends me to a rice paddy."

"Which," continued Smit, "brings me to Plan B for both Williams and me. Plan A is Ann Arbor and Janice for him, Ann Arbor and the SDS for me. And jobs, of course, to pay for the pizza and Cheetos. Plan B starts when we get our 1-A draft classifications and we pass the army physicals with flying colors."

"Or not," Williams chimed in. A smirk.

"Or not.

"Anyway, we climb into my fake Mercedes (a wink), drive over the Ambassador Bridge to Windsor, take a left north-northeast, and head into some obscure part of Ontario where we get new jobs and drop off the radar for a long time."

"You'd dodge the draft, in other words?" Nancy said. "Isn't that illegal? Won't you get caught?"

"Illegal?" returned Smit. "Yes. Caught? Not likely. Not according to my sources in the SDS. There's quite a bit of sympathy in Canada for conscientious objectors, Canada having a very different view of foreign policy than the U.S. Plus, I have a cousin who lives up there and she's promised to help. I think we'll be fine. At any rate, we *do* have choices, and we *will* exercise our right to choose."

Smit looked directly at Lucy then, and said, smiling, "You know, Sister, there are a lot of nuns in Canada. Maybe there's a school where you could teach *catacombs* or something" (a slight smile).

Lucy burst into laughter. "If you mean *catechism*, that's probably true. But I have my sights set on a much different path than teaching catacombs."

Lucy let that teaser hang in the air as she rose and strolled into the kitchen to bring in more crackers to replenish the tray. All eyes followed her in silence as she sat back down and drank a long sip.

Visibly eager, Smit leaned forward and stretched his

neck her way. "And what would that path be, if you don't mind me asking, Mother Superior?"

Lucy turned her head slightly to the left and then right as she looked at Smit first, then Williams, then Nancy. "Chicago. I've made contact with the woman Smit connected me with at the ACLU there. Her name is Frances Adamson. She says she knows people who say the president is going to sign into law the Civil Rights Act this year, by summer at the latest. That will really energize the movement and give credibility to the civil rights of *all* people, regardless of their color, gender, ethnicity, everything. She says it's just a matter of time before Washington begins looking seriously at women's rights, Indians' rights, even the *rights of people in mental hospitals*.[25] When I heard that I nearly fainted! And, when I told her about my history in civil rights, and about what I had been researching here, she invited me to come to Chicago to interview for a job in the ACLU office in Cook County."

---

25 "Spearheaded by the New York Civil Liberties Union's (NYCLU) Mental Patients' Rights Project, the shuttered world of people confined because of mental illness and developmental disabilities was one of the next major enclaves targeted for legal action. Bruce Ennis, Director of the Project, was a prime participant in several landmark cases that became the highpoint of the civil rights movement for people with mental disabilities. In *Wyatt v. Stickney* (1972) and *Wyatt v. Aderholt* (1974), Ennis challenged the conditions of hospitalization for those with mental illness and developmental disabilities, leading to significant reductions in the institutions' populations; major increases in expenditures for mental health and rehabilitative services; improvement in psychologist-patient ratios; significant reductions in the abuse of patients; and the adoption of the then-innovative concept of specific treatment and rehabilitation plans for each individual" ("ACLU History: Mental Institutions," Accessed February 6, 2020, https://www.aclu.org/other/aclu-history-mental-institutions).

Nancy threw up both hands and clapped wildly. Williams' face lit up with a broad smile as he raised a glass to Lucy. Smit's expression was neutral.

Lucy continued. "So, I'm driving to Chicago next week for ACLU orientation with the Director of National Initiatives. Frances briefed him on my background, and he said he was very interested. So yesterday, I got a call from him, a telephone interview. He said he could foresee a time, not too long from now, when disability rights would become one of their national initiatives. Then he asked, how soon could I start? I couldn't believe my ears!"

Williams clapped again, said, "I'd say you have a new job. Slam dunk! Shoo-in! Bullseye!"

Nancy joined the chorus: "Congratulations, Lucy."

Smit's furrowed brow revealed his inner turmoil—happiness for Lucy's great opportunity offset by the fear that he may never see her again. Faking joy miserably, he raised his glass too, winked one eye and nodded to her.

"Were our Dr. Turner to find that out," Smit said, "he would not sleep well for quite some time. The last person he would want advocating for patient rights out of an ACLU office would be Sister Lucy Greene, S. S. J. Congratulations."

The clapping and toasts lasted only a few moments before an eerie silence set in again. Another pensive stretch ensued as they each reflected on the events of the past month. They were all thinking the same thing.

Smit was the first to speak. "There's nothing we could have done," he said. "He had all the angles figured out. Williams and me with the homosexuality claim. Lucy with the mild accusations and hint of wrongdoing. Mr. Oakes and his secret writing project."

"There's no way to prove he did anything wrong either," said Williams. "He's sure about that or he never would have treated us with such arrogance. He'll just go on doing the same old things."

"What bothers me the most," said Nancy, "is that he's only one person, a very influential person, sure, but what's on the horizon? Is he a harbinger of what's to come as more drugs come on the market, more doctors get involved with the drug companies, and on and on? Drugs that we can't even imagine now. The pharmaceutical companies that produce those drugs, they'll do anything it takes to sell their products. It's all business to them."

"Capitalism raises its ugly head once again," chimed in Smit.

"Power corrupts," echoed Williams.

Nancy continued. "It's like cigarettes. We in the medical profession have known for at least ten years that smoking is linked to cancer, but the tobacco companies deny the science and brazenly market their brands to make them sound sexy, or masculine, or feminine, or just plain fun. I'm afraid we have entered an era where the drug industry will grow exponentially, their budgets for marketing and packaging medicines will explode, and their willingness to penetrate the ethics of medical professionals will run amok.[26] I fear

---

26. Three brothers—Arthur, Mortimer, and Raymond Sackler—were doctors in the mid-20th century who founded the first big pharma company, Purdue Pharma, the company that developed and marketed Oxycontin in the 1990s. All three had expertise in marketing their products, but Arthur was the genius, as this article in *The New Yorker* points out:

"[I]n selling new drugs he devised campaigns that appealed directly to clinicians, placing splashy ads in medical journals and distributing literature to doctors' offices. Seeing that physicians were most heavily influenced by their own peers, he enlisted prominent

the future—for our patients, for our doctors and nurses, and for our moral and physical health as a nation."

Lucy would have the last word. "That may well be what happens, Nancy. But it won't be forever. I'm hopeful. We must *all* be hopeful—and vigilant. We must remember what Dr. King said about the moral arc of the universe. We must remember that quote from Isaiah about how we position ourselves in an unjust world: It was something like, 'Learn to do good; seek justice; correct oppression.' I say, *never, ever* give up. Things *will* turn out for the better. The world may turn darker, but we know there will always be light."

It would be the last time they would spend together.

Lucy found some music on the radio and they danced around moving boxes and piles of books. Williams found

---

ones to endorse his products, and cited scientific studies (which were often underwritten by the pharmaceutical companies themselves).

"In the early sixties, Estes Kefauver, a Tennessee senator, chaired a subcommittee that looked into the pharmaceutical industry, which was growing rapidly. Kefauver, who had previously investigated the Mafia, was especially intrigued by the Sackler brothers. A memo prepared by Kefauver's staff noted, 'The Sackler empire is a completely integrated operation in that it can devise a new drug in its drug development enterprise, have the drug clinically tested and secure favorable reports on the drug from the various hospitals with which they have connections, conceive the advertising approach and prepare the actual advertising copy with which to promote the drug, have the clinical articles as well as advertising copy published in their own medical journals, [and] prepare and plant articles in newspapers and magazines'" (Patrick Radden Keefe, "The Family That Built an Empire of Pain," *The New Yorker*, October 23, 2017, accessed January 23, 2020, *https://www.newyorker.com/magazine/2017/10/30/the-family-that-built-an-empire-of-pain*).

the University of Michigan men's basketball game on the television and tried in vain to explain to Nancy and Lucy the intricacies of the full court press.

Tom Oakes never showed up.

Nancy was the first to leave.

Williams went out to the street to warm up the car while Smit hung at the door. Alone with Lucy at last, he muttered something about regret this and sorry that, but in the end, she pulled his cheek to her lips and kissed him lightly.

"You have challenged me, Smit, "she said, smiling. "And I will always love you. In my way."

He stood there, speechless for once, holding back the tears. "I will love you too, Lucy. In my way."

On the following Monday, Lucy packed up her car and headed south to Kalamazoo, where she would spend a few days at home before driving to the Sisters of St. Joseph convent in La Grange, Illinois, just outside of Chicago. There she would take up residence before starting her new job at the ACLU in downtown Chicago.

On that same Monday, Smit and Williams returned to Ann Arbor.

Nancy Brownell went back to work.

Chapter 26

THREE DAYS AFTER THE PARTY AT LUCY'S FLAT, OFFICERS TONY GRYMES and Bill Demond of the Traverse City Police Department parked their black and white squad car in front of Building 50. A group of patients in thick winter clothing and rubber galoshes huddled together at the entrance as the officers made their way through foot-high snow drifts to the front doors of the building. It was just after 8 a.m.

"You the FBI?" shouted Muriel Putney from the huddled group. "'Cause if you are, then you can waltz right up to Ward 5 and arrest that SOB Mrs. Glaussen on account of she stole my brown purse with my candy in it. And while you're at it, toss that snotty nurse Johnsen in the slammer too 'cause she's in cahoots with the Nazis."

Muriel shook a mittened fist at the officers as they approached. Grymes and Demond glanced at one another, said nothing.

Muriel stepped forward as the others stepped back a bit. She called out, "You FBI got my letter about the toilet paper? Ain't no better since, lemme tell you. Hard as sandpaper. Falls all apart in your hands too. And never enough. Got to beg for each square, lemme tell you. That's how they treat us here. You come to liberate us from this hellhole?"

The officers made their way past the small crowd without comment. Muriel stood there waiting for an answer as the door closed behind them.

"A-hole FBI," she shouted to the others, jerking a thumb

over her shoulder toward the door. "I'm writin' to the CIA now," she announced. "We'll see who gets the attention now the big boys are involved. We're gonna have the Marines in here to clean up this mess, lemme tell you!"

The officers went up the stairs to the second floor. At the top, Demond remarked, "I hate getting calls out here. This place gives me the willies."

"My aunt Beatrice was committed here," said Grymes as they walked. "Ten years ago." "She was my favorite aunt. Her old man, my Uncle Ned, he got hot for some barmaid and before we knew it, he had Aunt Bea committed for, shit, I don't know what. She was a good woman, he just got rid of her, just like that. Then he moved to Tennessee, with the hussy. I was only sixteen, nothing anyone in the family could do about it all. He had a lawyer make it legal. She died here. Didn't take long."

Demond glanced sideways at his partner. "If I had an aunt in here, I'd have bad memories too," he said.

"It's not that simple," said Grymes as they walked. "We hated that she was in here, but they treated her good. She tried to adjust, she really did. But in the end, she just lost her way, and her heart gave out. Broken heart is more like it. I think about finding my uncle with that whore, and slitting his throat, the miserable bastard."

"Here we are," Demond announced as they approached an office door with the words DIRECTOR OF COMMU-NITY RELATIONS on it. A small group of nurses and other attendants stood nearby. Nancy Brownell emerged from the group. She said she found him earlier that morning. She made the call.

"His name is Thomas Oakes. He is—was—our Community Relations Director. I tried to rouse him," she said, "but he didn't respond. I couldn't find a pulse. That's when I called the station. I didn't touch anything else."

"Thank you, ma'am," said Grymes.

"And, I called Dr. Anderson. He's the chief medical superintendent here, but he's giving a speech downtown at the Rotary breakfast. His assistant said he'll be here by nine."

Officer Demond tipped his cap in her direction and thanked her for being careful. Both officers pulled off their gloves and overcoats. Nancy took them and placed them on a nearby bench. The cops went inside. Nancy remained in the hall with the others.

Tom Oakes was seated in his desk chair, his torso slumped from the waist up on the desktop. Both hands were on his lap. His head was turned to one side.

Grymes felt Tom's neck for a pulse.

"No pulse."

He turned the head slightly to get a better look at his face and then put it back. Demond took out a notepad and recorded as Grymes dictated.

"White male, estimate height, 6 feet. Estimate weight, 195. Looks to be age 50-55. Unshaven. Casual dress. No sign of trauma."

Both officers glanced around the room. Other than the normal disarray of an office where someone worked, nothing seemed out of place.

"No sign of struggle," said Grymes.

"Got that. Nothing broken or thrown around, as far as I can see," said his partner.

Then Grymes said, "Bill, we got a bottle of Kessler's on the desk, looks half-empty."

"Looks half-full to me," said Demond, grinning. "But that's just you and me, Tony."

"Very funny. Check out the vial over there."

Demond reached for a medicine vial and held it up to the light to read.

"Phenobarbital.[27] Empty. Says it's from the hospital dispensary. No date."

"All right," said Grymes. "The lab boys will be interested in that. Just note that it's here and there's no date on it. They can do the rest."

Demond's eye fell on a single piece of paper sticking out from a book. He picked up the book and turned it over to check the title. Grymes looked up and waited.

"*How to Write A Blockbuster Novel*," Demond read. "Guess our boy here had some aspirations."

Grymes was growing impatient. "Cut the jokes, Bill. The note, what's in the note?"

Demond held the paper up to the light. "Handwritten. Hard to make out some of the words. Gimme a second."

Then, "Okay, I got it. Here's what it says."

To whom it may concern: No one is responsible for my dying except me. I took the pills from the dispensary when I had a chance, so don't try to blame anyone there. I stole them when no one was looking. I mixed the pills with the whiskey. I don't see any point in dragging this life out anymore. I've been a failure in just about everything, and a

---

27. The impairment of brain functions caused by phenobarbital and alcohol can lead to the inability of the brain to react to internal stimulus. Activities such as breathing, pumping of blood from the heart and other automated bodily functions slow down leading to possibly hypovolemic shock, coma or death (*https://alcorehab.org/mixed-with/barbiturates/*).

damned fool for thinking I could be anything else. Ask Dr. Turner, he knows. He'll tell you what a schmuck I am. Ask Lenore too. She's my ex. She called me worse names. Some of those were true too, I guess.

There was a time when I thought I could be a better man. That was when Sister Lucy came here. She made me feel good about myself for the first time in years. It's because of her I thought I really could become a real writer. She brought out some parts of me that had been lost for a long time. But I let her down just like I let others down. I would appreciate if someone would let her know that I took my life by my own hand. Taking my own life is the one thing I've done well in a long time, and no one can take that accomplishment away from me. Maybe that's a morbid thought, but it's true.

Tell her I'm sorry I didn't clear my desk off. That was foolish.

My last wish is that you investigate Dr. Alan Turner. What he does for the drug companies and what he gets in return. How he treats patients like lab rats and how he tries out drugs on them that aren't proven safe or that have horrible side effects. How he wants desperately to impress the drug companies by writing articles praising the medicines as wonder drugs.
I know, because I ghostwrote those articles for him, though he claimed all the credit for them. Go to his superior, Dr. Anderson, the chief medical superintendent. He has responsibility for the ethical obligations of his medical staff. I suspect he will be very interested to learn of Dr.

*Turner's extra-curricular activities, especially those for
which he receives money and gifts.*

Grymes turned to his partner. "Bill, this guy, whoever
he is, had a dream and then he lost it, or he had it stolen. I
don't know. It's ironic that here, in this place, this guy lost
his way. Reminds me of my aunt."

"Well, he's looking at the radishes from below now," said
Demond as he put his notebook in a coat pocket. "Foren-
sics can take it from here. Looks pretty cut and dried."

"His suicide does," said Grymes. "Not this note. It's
anything but. I'm gonna grant this guy his last wish and
wait for this medical superintendent to show up. He needs
to see what this poor fellow has to say about this Dr. Turner.
That seems the right thing to do."

Afterword

THROUGHOUT THE LATTER PART OF THE 1960s, AND IN THE FOLLOWING decades, awareness of disability rights would develop slower, but in step with the anti-war movement, the women's movement, and the gay rights movement. Rights groups would mount court cases that would establish and protect the rights of mental patients in state institutions. Throughout the 1970s, mental patients' "liberation groups" would form throughout the country. Former mental patients were the organizers and spokespersons. The Insane Liberation Front started in Portland, Oregon, at about the same time that the Mental Patients Liberation Front began in New York City. In San Francisco, the Madness News Network began a newsletter that quickly went national and then world-wide. By the end of the decade, the patients' rights movement merged with the inevitable closing down of the asylums. Through "deinstitutionalization," former patients were transitioned into the community mental health system that had evolved out of the 1963 Community Mental Health Act signed into law by President Kennedy. Some believe that deinstitutionalization brought with it a host of other problems:

> "Deinstitutionalization was successful in the small
> but literal sense that many long-term residents
> of state hospitals were discharged, and that some
> money was probably saved in the process. But

310

deinstitutionalization failed to resolve many other important problems. These problems include failure to provide alternative care in non-institutional settings, failure to reintegrate chronic mental patients into the community, failure to dramatically improve their quality of life, failure to reduce their dependency on mental health and welfare institutions, and often failure to provide simple custodial functions for needy patients" (George Paulson, *Closing the Asylums* [Jefferson, North Carolina: McFarland & Company, Inc., 2012]185-86).

RICHARD VANDEWEGHE is Professor Emeritus of English from the University of Colorado, Denver. He has published numerous articles and two books—*Engaged Learning* (2009), a theory of instruction and practical guide for learning across the curriculum; and *Jimmy Quinn* (2018), historical fiction that is Book One of the Traverse City State Hospital Series. *Jimmy Quinn* was nominated for the Michigan Notable Books Award and the Next Generation Indie Book Award. *Lucy Greene* is the second novel in the series. Richard lives in Traverse City, Michigan.

Made in the USA
Monee, IL
06 September 2022

13391777R00194